THE NOWHERE MAN

Books by Roy Holland

Insights and Outsights: Poems by Roy Holland
   Cape Town: David Philip. ISBN: 0864861214

Just A Bit Touched: Tales of Perspective
   Writers Club Press.   ISBN: 0-595-15874-9

Flakes of Dark and Light: Tales from Southern Africa and Elsewhere
   Writers Club Press.   ISBN: 0-595-17423-X

Pivot of Violence: Tales of the New South Africa
   Writers Club Press.   ISBN: 0-595-15821-8

*News From Parched Mountain: Tales from the Karoo in the new
South Africa*
   Writers Club Press. ISBN: 0-595-14612-0

*The Awaking & Making of Paul Gauguin –
Conversations with Himself: A Play for Voices*
   Diadem Books, 2008

Alan Paton Speaking: The Lintrose Conversations
   Edited by Charles Muller. Diadem Books, 2008.

The Jonathan Three (published by Diadem Books):

The Nowhere Man
Journey Towards Himself
Now Lead Me Home

THE NOWHERE MAN

THE JONATHAN THREE: VOLUME 1

Roy Holland

DIADEM BOOKS

Published by Diadem Books

For information, please contact:

Diadem Books
Ocean Surf
CLASHNESSIE
IV27 4JF
Scotland UK

This is a work of fiction. Characters and situations are entirely a result of the author's imagination.

ISBN: 978-0-9559741-0-6

1

Travelling to work each day, between Shirley Station, where he got on, and Tyseley Junction, where he got off, gave Arnold Jonathan Godley a chance for a spot of serious reading. In moments less opportune, he amused himself perusing *Tit Bits* and *The Weekend Mail*. This morning, it was an anthology of extracts from *Works of Note*, collected by some famous bibliophile. A quotation had just taken his fancy. He put the book on the carriage seat beside him and relished what he had just read. Despite its old-fashioned language, it seemed to describe the contemporary world he experienced around him. '*Men be but fooles. And this may be most readily observed in their comings and goings, in that they come and they goe most readily, and yet in their coming they must soon goe again, and likewise in the manner of their going. Wherefore do I say, as may be readily perceived, that men be but the bloodiest of fooles.*' *DEMOGRAPHIES – Sir Charles Jopp.* He read it again, savouring the words. The world seemed not to have changed much in the four centuries since Sir Chas had written it! It set him thinking about his own ambitions.

He watched the fields of yellowing wheat go by, and the hayfields growing juicy and ripe. He was trying to get his priorities in order. He would have time to get them right before the man he called the 'Bank Manager' got into the carriage when it stopped at Yardley Wood

Station. He would be uninterrupted until then: British Rail rarely put corridor carriages on local lines.

He told himself his first goal was to get into a University to study literature. His second was to have some kind of significant relationship with sexy Alexis Treadgold. His third was to embarrass the Establishment in any way he could whenever he could. This usually meant harassing Burke, the Works manager, Treblitt, the Chief Draughtsman, and Dummock, one of his colleagues. But any other part of the Establishment was fair game if he got a chance. He seemed to devote most of his energies to number three, so he was thinking of altering the order of their importance.

He felt guilty that his father didn't figure in his list, but he still felt responsible for him. His father had invalided himself out of World War Two and the Royal Air Force, in 1945, by swallowing some sort of 'potion'. It left him with a duodenal ulcer and most of the nerves around his pelvis screaming for mercy. He had to spend his time in a wheelchair. But Jonty knew he got out of it occasionally when nobody was about to see him. His father hated "living off the Lickorish Stick", as he called it. His Mother had walked out on them the day his father got back into Civvies, about fifteen or sixteen years ago. They regarded her as Missing In Action and never discussed her. Jonty occasionally wrote for help to her *Doppelganger*, which, of course, never replied.

Today, the Bank Manager was having a day off: When Jonty arrived at Tyseley Station, Alexis was waiting for him. He put the book in his pocket and picked up his copy of *Tit Bits* and got off. They walked together up the steps onto the road bridge over the lines.

"I was wondering," said Jonathan Godley, " if I climbed up on the parapet like this...."

He stood precariously on the iron Victorian plinth, looking down at the silvered rails. A slight industrial breeze tousled his hair.

"And?" asked Alexis, looking up at him.

"Managed to jump into a few tons of anthracite in one of those trucks."

"Crazy man!"

"Injuring myself as little as possible, of course."

"What on earth for?"

"Get off work for a year. Make it look like an accident. Think of the compensation from British Railways."

"They'd certify you."

"Hey, that's not a bad idea."

He jumped down, like a mouse in slippers, and took Alexis's hand.

"Where were you yesterday, anyway?" she asked, on their way to Burke, Charles & Long's.

"Had another of my haemorrhages."

He glanced sidelong at Alex. Her left eyebrow rose slightly. "Had to pop into the Out-Patients at the General."

The eyebrow had risen another millimetre.

"All right, don't believe me. I shouldn't be carrying your toolbox for you like this. It could set me off again."

"Toolbox! It's my cosmetic case."

"Why is it filled with chisels, then? I can hear them clanking. With this gelignite fuse hanging out."

Alexis stopped dead still on the pavement. Jonathan forged ahead; in one hand the cosmetic case jauntily swung, his rolled copy of *Tit-Bits* in the other.

"Arnold Jonathan Godley!"

He stopped and turned round. "Why are you shouting at me like that?"

He was a slight small-boned young man. He had big grey eyes bright through frameless lenses, curly brown hair (tousled), gaucho moustache (prolonged), and a desire (chronic) to be unemployed, rich, and irresistible to women.

"Why do you always have to insult people, Jonathan Godley? There's something psychological about you."

"Me! Psychological. Me!"

He began to jerk his shoulders up and down. "Don't be silly! I always twitch like this. Insult people? Look at them all. They're not insulted. Are you?" he shouted suddenly.

One or two turned to look curiously at Jonty, but that was all. A thought appeared to strike him and a look of puzzlement appeared on his face.

"Or maybe they aren't people."

Crowds, on their way to the day's subtleties of crisp-making or sausage-filling, the allurements of moulding bakelites and plastics, of wire-chopping, button-pressing, wig-making, or the technological intricacies of motor-car-aeroplane-and-ice-cake designing, passed by unengaged by his antics. Instead, they all looked at Alexis, the men wolf-whistling in their minds, the women uneasy with envy or admiration.

Alexis was black-haired and slightly taller than Jonathan, with square shoulders. Jonty remembered noticing the first time his eyes had rested upon her — that was the word, 'rested'— she held herself so that everyone could see what she had and where she had it. Her emerald green tweed cape and dark green mini skirt focussed the men's eyes on her long calves and the curve of her thighs; and they didn't try to disguise what they would have liked to do with her.

"And if you do, I'll knock you down!" hissed Jonathan to a youngster just passing by — who merely chuckled and went on with what he was going on with.

Alex consoled Jonty by removing from under his arm the copy of *Tit-Bits*, replacing it with her own and steering him towards B.C & Long's.

"I don't know why I put up with such a rude and embarrassing man."

"No mystery! I'm very modest." He paused and looked quizzically at Alexis. "And very good at—"

"—Jonty! No obscenities. Anyway, it's other things that make you loveable."

"Such as?" He waited. "For example?" he persisted.

Her brow furrowed with agonised thought. She stayed agonised for too long

"Well?" said Jonathan.

"I'm thinking. It's not easy, you know, finding examples."

"All right, all right! I get the point."

"What about this? No career interest. No ambition. Getting on the wrong side of people. Lustful. Latent criminal tendencies."

"That's not bad for a start. Of course, it isn't true."

"What isn't?"

"No ambition."

"Oh?"

"Yes."

"What?"

"I want to be a millionaire."

Alexis stopped dead. Jonty watched everything Alexis had also stop, very much alive.

"And *I* want to be heavyweight champion of the world," she said.

Jonathan's eyes caressed her clingingly.

"You're going to have to work at it," he said. "But in my case — the best qualities of the best millionaires are already mine. What makes you think you can go fifteen rounds with Cassius Clay?"

"Okay, Aristotle Onassis, what're you going to tell Treblitt this morning?"

Jonty considered the question and began walking. "Come on! We'll be late," he said, thinking of no appropriate answer.

"I'm coming. What's the answer?"

"I'm working on it."

"Bet you are. Can't you tell him the truth for a change?"

Jonathan twisted his face into what he hoped was a wry expression, put his top teeth over his bottom lip, sucked in air through his lips and shook his head vigorously.

"He'd never believe it! Not from me."

"He might," said Alex with feeling.

"He'd ask to see the bruises". When Alex looked puzzled, he added, "From the blood transfusion."

"I said — the truth."

"The truth! To that brick-footed, pencil-counting, nit-picking, toffee-nosed, bog-trotting, twist-gut of a Treblittt."

"That's not fair. You know he's got a soft spot for you."

"Yes! Well-prepared, ten feet deep, and full of you know what. He'll say, 'Godley, when I say "jump", you jump. You can keep your clothes on. I've got the Maintenance Department standing by with shovels.' No thank you!"

"Arnold Jonathan Godley, you're just impossible."

"Wrong, my darling. I'm just possible. Lucky for you, unlucky for some."

The road was busy. They crossed over. Jonathan felt as if he were at the bottom of a canyon of bill-hoardings. He couldn't see the junction now. He looked at Alexis. She was everything that was fresh and new to him. Little flakes of soot touched willingly their cheeks like tiny oily fingertips out of the sharp morning air.

'No wonder she needs a cosmetic bag like a plumber's toolbox,' thought Jonty. 'Even I need one. Just smell it!'

The potato crisp factory was cooking crisps, the biscuit factory biscuits, the plastics factory plastics — the most appetising of the three. A thousand-folded chemistry of odours wound and unwound their skeins, knotting them finally round all available throats.

"Smell the Clean Air Act?" asked Jonty. "A world for sightless and perverted noses!"

"What?"

"It's best to stuff your nostrils with mixed herbs before you come out in the morning. I do."

Alexis laughed. "Don't be ridiculous."

"The world smells like a huge Sunday dinner, then. Lovely! Stuffing sage and onion up your nose alters the whole shape of your day. As well as your nose, of course. I'VE SIMPLY GOT TO LOOK AFTER MY T.B.," he said emphatically.

They were passing the long low-built Hardening Shop – an unlaunched trireme, with its rows of little windows for the galley slaves to breathe through.

'Breathe!' thought Jonty. 'A nasty joke! Half an hour in there and you feel as if your head has been wrapped in a towel, suspended over a vat of boiling vinegar, and gently basted until you are nicely cooked, fit only for pussy-cats.'

A comb of parking slots slanted diagonally towards the road, mostly empty: small wooden notice boards repeated twenty times the motto in neat white characters MANAGERS & DIRECTORS ONLY. Every slot displayed a metal plate. When Jonty reached the name of MAJOR H.B. KNOWLES — WORKS MANAGER, he stopped with a military stamp of his right leg, turned smartly to face the notice, and held out his right arm in a Hitler-salute. Slowly, he curled his thumb and third and fourth fingers into his palm, until only his index and second finger protruded in the shape of a vee. Then, very deliberately, he turned his palm and the curled fingers upward and jigged them twice jauntily. Finally, he swung his arm to his side and shouted, "Dismiss!"

He turned to Alexis. "I nearly forgot him. Army officer!" he snorted. "He's scarcely big enough to swing on the shit-house door."

"Don't be disgusting!"

"Sorry. I mean 'Die tur von die scheisenhausen'."

"What?"

"Just testing."

Suddenly, Alexis's white-jerseyed arms flashed through the slots of her emerald-green cape as she started to wave excitely to someone up ahead.

"Don't DO that," said Jonty vehemently, "You'll get a hernia."

"It's Isabel! I want to see her before she clocks in. Shan't see her all day." And she ran on in front.

"Phone her," called out Jonty, "she's on the switchboard."

Jonty watched carefully to see what her mini-skirt was doing.

"That's the point," came back faintly on the industrial breeze.

Isabel stood in front of the gateway that said WORKS ENTRANCE. Her hair was thick, long and luxurious. She knew it was her best feature. Jonty never understood why she had bleached or dyed it to a weak rust-coloured horsetail. He'd said she looked like a cigar-store Indian – only younger. When he had said that, Alex replied:

"You've never seen a cigar-store Indian."

"I have! Lots of 'em."

"Where?"

"The movies."

"Movies!" she said with incredible scorn, like this "Moo—oo—vies."

Jonty had never used the comparison again even though he'd liked it a lot at the time; at least, not out loud. Isabel was even taller than Alex. 'Geronimo-height', thought Jonty, but much slimmer with super-doopers that acknowledged her every step.

"But I'd still feel safer with the Indian on a dark night," he said under his breath.

Over his breath, he said "Hi, Butch!", approaching Alexis and Isabel standing together.

"What's it like among the poor-white trash of the Welfare State today?"

Jonty couldn't forgive her coming from such a good family, and for living in such a good area, and for telling him about it many times. Isabel turned regally toward him and raised her rusty eyebrows with careful elaboration.

"Who is this little man?" she asked.

'Goddamnit! She even bleaches her eyebrows,' thought Jonty.

"My gardener," said Alex, and they both laughed.

Jonty responded at once, as was his wont, sidling up closely to Isabel and whispering in her ear. "Yes, Madam, an' yuh want ter mind this fork I'm 'olding."

Her eyebrows were level with Jonty's hairline as she turned, and he saw how clear and green her eyes were, and the bluish makeup on the lids and the faintest touch of some other colour below. But she refused to meet his eyes and looked steadily into his forehead. They stayed like it for some moments, seeing who would win. Eventually Jonty asked: "Are you studying my acne?" and Isabel spluttered into a short laugh.

"Point, set and match," said Jonty.

"Jonty, why are you such a fool?" asked Isabel sweetly.

"We can't all be nature's darlings, can we, darling?"

"Oh, shut up," said Alexis. "Isabel and I want to talk."

"Very well then!" replied Jonty in offended old-maidish tones, "I'll go and read this new notice."

It was an old notice. And he walked towards the entrance. The two heavy wooden doors were shut across the entrance. A small doorway was let into the left hand side of one of them. The notice looked moth-eaten: NO UNAUTHORISED PERSON ALLOWED PAST THIS POINT. Archie Casbolt, the gatekeeper, a kind of Commissionaire, was standing beside it wearing one large blue uniform and two large blue stomachs.

"Where's the pint?" asked Jonty. He pronounced 'point' the way Archie said it.

"The what?" said Archie with much aggression. He pointed to the notice. "Because of the booze – that's what it means! Cheeky young sod," said Archie without much aggression.

"Major H.B. Knowles has authorised me to be a person," replied Jonty, gesturing again towards the notice.

"A big mistake, warn't it?"

"But only for five days out of seven, you'll be glad to know, Archie."

"Five too bleedin' many, then! Decided to come to work today, after all? Whassarnarrer? Couldn't you sleep or summat?"

Archie chuckled at his own brilliance, looking for applause to one of the toolmakers who was just arriving.

"Don't look at me," said the man. "We've got the wife's mother for a fortnight. She's got contagious schizophrenia. Prevents me from any kind of approval!"

Archie Casbolt grinned.

"Archie, you'll lose one of your chins if you go on doing that," said Jonty.

Then he was gone, through the door in a flash, before Archie could turn round to clip him.

Inside was a small cobbled courtyard, with several clocks placed at intervals round the walls, and under them the clocking-in mechanisms. Several short queues had formed in front of some of them. Jonty joined one.

2

"How's Howard Smedley Dummock this morning?" asked Jonty. Dummock, who was in the queue in front of him, didn't reply.

But he said over his shoulder, "Treblitt was asking about you yesterday."

"I wonder why?" murmured Jonty.

Dummock was a good-looking man of about thirty-five years of age, thin-lipped, thin-eyed, thin-nosed and thin-hoped. However, he fancied himself more than somewhat with women, with clothes and with his job, although none of them was a passion. They were extensions of his ego. Being good at women, clothes and his job was a matter of pride. His real passions were for chess, completing *The Daily Telegraph* crossword in record time, and reading Alexander Dumas (pere) at leisure. He had long piano-player's fingers, well-manicured, and he was reputed to be able to use them on the keyboard when he bothered to exert himself. His favourite boast was that he was the natural son of a Midland aristocrat with a pedigree that went back to William the Corncurer, as he called him. But despite his little black book with illustrations of baronial arms in to prove it, he had a square Teutonic head. Jonty wasn't impressed with that kind of proof. His head could have been Oriental, Negroid, Asiatic, or Frankish for all he cared.

The queues jiggled their way up to the clocks as people stamped their time-cards. Jonty stood in one and examined the back of Dummock's immaculate jacket.

"You can't force everybody into a suit like that, you know, Dummmock. You're lucky. If you had a chest, you'd suffocate."

"Envy will get you nowhere," Dummock replied without turning his head a fraction. "Lick up to me a bit. I might try persuading my tailor to open an account for you."

Then his head turned just enough to allow him to look sidelong at Jonty's feet. His eyes moved slowly and deliberately upwards: dusty suede shoes, bluejeans, T-shirt, brown velvet jacket.

"On second thoughts, it's hopeless, Jonty."

Dummock had now arrived at the clocking-in machine – a box-like body, a thick-lipped mouth on top for holding the time-card, and at one side, a lever to stamp your time of arrival. Above and over the box, a large round white-faced clock, yellowing a bit at its perimeter. The firm did not belong in the go-ahead-and-kill'em class. It was more of a stay-behind-and-wait type.

"Get a move on! There's a queue 'ere, mate," a voice called from behind.

"Now, now," cooed Dummock soothingly, "don't get hysterical."

He checked carefully his wristwatch against the large face of the timepiece, looking from one to the other with stubborn deliberation. Then he addressed the clock threateningly:

"If you stare like that, I'll shove this card in your mouth and pull your arm."

And he did. A woman giggled. Dummock turned round, stepped out of the queue and bowed. Jonty's card read 'Seven fifty-nine'. One minute early! The first time in weeks.

"Hey, Dummock! Half a mo'."

Jonty felt expansive enough to accompany him to the office. Dummock walked resolutely on. It would take more than a compliment on his suit to make him reciprocally expansive. But Jonty caught him. They were just about to go up the wide wooden loft-like stairs, through which Jonty had watched many a shapely thigh, when he heard a shout behind him.

"Arnie."

Dumnmock turned because it was a woman's voice. Jonty turned also, in surprise. Usually, people called him Jonty, never "Arnie", rarely "Arnold", sometimes "Niblo". So who was it?

Alex was hurrying towards them. She carried the emerald-green cape over her arm. In a tight white sweater, her breasts shone and jiggled like headlamps, dazzling Dummock, throwing him into a speed-wobble. But he recovered himself enough to say:

"Miss Vanity Fair herself."

Even Jonty was struck all over again by the weight of lust her breasts evoked in him, so much so that he made a mental note to re-classify them as soon as he could give his mind to it. She reached the two men breathlessly and held out her free arm, indicating:

"My cosmetic box!" she said affectionately compassionate.

Jonty looked down vaguely at the toiletry he still held. "Oh, yeah." He handed it to her, wonderingly. 'Yes,' he thought, 'they should certainly be upgraded. To Doopers, at least.'

Dummock's voice brought him out of his reverie.

"Oh, yours is it, Alex? I thought Jonty had developed a taste for jasmine-scented sandwiches."

"What?" Alex looked puzzled.

"You know," said Dummock, laughing. "A new lunchbox."

Alex looked down dubiously at her toiletry. "Oh, yes."

"What do you carry in that thing, Alex?" said Jonty. "It's given me chronic paralysis and water-blisters. Look!"

He held up one hand, like a claw.

"Never you mind. See you tonight, then." And she turned and minced away.

Dummock watched her with frank and open admiration. "What do you think it is she's mincing?"

When Jonty didn't respond, Dummock shrugged forbearingly and said: "Oh, well, if she wants to see me, I suppose I's'll have to go."

"Pack it up, Dummock. She's mine."

Dummock stood back, arms akimbo, and scrutinised Jonty in amazement. The amazement looked real, which wasn't good for Jonty.

"Yours! Are you serious? An exquisite bit of grumble-and-grunt like that? Yours! You're suffering from illusions of grandeur, my boy. Look at you! You're just a strip of fresh air and innocence. Take a tip from me, laddie, and leave her to the men. Our Miss Treadgold is not for novices. Deff-i-nightly not! She's stuff for the initiated. You just stick to carrying her makeup and you'll be all right, Arnie-boy."

For once, Jonty had been caught off balance by Dummock's rhetoric and sheer effrontery. Jonty had no reply. But he was busy wondering whether he should try stuffing Dummock's copy of *The Daily Telegraph* down Dummock's throat.

'If I fold it once and then roll it inwards from the outside, I might manage it,' thought Jonty. 'About the right diameter. No! On second thoughts, a quick Karate jab, straight fingers to the larynx would be better.'

"Don't mutter, laddie! You'll steam up your glasses."

'He's like an American TV lawyer about to expose a hostile witness,' thought Jonty. 'Better still. A British MP about to call for the resignation of the Prime Minister.'

"Mutter, mutter!" said Dummock.

Dummock approached Jonty and threw an arm round his shoulders.

"Come on, laddie. Forget it! I'm joking," he said, continuing to manoeuvre him up the stairway.

"Don't try out your Orson Welles voice on me, Dummock."

"Okay, okay! So I trod on a soft spot. Sorry! But, really, it does seem comical."

"What does? Your imitation of Orson Welles?"

"No. Alex. I never knew our Alex had a taste for—" He gestured at Jonty as if trying to scoop up a lot of air between widespread arms, jiggling his hands on the end of his wrists.

"A taste for what, Dummock?"

But Dummock had stopped, having run up a cul-de-sac.

"Like what?"

When Dummock had no reply, Jonty added:

"And you can pack up all this 'our Alex' stuff. See!"

"Jonty!" said Dummock decisively, "I think it's time you were told the facts of life. How long have you been with us, now?"

"Us?"

"Burke's, Charles & Long's."

Jonty disdained to reply.

"Well, I've been here about eight years," Dummock continued, ignoring Jonty's silence, "and I know pretty well everything there is to know about the depth and eligibility of every bit of bint in this factory. Put me in a dark room blindfold and give me a whiff of six pieces of fanny-fluff and I'll tell you whose is which."

He made a noise like a herd of buffalo coughing in Jonty's ear. Jonty looked at him scathingly.

"Take your arm away, Dummock."

"You're disgusted with me, aren't you, laddie?"

"What on earth gives you that idea, Dummock?"

"Well, let me tell you this. She's been here six months or so – a bit longer than you – and six months after she came.....No....I tell a lie....Five......and—"

He leaned over and whispered. Jonty felt as if hot lead had been poured into his middle ear, which was at this very minute, by way of his Eustachian tubes and oesophagus, finding its way to the chilblains on his toes. Strange burning sensations had set up in unlikely parts of his body. Then he felt very heavy all over and inert, as if gravity had laid a spell on him. He stood stock-still on the stairs and tried to turn a head that had gone solid on his spine.

Dummock watched him curiously.

Jonty managed to blurt out: "If you're lying, Dummock, I'll—I'll..."

"Not at all, Arnie boy. Ask Fisher! You know, Time-and-motion Fisher, not the accountant. And there's old—"

"Okay. Never mind the roll of honour. I get your drift."

"Don't worry about it, laddie. It's life. It's growing up. You'll soon get over it. What difference does it make to you, anyway?"

Jonty felt as though he needed a long period of notice to answer that question.

"Why not? Sweetness and light. You have to spread it around, you know, as good old Matthew Arnold was fond of repeating. Half-namesake of yours, laddie." Dummock drew breath and prepared to orate: "As I was saying to the wife's sister in bed this morning—"

"Cut the spiel, Dummock!"

After scrutinising Jonty's metal-coloured face, Dummock shrugged and went up the stairway alone, leaving Jonty still standing there, halfway up. Even Dummock could see that Jonty had received a blow. He did not begin to move until he heard a clatter on the stairs below him.

On his way to the Drawing Office, he began to work out his strategy in preparation for confronting Alex later that night. By the time he had reached the D.O., he felt slightly better. But he wasn't back to his old self, yet. He knew by the fact that, on entering, he had forgotten to deprive the notice on the door of yet another letter. It said: D.O. NO SMOKING. BY ORD.

If he'd been normal, he'd have flaked off another letter at least. It should have said: D.O. SMOKING. BY ORD. Or even: D.O. NO SMOKING. BY OR. Even a permutation like – He gave up. One chip of paint or plywood a day wasn't too much, was it? He'd hoped to have it quite unreadable in a week or two. But he couldn't go too fast. Treblitt might see it. Of course, it wasn't likely Treblitt would see it. He didn't look at doors at 9 30 in the morning when he arrived. No, he was too taken up with the state of his bowels at that time. And he certainly didn't look at doors when he went home at night. His main preoccupation would have switched to his stomach by then.

So, having convinced himself with his own arguments, Jonty decided to step up his campaign a little. He went back to the office door and surreptitiously pulled off a piece of white-painted ply the size of his thumbnail. It now said: D.O. NO SMOKING   OR. That operation helped Jonty's morale quite a lot.

He now felt strong enough to start work – nearly. He walked down the long office, between the rows of draughting machines and boards. The Senior Draughtsmen had positions near the windows where they were able to gaze into the street below. Draughtsmen and designers did a lot of gazing. It was part of the design process: it helped them to concentrate and visualize. Treblitt claimed, said Jonty, that designers who didn't gaze were falling down on the job. He hinted that Treblitt had been known to sack draughtsmen on the spot who were known to do insufficient gazing.

Most of the draughting boards had been uncovered by now and the draughtsmen were having their first cigarettes, soothing their lungs, coaxing their minds out of neutral, easing into first gear for reviewing the sections, elevations and projections they had drawn the previous day.

Three rows of draughting boards ran longitudinally from top to bottom of the office. None of the young men had positions near the windows. Junior Draughtsmen usually sat next to a corridor, or in the noisiest places near the print machine, or where they received full benefit from the effluvia that rose from the Hardening Shops, or, like Jonty, facing a wooden partition somewhere. As Jonty passed board after board, he nodded to a few Seniors, who scarcely deigned to notice him; sometimes one greeted him.

One by one, the latecomers arrived, shouting their depressed or bawdy or jovial greetings to each other, or muttering inaudibly, according to the way they felt.

"Back to the grind."

"I was just crossing the Coventry Road when the engine cut out on me."

"You don't look too good! Been on the nest again, Joe?"

"They've given me two buggerin' days to lay out the whole job and tool it up."

"Mmm! Sounds sexy."

Jonty was the youngest Junior in the office. His board was placed in the darkest corner of it. His potential for gazing was severely curtailed: two stretches of light beige varnish, one in front and one to his left. However, his sessions of gazing had yielded the interesting fact that the unknown painter of the front partition had managed to leave four-thousand-and-fifty-one bristles stuck in the varnish. Jonty hadn't started gazing in earnest at the other wall yet. But he'd had the presence of mind to jot down the total so far under the edge of the cartridge paper on his board. Just in case Treblitt crept up on him and challenged the quality of his gazing. Maybe he should work out the mileage in a painter's brush for Treblitt? Surely that would please the old nit-picking bastard? Assuming there were fifty thousand per brush, that would....

"Oh, to hell with it! Let him do his own cost analysis."

Jonty started to roll up the dustcover on his board. Dummock's draughting machine was behind and to the right of Jonty's, alongside the windows. Jonty glanced surreptitiously under his armpit at Dummock, disguised by the rolling-up operation. Dummock was wearing his white surgeon's overall again.

'It's a wonder he doesn't start affecting a stethoscope as well,' thought Jonty.

An immaculate narrow-shouldered Harris tweed jacket depended from a coathanger fastened to a small nail on one side of the support of Dummock's board. A green plastic shoulder-hood protected the jacket from factory dust. We can't have Herbert Smedley D's patina of perfection polluted by dust, can we? His elegant outdoor handmade shoes stood in their accustomed place beside his stool, the toes stuffed full of tracing paper. He had changed into the tatty pair of black walking shoes he kept at work. Dummock wasn't going to have the soles of his shoes ruined by oil and swarf on his trips to the machine-shops, was he? Oh, no, thank you very much, not at sixty-five sterling the pair!

Dummock took his copy of the *Daily Telegraph* from beside his board, opened it at the page he wanted, spread it flat, and started to cut out the crossword with a razorblade. He sat on his stool, put the newly cut newspaper square in a chunky red-covered manual called MACHINE TOOLS and stared at it with alacrity. He had begun his day's work. Plus or minus 10 minutes, Dummock was set for the next hour.

When Jonty had first arrived in the office, he had been puzzled that Dummock had spent so much time gazing at this illustrated manual of tools. Now he knew: the camouflage device of a professional time-server. If you happened to surprise Dummock working on an acrostic, he snapped the pages shut automatically—phut!—as fast as you could blink, and smiled at you through his thin eyes. *"Yes?"* he asked, bland as a poached egg. If you presented no danger, he'd open up the manual again and go on as if nothing had happened.

Jonty had his own obsessions to satisfy. He set about getting the angle of his drawingboard to the right slant, which was the best to hide what he was going to do. Then he took the largest print of a jig he could find and laid it on the board. Okay. He could use it like a tent and work beneath it. All he needed now was a clean sheet of scrap from his scribbling pad: this was the stationery he chose to write his letters on to the management. Or, to be more accurate, on behalf of the management.

3

After work, Jonty met Alex in one of their favourite haunts. The atmosphere was hot and close. They were sitting at one of the black-tiled tables which had small black skulls on them with electric bulbs inside. Other similarly lighted skulls stood on ledges around the walls. Much larger skulls were embedded in the walls themselves. Skeletons had been depicted under the lighted skulls in some kind of psychedelic paint. The only other decor was a variety of large potted plants dotted about which were not painted in psychedelic colours.

"So what did he say?" asked Alex.

"Exactly what I thought he'd say."

"What?"

"For one thing, he accused me of eating office pencils."

"Don't be ridiculous! And for two?"

"I'm not. He did. And he said I looked like a Carnaby Street rummage."

"Sometimes you do."

"Hey! Who's side are you on? And for three he said I was a born liar. Not in so many words, of course. He doesn't claim to be a gentleman for nothing."

"He's not stupid. He wouldn't."

"What? Claim to be a gentleman?"

"No, idiot! Call you a liar."

She then looked doubtful. "You did, didn't you, tell him the truth, as I asked?"

"Well—!" Jonty hesitated, because he had not yet told Treblitt anything, true or false. He was inventing the way he thought Treblitt would react. "Said I was lying, he did, and he was as happy as two Treblitts while he said it."

"Are you hiding something?"

Jonty decided it was time for a decoy manoeuvre so he began to suck in his cheeks, and went on sucking them in until his cheeks had disappeared inside his mouth. He then concentrated on making his eyes bulge, showing as much of their whites as possible, and trying, at the same time to force his head down between his shoulders so that his face would go black with the strain.

"Arnold," said Alex, nervously.

When he didn't reply, Alex shrieked: "Arnold! What are you doing?"

Several people turned to look at her in disapproval. Jonty took no notice. Alex began to shake him. She was disconcerted.

"Arnold!"

Jonty let the air out of his mouth with a Plop! Then he let his neck out slowly, without a plop.

"You nearly gave me delayed whiplash," said Jonty. "I was trying to stare him out."

"Who?"

He indicated the black-boned skull with its eyes lit up on the wall over her head. "Him."

"You fool," she said with quiet relief. "I thought you were going to give yourself some kind of a turn. Anyway it might be a 'her'."

"Ah! That's why I couldn't do it."

He took her hand and looked about him. The customers sat on benches along the walls and round the oblong tables. Unlike the potted plants, some of the clientele had psychedelic complexions that had not been painted on and were not due to the installations. Every so often the lights came up, making the nylon bras and panties glow through the girl's dresses with a fluorescent effulgence. It was good for a laugh, and the eyes of the men lit up with an effulgence that was not electrical. The place was full of all ages and all kinds, but mostly with those who looked like out-of-work-extras-for-crowd-scenes in political documentaries about the decadence of the West. It was one of the most popular hang-outs in Birmingham for the trendy young and not-so-young.

"They don't even have the prices up," said Jonty.

"What?"

"On the wall. There's no 'me-an'-you', but they do sell a kind of food here. What about a nice bat burgher and crumpet?"

They had dropped in for a coffee. It was an old Victorian cellar that had been converted. It was very twee. *Very twee.* Somebody had had the bright idea of calling it The Old Victorian Cellar. It is true, it was a lot like a cellar and even more like an old cellar; but anything less Victorian it was hard to imagine. Except in the way it expressed its preoccupation with death and keeping things generally underground. But Jonty liked it because it had no notices telling you what to do, no notices telling you what not to do, and no music.

"Can't you be serious for a minute? I want to talk to you."

'So do I,' thought Jonty, releasing her hand.

"You must have said it all wrong. Treblitt isn't a fool. How did you put it?"

"Oh, shut up! Have another swallow of that frothy insecticide."

"I won't shut up."

"Alex, you're looking superb," he said, taking her hand again.

Alex glanced uncertainly at Jonty.

"After telling me to shut up?"

"Exactly."

22

The blackness of the general decor set off her scarlet sweater-dress clinging perfectly over her breasts. Jonty watched them appreciatively. He was conscious of envying the edge of the table where they touched every time she leaned towards him to speak. What a set of doopers! He released her hand and touched the red chiffon scarf she had tied round her hair. This was another of his decoy movements for what he really wanted to touch.

"Sometimes I think you're almost beautiful, Alex."

"Thank you so much for the almost! I couldn't have managed without it."

But she had liked his comment all the same. Jonty was suddenly aware that she was one of the vainest girls he had met to date.

"Tell me what you said to Treblitt. Exactly said, I mean."

"I said: Yesterday my father tried to commit suicide."

"Just like that! How could you?"

"It just came to me."

"No wonder he didn't believe you. You should have wrapped it up a bit. Prepared him for it."

"Why? It's true, isn't it?"

"That's not the point and you know it. People don't try to commit suicide every week."

"My father does."

"Not EVERY week! But—"

"—Look, it's over! Treblitt's as happy as a breadfruit. Anyway, he preferred my second explanation. I gave him a choice of two, you see."

"Oh?"

"I told him I went for an interview for another job."

"You didn't!"

"Why, what's wrong with that?"

"Obvious. He'll put you out now when he gets half a chance."

"He would've anyway. Stop worrying. If there's one thing I've learned it's – always tell people what they want to hear. It makes them excited."

"You're not telling ME what I want to hear."

"You're not people."

"What am I, then?"

'Yes, I wonder,' thought Jonty.

"Look over there," he said aloud, but thought, 'Discretion is the better part, et cetera.'

"Where?"

"There."

He pointed to a man with a longish nose and well-formed lips that had superciliousness built into them. The man's hair was poor and his clothes expensive. They looked tailor-made. So did his hair.

'Come to think of it, what IS he doing in a place like this, anyway?' thought Jonty.

"That man," he said aloud.

"Which?"

"The one who looks like a churchwarden watching for a chance to slip the devil a quiet piece of folding money."

"What about him?"

"That's T.S. Eliot. I've seen him in here before."

"Is it? How do you—?"

But she caught him watching her.

"Well, why shouldn't he be? I caught a glimpse of E.M. Forster the other day, on the platform of New Street Station, with his rucksack. He was adding up his change at the ticket-off ice on the palm of his hand."

"Oh, what a liar! Aren't they both dead?"

"D H Lawrence told Forster he was. He said 'Forster, you're dead!' Anyway, there's Eliots and Forsters about by the dozen. The world is full of famous people. They just haven't become well-known. I can't help it if I'm observant, can I?"

"That's not observation. That's—"

24

Jonty interrupted her.

"—Like Dummock for example. Have you ever looked closely at Dummock's meatus?"

"His what?"

"Or scrutinised his concha?"

"Are you being vulgar, again?"

'Now I'm on to it,' thought Jonty. 'Get in when the enemy is least expecting it.'

He said: "People's ears give them away like nothing else."

Jonty leaned over and stroked the lobe of Alex's left ear. It was pendulous and fleshy and silky to the touch.

"Mmmmm! That's lovely," she said.

"Thought you'd like it."

Jonty half stood up and leaned across the table to nuzzle her right ear with his mouth and nibble the lobe.

"Must treat them equally," he said.

"For God's sake don't! It sends me all funny."

"It's only my tash that does it."

"No, it isn't. It's THAT! What you're doing."

"People have only got to take one glance at your earlobe and another at your meatus, to know that you like it a lot."

Now was the time, while she thought he was indulging her in an elaborate flattery.

"I can read 'em. It's sort of palmistry of the earhole. Yours is beautiful, but — wow! —don't you have to watch out."

She laughed with delight and some apprehension. He sat down, leaned back, and regarded her seriously through the top edge of his glasses. It distorted her doopers most entertainingly.

"Don't do that! It makes you look like Major Works Manager Knowles."

"Oh, my God! *Mea culpa. Mea maxima culpa.*"

He beat his breast. "I'll never do it again. Major Knowles! I couldn't live that down."

But he went on, pressing to his goal.

"If I wasn't such an expert on the physiognomy of earlobes, I'd say yours showed dangerous sexual tendencies."

Alex didn't look at all comfortable at this remark. She was uncertain how to react. So she went on smiling.

"Now, Dummock's got an interesting ear. Judging by the bulk of its concha, I'd say he was a first-class lecher. But taking the lobe into account, which is very disappointing — thin, undersized — I'd say he was just a sadist."

Jonty's latest observation began to alarm Alex. She sat up very straight and unconsciously moved as far back on her seat as she could.

'That must mean something, mustn't it?' thought Jonty.

"Are you sure you're not just kinky?" asked Alex." Are you a – a – What do the shrinks call them — fetishists, or something?"

'Oh, I see! Trying out your paperback education on me, are you? I don't scare easy, you know. Think I'm a secret ear-fetishist, do you?'

"Well, what's all this chat about Dummock's ear about, then?"

'One of those "about"s is redundant,' thought Jonty.

"I thought I'd made that obvious. It's about Dummock's ear."

"What else, besides his ear?"

Now that Jonty had reached the moment that he'd promised himself earlier in the day, he discovered to his surprise that he didn't seem keen on the slaughter, after all. He didn't own her, did he? He had met her only four weeks ago. They'd never made any promises of fidelity or long-lasting love to each other, had they? So what was he griping about? He was sure there seemed to be something there, but he didn't quite know what. He'd have to give himself a chance to find out what it was he was on about, wouldn't he? Yes, he would.

"Have another frothy insecticide," he countered.

"Never mind the coffee. You're leading up to something, and I want to know what it is."

'You're not the only one who'd like to know,' thought Jonty.

Alex's face was tense and they sat without speaking. Then she said with asperity, "I'm grown up, free and in charge of myself, so why am I getting steamed up about all this sex-stuff?"

Well, if he was honest, he'd have to admit that he didn't want used goods. Like most men, he preferred the commodities with the cellophane wrapper intact. But he couldn't tell Alex that, could he? No, he couldn't. Why, couldn't he? Well, for one thing, the Dummock nonsense would have to come out. And, for another, what would Alex think of his progressive mind? His progressive what? Oh, to hell with it! As so often in the past, Jonty found himself grateful for knowing he had a yellow streak, somewhere. Small, it was true, but unmistakably there.

"The trouble is, I'm a coward," he said.

Alex softened at this offering. It showed that he had no wish to hurt her, surely?

"You're not actually afraid of me, are you?" asked Alex.

"I don't think so. It could be that I'm afraid of me. Or it could be me telling you something that you could be afraid of. And me being afraid of that. I dunno."

They both knew that they had not made any kind of a contract, spoken or unspoken. She had never made offers to Jonty, of any sort, and he had never asked her for come-ons. They liked each other, that was all. She did his eyes good, and he made her laugh. He tried to do this as often as he could because there was something in her that made him want to make her laugh. She did his vanity good, and he satisfied her taste for clowning about. He was fully aware of not doing her vanity any good. They discussed things. They went about together. That seemed to be about the sum of it, didn't it? No it didn't! Or he wouldn't be some way along this jealousy tightrope, would he? And he wouldn't have found out, via Herbert Smedley Dummock, that he had actually got a fancy for her tucked away inside him, would he? What a bloody nuisance feelings of this kind were! Bugger Dummock and his lechery! Trust Dummock to get up his nose like this!

Alex sensed the dismay in Jonty and moved across to him and sat down. She put her hand through his arm and leaned her head against his shoulder.

"That doesn't sound like the Jonty we all know. I think I prefer this new one," she said.

"It's not a new one! It's an old one back on a visit."

"Well, tell him to come more often. Honest?"

"Honest! I like you a bit uncertain."

'I bet you do,' thought Jonty.

"Okay," he said, as if he had just reached a decision, "I'll tell you. After I'd left you and Isabel—"

Alex listened quietly, with her head still on his shoulder. Jonty reached the crucial point in his account, drew a breath and plunged on:

"—And Dummock said — well — in his words, that he'd been through you more times than he could count." He finished in a rush.

Alex jerked her head away from him, removed her hand from his arm and sat rigidly upright with a space between them.

"Oh, he did, did he?"

"That's what the man said."

He watched her. Despite the straightness of her back, her expression was impassive. He felt slightly encouraged to go on. Her passivity was, however, deceptive, and Jonty, unaware that the territory had been mined, stepped out jovially.

"Said you were the sort who just couldn't get enough of it. Ha, ha! A classical nympho, he called you."

Alex looked at him. Deliberately. He returned her stare. Her brown eyes now looked wild, and while he watched, her face tightened, bringing out the rather heavy lines of her jaw and nose and the hardness of her mouth that later (very much later) you might describe as rat-trap.

'A trailer for a forthcoming face. The middle-age of Miss Treadgold. Don't miss our next big feature,' thought Jonty.

She spat at him: "And you believed him, I suppose!"

"There didn't seem any reason to disbelieve him at the time."

"There's Dummock, isn't there? And me! That's two good reasons."

"I suppose so. But—?"

She moved still further away from him and started fiddling with her coffee cup. Neither spoke for some time. Jonty began to look around the Old Victorian Cellar, wishing he'd never started it, conscious once again that he could have become quite devout in his own cowardice. Why couldn't he just make the best of what he'd got, the way most people did? It was only a matter of time, after all. Sit it out, play a careful game, lead judiciously, and he'd have been counting the tricks in bed soon enough, according to all reports. Maybe he was concealing unsuspected puritanical tendencies somewhere? That would be just his luck, wouldn't it?

"I suppose your favourite bedtime reading is the diary of Queen Victoria," said Alex bitterly, as if she divined his thoughts.

"Oh, no!" said Jonty at once. "I don't like her style. It reminds me of the *New Statesman* book reviewer I used to read in my teens."

Alex's disdainful expression helped to change his mood. This was a time for sincerity, not flippancy, wasn't it?

"Yes, I suppose you're right. Why do I act as if I was born yesterday? That's my trouble! I think my mother must have been frightened by a Victorian Methodist," he added mournfully.

He knew he had been exposing his flank when he said it, but he hadn't been prepared for the speed with which she leapt to the attack.

"My God! Coming from you, that's priceless. Three jobs in twelve months. That's right, isn't it? Take time off from work when you feel like it. AND pick up your pay packet without a blink. You'd like to blow up the factory, put the management against the wall, and go on insulting people all over the place. Not to mention the way you upset Daddy the first time I take you home. And—" She paused to draw breath.

Jonty took his chance to use another decoy tactic from his repertoire. First he shuffled his bottom along his seat and glanced about as if he'd lost something. Then he leaned across towards the bald-headed man at the next table and said:

"Are you listening, Mr – er — er —? I think she's addressing you."

Startled, the man looked at Jonty for a moment, his eyes wide, and then glanced quickly away.

"You see?" Alex continued. "You're just impossible!" Her brown eyes were smouldering, smoky with anger. "And you talk about—"

"— Oh, I see! It's me you're talking to," Jonty said to Alex, then turning his head slightly towards the bald-headed man, added, "Sorry! I thought it was—" He turned back quickly when the man ignored him and went on speaking:

"Me! Have you ever heard me say those things? Have you?"

"No. You don't SAY them. But you do them!"

"Do them? Shoot the management? Me? I'm the one that invented 'Don't shoot the management, it's only doing its best'."

"Well, you ACT as if you believe them, don't you? And that's the same thing, as far as I'm concerned."

"No, not quite. You've emphasised the wrong bit. It's the AS IF you should stress. AS IF I believed them, yes! Yes!" he added vehemently. "And that makes all the difference."

"What difference?"

"Between life and art."

"You're joking! Life and art!"

"No, I'm not. Reality and make-believe, if you like that jargon better."

But, under his breath, he muttered: "'As if' makes art possible."

"Anyway," said Alex acidly, "what's all this got to do with Dummock?"

"That's what I'd like to know. Is it true, then?"

"What?'

"That you and Dummock—"

"What business is it of yours?"

"So it is true!"

"I didn't say so."

"No, and you didn't not say so, neither."

He considered the treble negatives in the sentence he had just said. When Alex disdained to reply, Jonty added: "Never mind the grammar! What's the answer?"

She began to arrange her belt of chained medallions around her waist with ostentatious care and searched for her Spanish Cape with pointed deliberation. She picked up her bag, put her head through the cape and stood up.

"Have you got an hidalgo to meet?" asked Jonty.

"I'm going. You can stay if you prefer."

"Well, did you?"

"What?"

"WITH DUMMOCK!"

"Don't shout! If you must know — yes, I did!"

"Fine!" Jonty stood up. "Wait for me. I'll come, too."

People were looking at them with curiosity and amusement as they left the Old Victorian Cellar together.

4

He began this one with: IT HAS RECENTLY COME TO THE ATTENTION OF THE MANAGEMENT. But he stopped to suck the end of his pencil while he wondered what exactly it was he was going to decide had been unavoidable enough to obtrude itself before the sight of that set of myopic, bungling, over-paid, over-dressed, over-fed and under-worked gangsters who called themselves 'The Management', and who would have died of shock if they had actually allowed something to capture their attention, never mind about forcing on themselves the managerial effort of actually noticing something. Manage! They couldn't even manage a quiet individual burp after a Works Dinner. At least, not without a handful of magnesia tablets to provoke the flabbiness of their stomachs into their journeys of protest. Even in the short time that he'd been with Burke's, Charlie's and Long's, Jonty had noticed the silhouette of Treblitt's stomach steadily advancing toward the edge of his whitewood desk. If he wanted to keep on reaching it, Treblitt would soon have to start moving back his chair a fraction each day and wearing his arms longer.

Jonty began to lose himself in the varied calamities, dilemmas and crises he devised for management in general, and for Mr Austin Treblitt and Major H.B. Knowles in particular. What about an astronomical drop in production over the last week? Or the naked body of Knowles's confidential secretary found in one of the vats of the Hardening Shop with a cherry-coloured ribbon round each ankle, the exact shade of Knowles's nose? Or the suicide of the Personnel Manager after a Board Meeting? Or suspected bestiality in the men's toilets? Or Austin Treblitt's embezzlement of the Drawing Office's Christmas Fund to satisfy the insatiable lust for luxurious living of some plump little doxy in Balsall Heath?

No. He rejected all of them. Too ordinary. You needed something subtler to do full justice to a firm like Burke's, Charles's and Long's. What about playing on the sympathies of the workers and announcing the staging of a public bastinado of the Chief Progress Clerk at the Christmas Party?

Jonty was startled out of his reverie of catastrophes by the powerful baritone of Dummock intoning to the whole office:

"Three down, eighteen across. Four-letter word meaning a sign of affection between a man and a woman. Anybody?"

Someone offered Dummock an answer he ignored. Jonty looked up to find him holding out his crossword, pencil poised, ready for the answer.

"Ah, got it," he cried exultantly. "Kiss!"

Then, slowly, like a Black Country preacher at an orgy, he surveyed them in great sorrow.

"Damned! You filthy-minded set of cripples. You couldn't raise a smile in a whorehouse."

And he turned back to his drawing board and his chunky manual of Machine Tools as if he'd simply paused to blow his nose. Everybody had got used to Dummock's outbursts of high-spirits and clowning. He was an excellent mimic. His satirical impersonations ranged from imitations of managerial personnel, through fictional and anonymous match-sellers and unfrocked priests (usually toothless, for which Dummock removed his top set), to sellers of obscene postcards and nonconformist ministers relating parodies of well-known Biblical events. These were interspersed with appeals for answers to imaginary crosswords that had multiple solutions, the most obvious of which were unprintable. This latest perpetration had evoked a few titters, but nothing to speak of. He had done better. What was worrying the maestro?

Jonty tried to get his mind back to the letter he was writing on behalf of the management. He wanted to get it finished before 9.30 am when Treblit came in on the dot of the half hour – promptly late. Treblitt would follow his ritual to the last detail, the point of which was to bring about the full and magical evacuation of his bowels. The Chief's health came *pro tutto.*

He'd got twenty clear minutes. Then, Treblitt would be arriving. His arrival wouldn't be easy. It never was. First, everybody would hear a loud 'clump' at the door of the Drawing Office. Treblitt managed this by allowing the toe of his lace-up boots to connect with the bottom of the door before his hand reached the door handle. His co-ordination was impeccable. He never missed. "Clump" he would go, every day of the week. Jonty wondered vaguely if he varied his performance for weekends, and what the bottom of Treblitt's doors looked like at home.

When Treblitt had actually opened the door, he flung it wide and wedged it with a small triangle of rubber which he carried in his waistcoat pocket. Then, his size tens splayfooted across the department's lino to his glass-fronted office. He never greeted anyone. That would come later. After he had made a successful foray to the men's toilets. However, he had been known to go all day without a single "Good morning". Everyone knew what that meant. He might just as well have issued a ten o'clock news bulletin about the state of his innards.

Safe in his office, you would see him take off his brown trilby hat, blow on its crown with slow deliberation and hang it up on the coat stand he had requisitioned as 'office equipment'. Next, he unwound his thick woolly rugby scarf, which he wore both summer and winter. It was an astigmatic creation of Mrs Treblitt's. It had thin wavering stripes of blue and white, more like an elongated humbug than a garment. But Treblitt gave it the full status of "rugger scarf" whenever he referred to it, although Dummock claimed he'd never seen a rugger match in his life, and Percy Jackson (who had a drawing board next to Dummock's) swore Treblitt believed that a rugby ball was a football that had gone misshapen in the laundromat.

34

After the scarf came the overcoat, a thick herring-bone job. He made a concession to the official announcement that summer had begun by discarding this article on the due date, but he'd never yet completed a whole summer overcoatless.

Last of all, he would remove his bicycle clips and arrange his trousers as best he could around the neck of his boots. Being a great believer in the beneficial effects of pedalling movements, Treblitt always cycled to work.

Finally, he hung his bicycle clips on a nail he had had knocked specially into his office door, which was, as yet, also propped wide open. Be prepared! Treblitt hadn't been a Boy Scout for nothing. Oh, dear no! Preparation was one thing Treblitt was good at. It was completion that he wasn't so good at, except in regard to his natural functions, which he was superb at.

The bicycle clips completed the first movement of the ritual. The second movement was, you might say, a surreptitious advance to the high altar. Paradoxically enough, this consisted in Treblitt's complete and utter immobility. He sat at his desk, obtruded his already protuberant stomach, clasped his fat soft hands across his navel, and contemplated his knuckles. His knuckles looked blurred through the fuzz of his moustache, which interested him. After a time he would close his eyes and appear to be fast asleep.

Newcomers to the Drawing Office were lulled into a sense of security by this period of absolute stillness. But they were soon rattled out of it by what seemed to have been occasioned by a minor explosion under Treblitt's chair, figuratively speaking. It would shoot backwards, teeter and topple. Meanwhile, Treblitt would erupt ataxically, his arms and legs appearing to be ready for blast-off, but, as yet, still attached to their ground stations, while the bulk and substance of Treblitt would be already off on a trajectory aimed straight through his office door for the propped-open door of the Drawing Office. In a twinkle, he'd be down the stairs and on course for the men's lavatories.

Behind him, there'd be a swirl of tracings and sketches on the boards he'd passed closest to and the smell of Cherry Blossom boot-polish.

That was the end of the third movement.

Jonty murmured to himself: "The Fourth Movement is, of course, familiar to everybody," and added the phrase IMPOSSIBLE TO DISTINGUISH BETWEEN DEATH AND NATURAL ACTION to his semi-completed letter on behalf of the management. Not that there was any connexion between Treblitt's daily communion and the letter, but he felt that it was appropriate in some elusive fashion. Jonty tried to keep his mind on the task of composition, but he found it difficult. Usually, he romped through a job like this, relishing every word. But that little contretemps the previous day on the stairs with Dummock had upset him more than he had realized.

"Must be going soft," he muttered angrily. "At this rate, I'll be a scoutmaster before I know it."

He tried again. But he had not been going long when there was another distraction. Dummock had set out his gruesome game of chess and was calling for an opponent, but not even Percy Jackson seemed interested this morning.

Dummock's chess set was completely homemade. It happened like this. At certain times of the year, wasps plagued the office, buzzing around heads, sizzling at the windows. When it wasn't "wapses" — as Dummock called them — it was bluebottles or the humble housefly. (A factory nearby that manufactured a well-known brand of jams was the culprit.) So when Treblitt was in conference, Dummock went in for a carnival of insect-trapping.

He kept his own special wire-mesh fly swatter in a drawer. (The plastic kind was no good; according to Dummock, only the wiry version could be wielded with right delicacy of touch, to simply stun them and not execute them.) When he saw a victim alight, or pause, or slow down, 'plop', he had one, down on its back, gyrating helplessly.

"That's a nice fat one. Make a good bishop."

"You're a sadist, Dummnock," said Jonty.

"Thanks for the compliment, I'm sure," replied Dummock. "But I doubt if De Sade would agree."

He was leaping here, pirouetting there, pointing here, and all the time 'plop' went the swatter. 'Plop'. 'Plop'. He never needed more than one swipe per insect. His aim was Olympic standard. As each one fell, in almost one continuous movement, he swept it into an empty jam jar and snapped on the metal lid which had breathing holes, and sighed with satisfaction.

His supply never ran out. He kept them in one of the drawers of his long table beside his drawing board. Even Jonty refused to contemplate how he kept them alive.

After his trapper's session, Dummock had gone into his fret worker's act; but it was a different kind of fret from the usual. He watched him setting about completing his 'chessmen'. They were made of cork and pins. Dummock had got himself a good supply of cork bungs from the Works Stores, the kind they used in the drums of the Hardening Shop fluids. The corks were about one to one and half inches in diameter, and two inches deep. From each bung, Dummock sliced several discs of cork, about the thickness of a matchstick, with his razorblade. He took one disc for the bottom and one for the top of his chessman, and after carefully pushing his straight pins through the top disc all round the circumference, he deftly pressed the other disc onto their points, and lo and behold he had a miniature cage.

It was wasps against bluebottles, buzzing angrily in the little arena of each cage.

"Anybody for chess?" asked Dummock once more. "What about you, Arnold boy?"

Jonty turned down a thumb emphatically, like Nero. "Not me," he said. "I'm not fond of death in the arena."

"Suit yourself." Dummock shrugged.

"Thanks," said Jonty. "I will."

Dummock tried again. There were no takers.

"Oh, well, I'll have to work out a few crafty moves of my own then."

And he opened the long drawer next to his board and began to study its interior intently.

Jonty hated insects. But all his sympathies were with the bluebottles, as repulsive as they were, because if the bluebottles lost the game Dummock put them in a jar full of wapses and tried to get them stung to death. No wonder he was fond of Bulwer Lytton, one of the nineteenth-century opium traders. Jonty made a mental note to ask

Dummock if he'd actually read De Sade, or if he was, once again, bullshitting.

Jonty put the finishing touches to the Management letter, for which they would show no gratitude, and stood up. The office clock said nine twenty. He'd have just enough time to rush downstairs and, after making sure that the coast was clear, pin it up on one of the most prominent noticeboards before Treblitt got in.

Jonty had his eye on the large posh noticeboard in the reception foyer of the Public Relations Office. Jonty had an enthusiastic belief in poetic justice, like Percy Bysshe Shelley, and one day Jonty intended to write an essay about it.

On his way out of the Drawing Office Jonty changed his mind about the foyer of the Public Relations Office. Not only would it probably be busy on a Monday morning, but his notice was likely to be seen only by management types, not the voters that made up Jonty's most avid reading public.

He went down the creaky stairs to the clocking-in area on tiptoe and peered round the corner of the wall. It was too late even for latecomers, and there was only one Treblitt, and the time-clerk wouldn't be collecting the cards until 9.35a.m. Another ten minutes at least. He could almost hear the four clocks ticking. Except for the dull whine of the machine shop to the right of the clocks, it was quiet. Treblitt's masculine haven sat to the left of the clocks awaiting his arrival.

Gingerly, Jonty extended the tip of his suedes downward and stopped midway, like a snapshot. What was that? The two rubber plants that the Management had placed on the black and white tiled floor to prettify the area went on ignoring him, and continued quietly to produce whatever they did or did not produce. 'Must have imagined the noise,' thought Jonty. He looked critically at the plants. If by some remote chance it WAS rubber they produced, Jonty felt firmly that it would be the kind that soon went porous and broke when you stretched it... Burke's, Charles's and Long's products did that — in one way or another.

Jonty completed his deferred downward step and surveyed about him. The door facing, which led to Archie Casbolt's cubicle for the Works Police, was firmly closed. The way seemed clear. Jonty tiptoed delicately down the remaining stairs and catfooted over to the large softboard beside the entrance.

The board was very full. Not a single blank space.

'Still, we all have to make sacrifices in the face of a greater cause.'

Pulling down a notice that warned people about petty pilfering, Jonty screwed it up and put it in his pocket for disposal later. Anyway, he needed the drawing pins to fix his own notice in a carefully prominent position. He had decided exactly where to put it as he was creeping down the stairs.

Jonty stood back and surveyed his handiwork. It wasn't quite right. He put it right and stepped back once more. He was satisfied. Although a long communication, Jonty smiled. He felt it had punch. He read it again, appreciatively.

NOTICE

TO ALL SHOP FOREMEN

IT HAS RECENTLY COME TO THE ATTENTION OF THE MANAGEMENT THAT EMPLOYEES HAVE BEEN DYING ON THE JOB AND EITHER NEGLECTING OR REFUSING TO FALL OVER. THIS PRACTICE MUST STOP FORTHWITH. ANY EMPLOYEE FOUND DEAD ON THE JOB, EITHER IN AN UPRIGHT OR A PRONE POSITION, WILL BE IMMEDIATELY DROPPED FROM THE PAYROLL.

IN FUTURE, IF IT IS OBSERVED THAT AN EMPLOYEE HAS MADE NO MOVEMENT FOR A PERIOD OF NOT LESS THAN TWO HOURS, IT WILL BE REGARDED AS THE FOREMAN'S DUTY TO INVESTIGATE. AS IT IS ALMOST IMPOSSIBLE TO DISTINGUISH BETWEEN DEATH AND THE NATURAL MOVEMENT OF CERTAIN EMPLOYEES. FOREMEN ARE CAUTIONED THAT THIS TIME LIMIT MUST BE RIGIDLY ADHERED TO. THE MANAGEMENT HAS NO WISH TO HAVE A STRIKE ON ITS HANDS. IT IS

GENERALLY CONSIDERED AN AUTHENTIC TEST TO HOLD A PAYPACKET IN FRONT OF THE SUSPECTED EMPLOYEE'S EYES. THIS TEST, HOWEVER, MUST BE APPLIED WITH DISCRETION, AS CASES HAVE BEEN REPORTED IN WHICH THE CONDITIONED REFLEX HAS BEEN SO DEEPLY INDUCED THAT THE HANDS OF SUCH AN EMPLOYEE HAVE BEEN KNOWN TO MAKE A SPASMODIC CLUTCH, EVEN AFTER RIGOR MORTIS HAS SET IN.

(SIGNED: MAJOR H.B. KNOWLES) WORKS MANAGER

Jonty had just managed to finish reading his handiwork when he heard the muffled voice of Archie Casbolt greeting someone coming in. Nipping smartly onto the creaky stairs and ascending fast, Jonty heard the well-known clumping begin to cross the tiles, and the tuneless humming that characterised most of Treblitt's conscious life.

But Jonty knew he was safe from detection for now, because Treblitt always stopped to read the noticeboard from beginning to end before going up to the Drawing Office. The humming clumps went across to the noticeboard. The clumping stopped. The humming went on.

Jonty bent low on the upper steps of the staircase. He could just peer below the joists of the floor at the top of the stairs. Directly in his line of vision were two gleaming Cherry-blossomed boots, an inch of dizzy-coloured socks, and two bicycle clips restraining Treblitt's already restrained fifteen-inch bottoms. Treblitt was in front of the noticeboard.

Jonty crouched lower. The whole of Treblitt appeared.

As usual, he was exhibiting the classic posture of lordosis: stomach forward, shoulders rounded backwards, neck thrust forward, arms hanging loosely, the knuckles somewhere in the region of the posteriors. He had pushed his hat (which bore a strong resemblance to that worn by the old-time comic, Bud Flanagan) to the back of his head, and had set about chewing the bedraggled ends of his moustache, which he was doing with relish. He was also humming

'Land of Hope & Glory' with relish, as his eyes went over the routine notices of factory life.

Treblitt's humming stopped. No wavering, no fading – just silence. The hope and the glory had dreadfully and distinctly gone. Jonty heard, quite clearly, a gulp; and then Treblitt's head jerked backwards out of his field of vision.

"My God! This is serious!" he heard Treblitt yelp.

It struck Jonty with a peculiar pleasure that Treblitt probably believed every word of it. Anything signed by Major H.B. Knowles? Even if it had been written on toilet paper, if it had somewhere in it the magic word 'Management', Treblitt would believe it, wouldn't he?

A renewed droning sound indicated that he was going over it aloud. Jonty couldn't wait to hear more.

"Treblitt's coming!" hooted Jonty, now at the door of the Drawing Office.

5

Men with rolled-up prints and newspapers were rushing about the office – thrusting, swiping, cutting, parrying, under desks, in corners, at windows, in the air, turning and hurling, whirling rulers, pencils, T-squares about their heads like Argentine bolasses. Whirr! Whirr!

"That damned young fool, Jackson," boomed Dummock in his Wellsian voice, "upset the chess board."

He was bending and ducking and swiping.

"The office is full of bloody insects."

"Open the windows, quick."

"Who's got an aerosol?"

"Where's the swatter?"

"Can't you use your fingers?"

"Ouch! The bastard's got me on the thumb."

The familiar clumping of size tens was heard in the corridor outside.

"Watch it! He's here."

Instantly, there were rows of immobile draughtsmen poring over drawings of suspension units and cylinder blocks with expressions in their postures and on their faces of agonised dedication. Backs, arms, and even the hair on their heads were showing effort and absorption in every detail. It was silent except for the buzz of wasps, bluebottles and houseflies; and the rather jerky breathing of some of the older draughtsmen.

The bangs and scufflings of Treblitt's first assault on the office door were heard clearly throughout.

"The debut of Rudolf Nureyev!" announced Dummock in a stage whisper.

The bent heads of the draughtsmen dropped an inch or two nearer their drawing boards. Jonty lowered his head with the best of them and squinted backwards under his lifted elbow. Treblitt was leaning over his stomach, groaning slightly with the effort of pushing his wedge under the door; his Bud Flanagan trilby slid gracefully downwards and rolled behind it. Barely audible sniggers came from various lookout points as the scrabblings for the hat floated through the office.

At last, Treblitt retrieved his headwear, stood up groggily, glared at the offending article, and made his way uncertainly ('A kudu wounded by Ernest Hemingway,' thought Jonty), towards his office. As he went, he brushed the knees of his trousers with his cycling gloves, walking gingerly inside his boots, that seemed today to be full of kudu feet and reluctance. Not like the usual gusto of his entry at all.

'Maybe my notice has upset him?' hoped Jonty.

Halfway there, he stopped. The habitual oblique angle of Treblitt's neck assumed the vertical. He was standing between two drawing boards in the middle of a row. His head moved jerkily about, watching something. He finished up looking straight at young Jackson, whose board happened to be nearby. Jackson was very nervous, but he managed to twitch in and out of a smile.

"Good morning, sir," said Jackson.

Keeping to his early-morning rule, Treblitt stared at Jackson without so much as a grunt. Then he resumed his kudu-footed way to his office. The atmosphere of busy-ness was oppressive. Arrived, Treblitt began his ritualistic disrobing. He managed quite well, until he got to his bicycle clips. They fell off their nail twice.

'Animism,' thought Jonty. Like Treblitt, they were ruffled. "All this exercise can't be good for his regularity, can it?" whispered Jonty under his elbow to Dummock.

"Put your saucer over that cup, can't you?" hissed Dummock.

Jonty's gaze followed Dummock's. Jonty looked at his unwashed cup — the khaki-coloured lees of yesterday's canteen tea were still in the bottom — standing on his long table. Three or four wasps were carefully exploring its perimeter.

'Good old Dummock. Trust him not to miss a trick.'

Jonty carefully lifted the cup, removed the saucer, and quickly capped it.

"Got 'em."

He turned round in triumph to Dummock. Treblitt was staring at him through his office windows. Jonty tried to appear as if he hadn't been noticed.

'What's up with him? He should be studying his navel by now.'

Jonty continued appearing to be looking right past Treblitt at someone down the office; he waved his arm to get attention and beckoned. As he did so, a wasp that had worked its way out from under the saucer began to zero in and divebomb dangerously. Jonty's faked beckoning turned into a genuine sawing motion of increasing distress, which he hoped was still near enough to some kind of sciatic beckoning to be mistaken for real. To Jonty's consternation, Treblitt started beckoning back.

'Oh, my crikey, he wants to see me.'

As he got off his stool, it crossed his mind to make a bolt for it, but decided in favour of valour for once. Jonty went towards the office. Treblitt was still waving his arm in and out. Jonty was nearly at the office windows when Treblitt spotted him. He paused, deadstill, and looked at Jonty with immense distaste. Jonty was unnerved. Jonty stopped in his turn, pointed his finger into his chest, gestured with his eyebrows and mouthed at the same time:

"Do you want me?"

Treblitt nodded and pointed to the windows that looked out on the street at the side of the office. Jonty went over, stood in front of them and pointed in his turn, feeling very stupid.

"These?" he mouthed.

Treblitt nodded. So Jonty started to open a window. Far from annoying Treblitt, it seemed to satisfy him, so he went on opening them until Treblitt sat down suddenly in his customary slump at his desk, which Jonty took for a signal to stop opening any more. This was Treblitt's full and unaffected response to the insect plague.

But in allaying one threat, Jonty had incurred another. Draughtsmen began, with exaggerated discomfort, turning up their jacket collars and muttering:

"Hey! That's bad for my asthma."

"Close them up! It'll give me the stone-ache."

"Brrrr!"

Now that Treblitt had gone into phase two, men all over the office began to erupt into short-arm jabs and galvanic jumps, in a contagious Saint Vitus's dance. Ebony rulers smacked down on shiny paper accompanied by expressions of satisfaction or disappointment. The expletives and blows, like crackerjacks and sparklers, caused Treblitt to shuffle his bottom restlessly and his eyelids to flicker.

"Don't wake him. It makes him bad-tempered."

"Yes! Quiet! Don't interrupt his communion."

As the wasps, flies and bluebottles found their way to the windows, the office got quieter, and the draughtsmen settled back on their stools in anticipation of Treblitt's coming sprint for the door. After ten minutes, Treblitt was still there. It was going to be one of those stubborn and unsociable days.

Jonty resolved to keep out of Treblitt's way, and had just made up a sheaf of blank papers with the copy of the letter he had specially written for such emergencies (using Work's Notepaper) displayed prominently on the top, and was fastening the sheaf to the clipboard he used as the sign he was on official business — in case anybody queried him — when Treblitt erupted. His chair shot backwards, sliding on the polished floor behind him. It was stopped with a thwack by the plywood wall of the office. The consummation promised to be unusually violent.

"Watch out for his slipstream."

"Jam your knees under your board."

"He'll move a six-ton press without blinking. You're right in his path."

Treblitt went out of the office like a V-2 rocket. His exit was accompanied by sighs of relief, carefully phrased obscenities or pious expressions of thanks, according to individual faith or temperament. It was as if some great national crisis had been averted. Perhaps it had. Daily newspapers — Expresses, Mails, Mirrors, Guardians, Chronicles, Heralds, even Morning Stars, Times and Telegraphs — appeared like large speckled oblong mushrooms all over the office. Dummock's stubby red volume of Machine Tools emerged from its hiding place and he knuckled down with satisfaction to his work. There was an air of contentment everywhere.

Things were back to normal.

Read Jonty, softly aloud from *Tit Bits*:

A DETECTIVE COURSE founded on 120 years personal experience of criminals and police methods. Individual postal tuition. EX-INSPECTOR DOOK (NETHER MERTON POLICE). 1 Old Summer Lane, Birmingham.

"Looks interesting. Mebbe I could—no – nooo! I'm not the policeman type. Am I?" Wishing he were, he began to muse, seeing himself as a Private Eye, a Brummagen Philip Marlowe:

"Okay, Jonty. Get out." I got out. He looked like any other cheap punk, only uglier. I catalogued him. He had six inches and 200 pounds on me. "Finkstone wants to talk to you, Jonty," a voice snarled through its adenoids. "Now, there's a famous name, Finkstone. Don't know the guy. What is he, royalty?" I said. "And put the heaters away.

I use razor blades." "Wiseguy, huh?" snarled Adenoids. I ignored him and took an inventory on the other shmock. His biceps were as thick as my thighs. He wasn't as pretty as Punk Number One. Just a lot bigger. I figured that a quick karate chop to his breadbasket would give him only a momentary diversion. So I had to work on some other kind of insurance. "Okay, Jonty. Get in." I got in. "Finkstone said to give you an invite to lunch," snarled Adenoids. He was the talker in the trio. "Oh, yers! Decided I'll be good for his digestion, I suppose?" "Thassright," said Adenoids. "He's having YOU for lunch." And he hit me. 'Curtains for Jonty, P.1.'

Jonty wrote a few lines on his memo pad.

> Dear Inspector Dook, I've decided not to take your detective course and could you please return my deposit?

Jonty chuckled and went on reading his weekly copy of *Tit Bits*. In every issue, the advertisements inspired Jonty to new flights of invention. He felt in a remarkably decisive manner that he was a small square peg in a very large round hole. Whenever he opened a newspaper or magazine, he turned first to the Classified Advertisement columns. He was beginning to apprehend that Jonty-shaped jobs were rare or even nonexistent in the world.

He turned over the page. Here was another wonderful offer!

> POEMS WANTED for pornographic anthology. £500 in prizes. Legal defence undertaken if required. Terms arranged. Royalties paid. Send MSS in plain wrapper to the following adres.

'Can't spell address,' Jonty smiled. Jonty thrust his copy of *Tit Bits* out of sight, lickety-split. He had heard Treblitt returning from his contemplation of the fundamentals in his life. Now, however, there was sprightliness in his Cherry Blossomed bootsteps and he had lost all trace of having them filled with kudu-feet.

"Morning, Jackson," said Treblitt airily, oblivious of his earlier reaction, as he breasted Jackson's board.

Jackson's smile switched on and shone steadily.

"Good morning, sir."

The day had now begun in earnest. 'Nothing succeeds like success,' thought Jonty, and began to review his list of failures so far at Burke's, Charles & Long's. His meditations were shattered by Treblitt's next remark.

"Oh, Jonty, I'd like to see you. Come in three minutes, at ten, will you?"

Jonty groaned.

"He got you that time, Arnie boy," said Dummock in a stage whisper, not even bothering to look up from his crossword.

Jonty responded by turning round on his stool and gibbering like a chimpanzee, while scratching himself frantically with a pronounced simian swing. It gave him marginal relief, only.

"Now, now, Arnie boy, ancestral rituals won't help in this case."

Jonty muttered a rude word under his breath, after which he felt slightly better and decided to get on with a bit of drawing — in case Treblitt showed the presence of mind to ask him how his tracing was going.

Jonty got off his stool in what he fancied was an apelike crouch and lumbered over to the bureau where the tracing roll was kept, swinging his arms and leaning on his knuckles. He could not help feeling disappointed when Dummock disdained to notice him. Extracting the roll, and cutting the paper to size on the guillotine, while still pretending to be an ape, proved too difficult even for Jonty. So he decided to play it straight.

Back at his board, he lined up the blueprint with his T-square, pinned the sheet of tracing paper over it, put a new chisel-edge on his 3-H pencil and prepared to draw the all-important centre lines of the elevations and sections exactly, according to the specifications set out in the manual Treblitt had presented him during his first week with the firm, DRAWING OFFICE PRACTICE by C. AUSTIN TREBLITT. Jonty wasn't going to leave anything to chance. No thank you! Not with an 'interview' coming up. The least he could do was to display the manual conspicuously, in case Treblitt came up on him from behind (which was just what his distorted mind would think of) and boom in his ear: "Finished it yet, Jonty?" Jonty blew the graphite dust from his chisel-edge and began—one long line, one very short, one long line, one very short, one long.

Ten o'clock!

Jonty climbed painfully off his high stool, already preparing himself for what he was going to tell Treblitt about the day he'd been absent. He decided he would have to have had sciatica. Jonty set about straightening his right leg until it was rigid and then began to step-and-carry-it with great care across the office towards Treblitt's citadel.

"Take cover, boys," said Dummock. "Here comes Hopalong Cassidy."

"Oh, so you've read two books, Dummock? A Bulwer Lytton AND a Clarence E. Mulford," replied Jonty. "No wonder you're so good at crosswords."

A few wry and amused glances were bestowed upon his progress, but he ignored them.

Jonty knocked at Treblitt's door and went in.

Treblitt had a technical magazine open on his desk, and he was gazing raptly at their coloured diagrams in double-spread and smoking his Sherlock Holmes pipe. Jonty stood silently in front of the desk, listing heavily to port. Treblitt did not appear to have heard Jonty enter, nor to have noticed him, for he went on reading. He was humming 'God Save the Queen'.

Jonty began to feel aggressive because of the pain that had started in his hip with the effort of holding his pose. He gazed at Treblitt's large pasty face hanging over the magazine and got only a slight satisfaction in regarding the sore-looking pouches.

6

'If a breadfruit had a face,' thought Jonty, "It'd look very like Treblitt. But with more intelligence. I wonder if it's possible to grow hair on a breadfruit and train it to smoke a pipe?'

Jonty began to wish he'd chosen something internal, a disablement that didn't show, like migraine, or the benz. Jonty tried out a short hacking cough.

Treblitt raised his head very slowly, like something coming up from a waterhole in the Namibian Desert. His eyes came back into his sockets from the innards of technical complexities unguessed at by the *hoi poloi.* When he had focussed on Jonty, he started nervously. It made him sit up and take his pipe out of his mouth.

"Well, Jonty?" he asked with irritation. "What are you doing here?"

"It's ten o'clock, sir."

A look of blank incredulity went across Treblitt's face, making him look more than ever like a breadfruit.

"Do you mean to tell me, Jonty, that you crept into my office just to remind me of the time?"

"No, sir, only—"

"—What do you think I've got this clock for, Jonty?"

Treblitt indicated a small travelling clock standing near his desk lamp.

"It's to tell the time by, sir."

"Jonty, you amaze me."

"Yessir."

'The silly sod's forgotten,' thought Jonty, and a sudden shaft of elation went through him. Treblitt's absence of mind was notorious among the draughtsmen of Burk's, Charles & Long's. It must have cost the firm thousands. Jonty now felt that it was safe to relax his rigid leg and stand normally again. He changed his position as inconspicuously as possible. The relief was wonderful. Next, Jonty changed his tack.

"What I meant to say, sir, was, I need another 3-H pencil. My other one has just worn out."

"Oh, I see! That's what you're after, is it?"

Treblitt, feeling himself no longer challenged, put his pipe back into his mouth. "3-H pencil – doesn't sound much like 'ten o'clock' ter me. Does it ter you, Jonty?"

"Nossir."

"So why say it, Jonty? Why say it?"

"Dunno, sir. Wasn't thinking, I suppose."

"Situation normal, hey, Jonty?"

Treblitt kept all the pencils locked up in a bottom drawer of his desk and doled them out one by one, to all the draughtsmen, senior and junior alike, as if they were molecules of uranium.

'Oh, well,' thought Jonty, 'it saves the firm a few shillings a week and helps to make up for the heavy losses sustained in battle due to loss of memory.'

Treblitt took out a little black pocket-book and consulted a page, two pages, a third.

"Let's see. When was the last time you had a 3-H, Jonty? Mmmmm! What do you do with 'em? Eat them?"

"Nossir. They give me indigestion."

It was out before he could stop it. But Treblitt had not expected that answer, so he hadn't heard it.

"What?"

"Worn out, sir. Used up."

"Jonty"

"Yessir?"

"Jonty. The date here — "

Treblitt tapped his little black book.

"I — I — lost the other one, sir."

"Carelessness! Sheer carelessness, Jonty. You're never going to make a draughtsman if you haven't got any respect for your tools, are you?"

Treblitt waited for a moment to hear Jonty's reply, but when nothing came he bent over and unlocked the bottom drawer. He fiddled about inside for a while and then took out a pencil. His face was on the way up when it stopped with a little jerk, and pink began to tinge his pallor. Jonty had heard a slight 'click' only a moment before, and was wondering if Treblitt had managed to slip a disc, when he realized what was wrong. Treblitt had caught the bowl of his Sherlock Holmes' pipe under the lip of his desktop; but he couldn't move back on account of his general stiffness and the size of his stomach. The glimmer of pink deepened a smidgen. He was beginning to show signs of distress.

"Use your hands," Jonty offered sympathetically. "Take your pipe out."

Treblitt gave a sudden jerk and managed to free himself. He had a short straight mouthpiece sticking out of his face. The curved lower half of the pipe had come away and dropped to the floor of the office. Jonty went down on his knees. Dark flakes of Balkan Sobranie and ash scattered themselves around Treblitt's gleamingly polished boots. The horn of the pipe lay on its side in conspicuous abandon of its usual Holmesian panache.

"Leave it, Jonty!"

Jonty raised his head and looked over the desktop, straight into Treblitt's eye-pouches. He looked very weary.

"Get up, Jonty."

Jonty got up.

"It's a funny thing, isn't it, Jonty, but whenever you're about, things seem to go wrong."

Jonty's fist impulse was to make a very rude gesture indeed, but he restrained himself, remembering his absence the other day. He didn't want to provoke Treblitt into any kind of a retaliation. Jonty contented himself with humming the tune of a TV commercial that had got the words: 'Destroy your facial hair with our atomic aerosol.'

Treblitt scrutinised Jonty with narrowed eyes.

"What was that you said?"

"I didn't speak, sir. I was humming."

"Mmmmmm!"

Treblitt handed Jonty his pencil with great reluctance.

"Thank you, sir."

Jonty turned to go, and went towards the door. He opened it, and was about to close it, breathing relief in three dimensions when Treblitt, in his most dulcet tones, said: "By the way, Jonty, why didn't you come in the other day?"

'Why, the old bastard!' thought Jonty. 'He's been having me on.'

Jonty turned, closed the door again, and confronted Treblitt. Was that a gleam of triumph above one of his pouches?

"Well?" said Treblitt.

Jonty remembered Alex's words: "Tell him the truth for a change."

Jonty drew a large breath and began.

"It's a rather delicate matter, sir. A bit difficult to explain."

"I've no doubt it is, Jonty. But—just a little suggestion from me—try, Jonty, try."

"Yessir. Well—er—"

"Go on, Jonty."

"Well, it's my father, sir."

"Oh?"

"Yes. He tried to commit suicide."

Treblitt took the remainder of his pipe out of his mouth and placed it carefully on his desk. He breathed in—deeply. The frayed edges of his Old Bill moustache shook with emotion.

"Jonty! I don't ask much from you, do I?"

Without waiting for Jonty to disagree with him, he continued. "After all, you come to work looking as if you'd just been to a Jumble Sale in Carnaby Street—that is, when you remember to come at all— you write rude anonymous letters to the management—"

'Oh, so you know about that, do you?' thought Jonty.

"—Oh, yes, Jonty. We know! We've been watching you. You hardly produce a drawing worth looking at, still less sending through the copying machine, and you spend hours on the factory roof reading comics."

"They're not comics, sir, they're—"

"—Never mind what they are! And now, you come up with this fantastic story about your father. You should be ashamed of yourself. That is the worst thing of all. Do you take me for a fool, Jonty?"

Jonty thought seriously about that question while Treblitt watched him. Finally, Jonty said: "No, sir. I don't think you're a fool."

"Thank you, Jonty. It makes me feel so much better to know you don't disapprove of me," he said heavily. "Now—what's the truth?"

Jonty's engine was racing madly: he said the first thing that came into his head.

"Well, as a matter of fact, sir, I went for an interview."

Treblitt sat bolt upright in his chair, which Jonty thought was a real achievement for him. He smiled expansively.

"I'm delighted to hear it, Jonty. I like to see a young chap trying to better himself. Any luck, may I ask?"

"Dunno, sir! Got to wait for the results."

"Yes, yes. Naturally. Ah, well, Jonty, I wish you luck, all the luck in the— It won't be necessary for us to—er—" Treblitt added in an undertone. Then, more loudly, "Well, well! But remember, in future, Jonty – that is, if there is any future for you here—" Treblitt laughed, shaking his stomach.

'That must be good for his bowels,' thought Jonty.

"Just take the trouble, next time, to inform me BEFORE you take time off for interviews, will you, Jonty?"

"I will, sir. I will"

"Good. Off you go!"

Treblitt was quite radiant with goodwill at the thought of losing Jonty to one of Burke's, Charles & Long's competitors. He resumed his humming of 'God Save the Queen' and, as Jonty allowed himself on his way to the door to draw at last his leftover breath of relief, Treblitt took up his double spread of diagrams and settled back on his lordosis.

Jonty had made it again.

7

Jonty had arranged to meet Alexis to go to Barry Crehan's pad – the first date after the fiasco in the Victorian Cellar.

Alexis lowered her well-shaped bottom into the driving seat of the plum-coloured Sprite and Jonty closed the car door with just the right clunking noise. He was slightly conscious that the scarlet of her dress and scarf against the plum of the car was disturbing, but the flash of the paler insides of her tanned thighs excited him and counterbalanced his discomfort. He walked behind the car to the passenger seat. As he got near to the exhaust pipe, the engine broom-broomed and spluttered something hot and damp onto his jeans. He bent down to brush it off. When he had straightened, the palm of his hand was filthy with carbon. He had just put his hand on the handle of the passenger door when he was nearly jerked off his feet by the Sprite accelerating away. He caught sight of Alexis's face through the open window turned slightly towards him, still angry.

"You can walk to Barry's!" she shouted, and was gone. He watched her taillights slew out of the car park onto the dual carriageway of the Bristol Road and disappear in the direction of Selly Oak.

Surprisingly, he felt relieved.

It was Autumn, a good time to walk. The way the sodium lamps lit up the branches of the limes and beeches, and the leaves falling, woke feelings in him he could not describe.

"There's always a lot of leaves in the Autumn," he said aloud, for no reason that he could see. "But they're mostly on the ground."

This observation somehow reminded him of a time in his boyhood, early in his teens, when he had first read the Four Quartets, and when his mother was 'alive'. But Jonty would scarcely admit to feelings like these, even to himself.

He began to walk more quickly, kicking his feet through the damp fragrant leaves.

'What's it all for?' he mused. 'What's this smell for? What am I for?'

'Dear Mother', he wrote in his mind to a ghost who was still alive, 'I am now twenty years old and I've quarrelled with a nymphomaniac who's squirted me with her exhaust. It didn't hurt. She told me she's been to bed with my best enemy, a married man of thirty-three illegitimate years who wears shirts the colour of aubergines, hand-made shoes the colour of loganberries, and lapels as wide as his morals. It did hurt. I'm not sure if he wears his shirts and lapels in bed, but I'm sure about his shoes. He fills them with mothballs and puts them under his pillow. I've got to walk all the way. Don't worry about me. I like walking. I'm fine. The Old Man's fine, too. He drinks himself to sleep every night and tries to do himself in every Friday so's he can have a quiet weekend. It's Autumn. Whatever they try to do to us, we'll beat 'em in the end.

Love, Arnold.

P.S. I'm thinking of changing my job, but I can't think of one I can change it for. I always read the ads hoping to see one that says ARNOLD JONTATHAN GODLEY WANTED. DUTIES: BEING JONTY. AT LEAST £6000 PER ANNUM. INCREMENTS MONTHLY. No luck as yet. What's it like where you are?

Your loving son. '

He was passing a pillarbox. He wondered why he should not post the letter he'd just composed to his absent mother. The crimson paint of the pillarbox had turned a muddy brown under the sodium orange glow of the street lamps. He put his empty hand into the slot, and laughed, posting the imaginary letter.

'That'll give the GPO a headache,' he thought. 'But who knows? Technological advances. Satellites. Telepathy. It's wonderful! One more abortive attempt? Pillar boxes – the thousand and oneth way of staying incommunicado?'

Jonty felt overwhelmed by a sensation that his life had been full of moments such as these. He was trying to say something, but no-one was listening. Or, if someone was listening, the listener didn't understand him. What Jonty was trying to say, he could not have defined. But he felt with a profound conviction that what he had succeeded in so far saying, he had articulated without utterance in words. Or, perhaps all the auditors were, in truth, stone deaf? Jonty discovered he was laughing aloud as he remembered how he often turned down the telly and watched them mouthing away mutely. Now, he realized why he found it so funny. It was just like life, wasn't it?

'Like that time I went to see Friend Lacestone. When I was a kid just out of school!' mused Jonty. 'What a joke that was! Called himself the Youth Employment Advisory Officer, he did. Advice! Couldn't advise a pimple to burst. Offered you choices from a set of organised insults. Take this one! Insults Unlimited! See yourself in the Big World! Here's a slot! Here's another! Take this niche! Or this! Or that! I told him, they're all entrance tickets to limbo. But he didn't understand me, Hadn't got his dictionary handy. "Work hard", "keep quiet", say "pardon when you belch", say "sir", and totter up in fifty years to get your gold watch – when time isn't what you've got. Not bloody likely, Professor Higgins! Vacancies for Young Men. Exactly. Vacant is what they are.'

That was soon after Jonty had left school. The interview had gone like a well-rehearsed music hall sketch.

"Come in, Mr Godley! Sit down. Do you smoke? No! I'm glad to hear it. Very glad. The Young show a lot of sense these days. I do! Smoke, I mean. Started twenty years ago. Now I can't give it up. Terrible! Terrible!"

Lacestone was a short man, built like a steam pudding, wearing ill-fitting trousers. But then, what tailor in his right mind caters for steam puddings? Not only were they too big, but their bottoms were too wide, and their turn-ups were too turned up, and they flapped round his ankles too much when he walked over to the filing cabinet to get Jonty's file. Jonty felt that 'walk' wasn't quite the word. It sounded like hyperbole, or a bit of insincere flattery. Lacestone moved like one of those toy men, Kellys, aren't they, with large wooden convex shoes that will only go downhill? It seemed that he couldn't bend his knees more than a fraction. What was it, arthritis or sheer affectation?

"Now!" said Lacestone. He sat down and opened the file. His nails and the insides of his fingers were the same colour as his teeth. What had he been smoking for twenty years — army blankets? A parade of deflationary images began to march through Jonty's mind, one-two, one-two. Halt!

Lacestone's high tones came in on him as he read from Jonty's file.

"That's right. Billesley Primary School... then a Grammar School scholarship... quite good at French... aptitude for... whose behaviour was... mmmm... not always willing... to... mmmm... absenteeism."

Unexpectedly, Lacestone looked up at Jonty and caught him watching him. Lacestone's eyes were startlingly blue and piercing.

"Were you a sickly child, Mr Godley?"

"S — sickly?"

"Yes. A lot of illness. That kind of thing."

"Not that I know of," said Jonty.

"Hmm! Just curious. I wondered why you – irregular attendance. – your – Oh, well, never mind, never mind."

The recitative of phrases from Jonty's school reports went on in Lacestone's unoperatic falsetto. Jonty stopped listening. Instead, he started to look round at all the posters on the walls of the office. Soldiers, sailors, railway workers, nurses, machine operators, mechanics, tool makers, bricklayers, and on and on — were inviting the Youth of Britain (in exhortations believed to be enticing), to become over-worked, under-paid, empty-headed and quick-about-it.

'Some hopes,' thought Jonty. 'Look at 'em! Smiling at shovels, saluting bosuns, sitting outside bell tents. Whatever next?'

He regarded steadily the brightly coloured posters crammed with 'job opportunities'. He wore an expression of pure and ecstatic cynicism.

Lacestone had left his operatic mode and was finishing his recital of Jonty's past in a thin high wine, the voice an educated gnat might use if really pressed to the dress rehearsal. Lacestone was a friendly man and smiled amiably at Jonty.

'If he feels like smiling,' thought Jonty, 'he's got the wrong report. Must be somebody else's. Maybe I can get a job under false pretences, then?'

"Now, Mr Godley," Lacestone had intoned, "I'd like you to tell me what kind of ambitions you have got, if you would. A young man of sixteen or seventeen must be full of bright ideas, I'm sure."

'Not this young man,' thought Jonty.

He looked round at the posters on the wall. Jonty was particularly impressed by a poster that showed a group of healthy-looking youngsters with shining, vacuous faces standing round a toolmaker's lathe that had empty chucks, but which seemed to delight the toolmaker and made him look more like Gerry Colonna than he obviously tried to be. The most interesting thing in the picture was the toolmaker's moustache.

"Well, there's nothing in this little lot, for a start," said Jonty, gesturing towards the poster. "But I wouldn't mind studying for a moustache like that. Do they give courses at night school, then? I suppose you couldn't make a profession of it, could you?"

Lacestone seemed somehow to be gaining density with the effort he was making to remain friendly with Jonty. Gravity held him more deeply in his chair. Perhaps Jonty was the kind of challenge he honed the edge of his dedication on?

"Noooo!" he smiled. "Probably not. But there are plenty more, plenty more. Just an idea! Give me something to go on."

Jonty was silent.

"We must start somewhere, Mr Godley."

"Yes, I suppose we must. All right, then. What about a success?"

"What!"

"I'd like to be a success. Like all those models in the Miss Universe competition. That's what they all want to be." Jonty added ingratiatingly, "You know".

"Ah, Mr Godley, I DO know. Naturally, we all want to be THAT, don't we? But what do we want to be a success AT, eh? We can't be a success in a vacuum, can we?"

'I don't see why not,' thought Jonty. 'You've managed it well enough.'

Then he said, aloud: "That's what the Beauty Queens want, isn't it?"

"Yes, perhaps. But we aren't beauty queens, are we, Mr Godley?"

'Well, you certainly aren't,' thought Jonty, 'not with ears like that. No lobes to speak of, just one sweeping curve of pinna. What a piece of gristle is man! What a face! What a suit!'

When Jonty remained silent, Lacestone revved up his gnat voice again. But Jonty could not tune in his attention quickly enough and only caught the tail end of Lacestone's remarks.

"...so we'll just think for a moment, shall we?" Jonty accepted his offer and thought in silence.

"Well, Mr Godley?"

"Pop groups!"

"Ye—e—es?"

"Any vacancies for them, then?"

"Er — groups – that's hardly the sort of thing we —"

Lacestone began to riffle through the notes on his desk in front of him. Jonty watched Lacestone's fingers with attention and was beginning to formulate a telling metaphor in his head when Lacestone said: "There's a nice little job here for an Apprentice Doorman at the Alexander Theatre. That's the nearest I can get to a pop group, I'm afraid. Will that do for us?"

Lacestone looked up, opened his clear blue eyes widely and smiled.

'Well, it might do for you but it won't do for me,' thought Jonty. 'And another thing, all this "we" stuff is getting up my wick.'

But he said aloud:

"What do you have to do at a job like that?"

"Do?...Do?...Well, I suppose... we just... look after… doors. So's the theatre's safe," he added lamely. "Don't we?"

61

"Look after doors!" said Jonty with unassumed indignation. "Any idiot can do that. What they want an apprentice for?"

"Hmmm! Er — yes! Apprentice means here—I'm afraid—junior. He earns — he gets less pay."

"I s'pose the Senior Doorman opens it for the fobs and the Junior for the rabble. Is that it?"

Lacestone lit another cigarette from the one he had smoked down to a couple of millimetres from extinction and thumbed the nub end into the ashtray in front of him: it looked like a miniature byng. He smiled at Jonty, khakily. Jonty still had his eyes on the byng.

"Yes," said Lacestone,"I suppose that's about the size of it."

It took Jonty a moment or two to realize that Lacestone was replying to his previous question, and not describing the ashtray.

"But do we play any instruments, Mr Godley? Are we musical in any way?" he went on.

"I wasn't actually thinking of teaming up with you or anybody, Mr Lacestone. I was thinking of going in on my own."

"Eh?"

This time Lacestone looked at Jonty quite blankly. His mouth fell open a little. The fresh cigarette stuck out from his lower lip, adhesively. A wisp of smoke wavered upwards.

"I was thinking of starting a new trend," Jonty continued blithely. "A pop group of one. I was going to call it THE ALMOSTS. It's a good 'un, that name, isn't it?"

"The Almosts!"

The cigarette waggled at him neurotically, like an admonition. In the mass of British youth interviewed by Lacestone, he hadn't met one like Jonty before. Lacestone simply couldn't help it. He blurted out:

"Jonty, I've never met one like—"

But Jonty was ahead of him. "Ditto!" he said, happily.

"What?"

Lacestone collected the pieces.

"Oh, sorry, Mr Godley! It just... it was a... what I meant was... you seem to be very... musical. Singer or instrumentalist?"

"Neither!"

"Neither?"

"Neither. But these days, ANYTHING goes." Lacestone laughed derisively.

"Even these days, you've got to have SOME talent."

"Oh, yes?"

Jonty paused for a moment.

"What about a conductor, then?"

Lacestone started to shake his head from side to side and went on shaking it. Then he stopped shaking it abruptly and said with a new alertness:

"You mean 'bus conductor', of course!"

"No. On the Proms, or something."

Lacestone shook his head again, this time vigorously. Jonty thought: 'If you're not careful, you'll rupture yourself.' But aloud, he said: "I practise in front of the telly."

The head-shaking went on, as if it couldn't stop.

"What about a pilot — Jumbo Jet?"

Shake-shake. Was Lacestone practising some kind of self-hypnosis?

"Stockbroker?"

Shake-shake-shake-shake.

"Seal-hunter?"

The shaking stopped, and Lacestone sat back, smoking like Vesuvius, with a glazed, seraphic smile on his lips.

'So it WAS hypnotism,' thought Jonty.

"Pope?" he suggested.

"NOT—A—CHANCE," said Lacestone very quietly, but with immense deliberation.

"All right, then. I'll settle for the Doge of Venice."

Lacestone sat forward aggressively, stretched out both arms sideways, and putting the ginger-coloured fingertips of both hands on his desk he crouched over them, as if he was about to do some kind of spider dance, while contriving to remain seated. He hissed at Jonty: "I'm afraid you're living in cloud-cuckoo land, Mr Jonty."

"Oh, so that's where I'm living, is it?"

"It is! Let's face it, Mr Jonty."

'Inside as well as outside with gold leaf,' thought Jonty.

"That's not easy, Mr Lacestone, facing it," he said aloud.

"Of course it isn't easy. I didn't say it was easy, did I?"

Lacestone was showing signs of strain. "But we simply have to face it." His voice had risen a tone or two.

"We have to start at the bottom."

'If we're going to use gold leaf, it'd be better to start at the top,' thought Jonty.

Lacestone kept on going. "We have to have some qualifications, don't we, experience, training!"

It wasn't a question, although Lacestone pretended it was.

"Well, I don't mind being an apprentice stockbroker. You can't need much for that, surely?"

"There's no such thing as an apprentice stockbroker! It's a job you can't train for."

"Oh! Why not?"

"Well, you just can't! Like all the others you've mentioned. Such jobs are not offered to beginners on the open market."

"Well, Mr Lacestone, if all you can offer me are jobs like delivering bread and polishing doorknobs and filing letters when I keep seeing all these other posh voters with lots of rolled umbrellas and banknotes, there must be something wrong with things, mustn't there? Hey, mustn't there? I'm not asking to START at the top, only TRAIN for the top. See?"

"I see your point very well, Mr Jonty. But we've got to face – er – "

"Yes?"

"—Facts."

He picked up Jonty's file and waved it at him.

"No General Certificate of Education. No certificate of any kind."

"Yes, but I WAS a Patrol Leader in the Scouts." Then added: "Jaguar troop."

Lacestone ignored him.

"Bad attendance. Actually, a truant, weren't you? C-stream, where they put the 'academically uninclined'. Isn't that the phrase? And the Headmaster's report, well, it reads more like a Probation Officer's casebook than – (Et cetera, et cetera)...Facts, Mr Jonty, facts!"

"Irrelevant."

"'Fraid not. There it is. Sad but true. And if you add to that," said Lacestone, striking the file a sharp blow with the back of his hand, "the fact that you haven't a clue WHAT you want to do with your life — well — there you are, aren't you?"

"Where's that?"

"Exactly my point. Where are you?"

Lacestone took out a fresh cigarette from the packet of Woodbines on his desk and applied it to the thin glowing slice of an end resting in a permanent little hollow worn into his lip. He puffed vigorously.

'Well,' thought Jonty, 'I'm in your exhaust, at the moment.' Then aloud: "But I know what I DON'T want to do, Mr Lacestone."

"Perhaps, perhaps. But — it just won't do, I'm afraid."

"Then I'd better tell you what I really want to do, hadn't I?"

Lacestone sat bolt upright at that, or as nearly bolt as the backbone of a steam pudding will allow.

"Oh, what's that?" he said, dropping his voice several tones.

"A poet! I want to be a poet."

Lacestone lost all his bolt-ness in an instant, collapsing into uncontrollable laughter. He became a cloud of smoke with a sense of humour. Jonty got up and left, and never went back.

That was how it went, wasn't it? Jonty kicked his feet through another bunch of soggy leaves. It all added up to not getting through what you wanted to get through to people you wanted to get through to. Now, there was this present balls-up with Alexis. However, her case was different.

8

'The trouble is cases are always different. Nature has built the differences in on purpose,' thought Jonty, 'so you can't learn to cope with life until you're on the way out.'

What did he want to get even with Dummock FOR? Just because the man was a natural-born, non-shrink, hundred-per-cent, man-made, rust-proof, double-dyed bastard? A no good reason to get even with him for, was it? Maybe not. But it was a bloody good excuse, and Jonty promised himself to think something out in that direction in the not too far distant future.

But in the meantime, there was still his attitude to Alex to work out. What exactly was it that he wanted to get through to her? Good question. Did he want to show her he was jealous? Had he become keen on her without realizing it? Or even partly realizing it? If so, he needed his head examined. It wasn't doing its job. Maybe it was vitamin deficiency? After a moment or two's consideration, Jonty decided that he wasn't all that keen on her after all. At least, not for any permanent arrangement. As for a bit of – well, naturally – she was a spot of hundred-per-cent. What was it then? Had Dummock's juicy titbit of information upset him more than he cared to accept? Jonty had to admit to himself that this seemed to be the most likely explanation.

In that case, what in the name of the Moderator of the Church of Scotland did he think he was playing at? Who did HE, Jonty, think SHE, Alex was – the Singing Nun? He was part of Modern Youth, wasn't he? Didn't he represent a bit of the permissive society? Hadn't he been taught the facts of life by Bernard Levin and David Frost? Otherwise, what WAS the good of the Press and the Telly? Wake up, Jonty! The reign of Richard Dimbleby is over! And now that Lord Reith has disappeared into the mists of the Scottish Highlands, Aunty Beeb is out of purdah. Why should I get so all-fired-up about a bit of perfectly normal nymphomania? You see it about everywhere these days. It's at the height of fashion and uses vaginal sprays of a delicate fragrance, doesn't it? Yes, it does. Jonty had to admit that he hadn't got much of a case.

'However,' he said to himself 'that doesn't alter the fact that I AM angry so I'll just have to BE angry, and face the fact that I'm irrational as well.' Having reached his conclusion, Jonty decided that there was no longer any need for him to write an IS THIS NORMAL? letter to Godfrey Wynn and get a guinea when it was published. What was wrong with being irrational, anyway? All the best politicians were, weren't they?

He looked around him. Damn! He'd come too far. He was very close to the University. The buildings stood out on the hill a little way ahead. He had come a good mile beyond the point on the Bristol Road he wanted. He could see the lights of Selly Oak behind the University, and behind those the lights of Harborne.

Oh, well, he didn't mind, really. Walking alone at night in the city streets under the light of the lamps gave him a sense of – he wanted to say *liberation* – but it sounded pompous. A feeling of — something. Perhaps anonymity was a better word to describe it?

The sodium lamps seemed to do something to the air, turned it into a kind of orange lymph that you could move through painlessly and still feel enclosed by. It was safer than daylight. People went by like pieces of coloured darkness, and you didn't even have to look at them. He could hear the leaves falling onto the Autumn ground, too. That is, if you ignored the burping of the motorbikes and the flatulence of the passing cars. If you stood close up to the trunk of one of the big plane trees, you could even hear the little tearing noises they made when the leaves came away from the cork rings on their stems. At least, that's what he told himself he heard. If he had heard anything at all. You

67

couldn't be too careful. Things made noises like other things, just to fool you. And things made shapes like other things, too. You believed you'd seen a flying saucer when it was only a cloud of Black Magic steam from the Cadbury works in Bournville blown over on the wind; or the general fog that emanated from the minds of the employees of Burke's, Charles & Long's . Things were never what they seemed; and they weren't even what they seemed to seem, which was a damnsight worse.

Jonty's mind went back to his encounter with Lacestone. Lacestone was all right. He did his best. And he did what he was paid to do, which was more than Jonty could say for himself. How could Lacestone be expected to fit Jonty into a scheme of things that wasn't designed to have Jonty fitted into it? Jonty knew he had been especially born not to fit into things, even though, if he had been consulted about it, he'd have given his full support to fitting in. He could say, in all honesty, couldn't he, that he had tried to fit, but all his knobs and edges and corners got in the way?

But that interview with Lacestone had been seminal. 'It scared the marrow out of my innocent growing bones,' he said to himself in self-defence.

He recalled with pleasure the three years afterwards, spent bumming around from one casual spell of employment to another — dishwashing, roadsweeping, doormanning — all the jobs that Lacestone had wanted to give him a career in. But he'd used them the way he wanted to use them, not allowed them to use him, keeping body and soul together his way, or keeping together whatever it was life had put together in his frame.

Three glorious years of free reading in practically every Public Library in Brum! Jonty knew which branch had which book on which shelf on any bus route a fourpenny ride from the city centre. How he'd whipped through them: Freud, Adler, Jung, Macdougall, Spearman, Melanie Klein. He read them as if they were novels. And the literary critics: Leslie Stephen, Edmund Gosse, Leavis, David Cecil, Kenneth Burke, Edmund Wilson. On and on! And T.S. Eliot, Dylan Thomas, W.H.Auden, Wilfred Owen, Edward Thomas, Robert Frost, Marian Moore. That was living! Especially Eliot, churchwarden *manque*, frightened of girls, fascinated by the sordid and the elegant, cane and gloves, dressed like a dandy, connoisseur of gin and sin. He'd read the

French novelists, the Irish, the American, the English, even Swedish. Who hadn't he read?

All that time, he'd lived at home and looked after his father. He did the necessary bit of shopping and housework and eked out his father's pension with the odd job, and they'd managed fine. His dad had been quite happy. At first. But woe, woe, woe! Or rather, howl, howl, howl, as King Lear put it. Governments may come, and governments may go, but inflation goes on forever. That is what had 'tatered' him. His father's first necessity, Ansell's beer, the water of life, had been in serious jeopardy and he'd simply insisted that Jonty find a permanent job. Work! His nemesis had finally overtaken him. *'Work! the very word is like a knell to toll me back to Burke's, Charles & Long's.'*

Jonty stopped walking. He happened to be in front of a privet hedge that was thick and luxuriant and high, and so he punched it very hard from exasperation as sheer and steep as it comes. Having done that, he felt better and looked about him.

He was nearly there.

♣

"What'll you have this time, Jonty, old son?"

Barry Crehan got up reluctantly from the Bauhaus chair where, for the last fifteen minutes, he had been ogling Alexis's mini-skirt, hoping to catch some brief news of her Paisley panties. He went across to where Jonty was trying to make himself comfortable in a small chair made from a cider barrel which Crehan kept for people he wasn't keen on. Crehan leaned towards him. Jonty tilted his head back painfully, and found he could see straight into Barry's more than usually hairy nostrils. They looked like Victorian coal-holes, complete with gratings. During Crehan's quarter-hour performance Jonty had been restraining himself from going into Barry's superbly planned kitchen, grabbing a packet of mixed spices, returning, and stuffing them, still in their unopened cellophane, up Barry's nose. It would have been easy. But, in the circumstances, struggling to offer his empty hand-fired pottery jug for a refill, he settled for unjamming his arms from the cider barrel.

" A pint of egg-nog," he said to Crehan.

"How to save 8000 calories without really trying," said Crehan. "You'll be lucky! A Double Diamond okay?"

"Okay! I2000, then"

When Jonty had eventually reached Crehan's after his two-mile detour, Alexis's plum-coloured Sprite was standing in the courtyard, outside the converted stables that comprised Crehan's pad. As soon as he walked in, Alexis said:

"So the Great Screen Lover decided to come, did he?"

And they all laughed. That's how he knew that Alexis had told them about their quarrel.

'Bet I know which bit she left out,' thought Jonty.

"You can laugh," he had said to Alexi's friend, Isabel, "sitting there in that floppy orange hat and granny boots, with that heavy string sack down to your ankles. That's not funny, I can tell you."

"It's knitted tweed!" she said, with indignation. "And it's only calf-length."

"Knit one drop six, by the look of it."

"Don't let him faze you. He's rude to everybody. It passes for wit in his tiny mind," said Alexis to Issy, but she was watching Jonty.

Then they all continued discussing Enoch Powell's latest exploits as if Jonty hadn't arrived. Since then, Jonty had made two attempts to seat himself beside Alexis on one or other of the numerous sofas, divans and beds that Crehan had carefully arranged in the space of his vast den. But, each time, she had managed to find some pretext to move off. And, as each move had facilitated Alexis's fanny-flashing exploits, Jonty thought he had better stop trying to get close to her, in case matters got out of hand. He was going to be very interested to find out when Crehan and company would actually deign to let him arrive. He had put up with Crehan's manoeuvring him into the barrel, although Jonty would have preferred to have got Crehan across it. At the moment, he was occupying himself with cataloguing in silence the punctiliously arranged items that Crehan had about him, and trying to find out exactly how Crehan had succeeded in achieving that blend of sophistication and educated corruption which was so dear to Crehan's heart, and which Crehan aimed at, and which Crehan knew he was good at.

Of course, the carefully unmade bed that Issy was reclining on played a big part in things and Issy reclining played an even bigger part in things. The lavender sheets were spotless; and Crehan's judo-style Paisley sleeping suit, flung with the greatest regard for effect, and balance of colour, was probably taken fresh out of the drawer that very morning. (Jonty felt that calling them 'pyjamas' was irreverent.) Furthermore, they probably imprisoned a delicate blend of incense and vaginal deodorant that had taken Crehan considerable experimentation to arrive at.

Then, there was the table. Its legs had been beautifully fashioned out of the disused blades of piston-type airscrews. By Crehan, presumably. Resting on the table was an oak tray of deliberately unwashed breakfast things, all of the best Scandinavian crockery. And then there was that monstrous drinks cupboard: many an immigrant family would have been glad to occupy. An unscrupulous landlord could have made a good rent on that alone. And the fridge. Look at it! You could park a Mini inside, as long as you remembered the anti-freeze for the engine. Jonty's eyes moved to the stinkwood coffee-table. With silent and glossy panache, a clutch of Weidenfeld publications, each the size of pavement slabs, flaunted themselves in appropriate modesty. It was vintage Crehan all right!

Jonty shook his head with some sadness as he thought of the grubby-wood table on which he and his Dad usually ate. True, their pink tablecloth did get changed daily — when his father bought a newspaper to follow the gee-gees with.

Jonty let his eyes wander.

Scattered about was all Crehan's photographic equipment: floodlights, reflectors, tripods, cameras, and what-have-you. And they weren't expanded polystyrene models just for effect, were they? No, they were real and functional and expensive. (Crehan had once used such a stratagem to fake an Epstein bust.)

But perhaps the largest contribution to the effete decadence Crehan aimed at was made by the room itself. Converted riding stables? On second thoughts, it could have been a refurbished granary barn. It extended so far into the middle distance that even the colonies of thick-leaved pot-plants growing up things, and in and out of things began to fade due to aerial perspective. Or was it simply cigarette smoke? Or maybe the heat-haze caused by Crehan's, fiercely effective oil-burner, that seemed to be fashioned out of bronze or rolled gold or something, about the size of the Selly Oak Crematorium?

Jonty was struck by the sudden realization that a man as successful as Barry Crehan must have something special about the physiognomy of his ears. Jonty reminded himself to get a good close look at them, sometime. The trouble was going to be finding them under all that hair. You couldn't call it long for these days: he hadn't got as far yet as belting it round his waist. Nevertheless, he could have got away with wearing shirts without collars, if he'd wanted to. But he didn't want to, as was evidenced by his wearing collars all the time; and that must indicate something pretty fundamental about the man, mustn't it? What was it? That was a question worth pondering—another time.

For now, he swallowed what was left of his Double Diamond, and waved the hand-made pot in the air to try to catch Crehan's eye. It wasn't going to be easy. Crehan was gazing abstractedly in the region of Alexis's genitals again, as if pondering his problem, or even pondering her problem, while Alexis talked at him with animation. Yet Crehan suddenly looked up, straight into Jonty's eyes, taking him off guard, without saying a word. His stare moved to Jonty's hand waving the pot in the air.

"Arnold, what do YOU think of all this paper underwear craze?"

When Jonty didn't reply at once, Crehan said: "Fill it yourself! You know where it lives."

Jonty let the pot descend slowly to a more usual position. 'Oh, so they've let me arrive at last, have they?' he thought.

"Thanks," said Jonty

"What's the answer?" asked Issy.

Jonty stood up and looked at her. She'd taken off her floppy orange hat and Jonty was struck once again by how golden and lush her hair was. You had to hand it to Crehan, his lighting was really very good.

"Don't ogle me like that!" said Issy, and laughed, a little drunkenly Jonty thought. "Answer my question! That's the third time I've asked you."

"What question?"

"Cripes! You're impossible. THE PAPER UNDERWEAR."

"What's paper underwear got to do with Enoch Powell?"

"Enoch Powell! The man's gone mad."

"You want to be careful. You're slandering one of our most notable public figures," replied Jonty.

"Not him, YOU!" shrieked Issy.

Jonty ignored her and went across to get himself another Double Diamond from the enormous fridge, returned and lowered himself into his cider-barrel with as much ostentation as he could muster, fully aware of Crehan's mild antagonism to him. No-one said anything. They watched him until he was once again jammed solid in his seat.

"Now!" said Jonty. "Back in the stocks."

"The real question is," said Crehan in his lilting Highland brogue and with quiet deliberateness ignoring Jonty's comment, "What has Enoch Powell got to do with paper underwear?"

"That's what I said."

"No, you didn't," put in Alexis sharply, "you said it the other way round. There's a difference! We're not that drunk."

'Oh, so it's like that, is it?' thought Jonty. 'As long as we know where we stand. Or sit. Or lie, depending on our circumstances.'

"Exactly!" said Crehan. "Exactly!"

"For God's sake stop your waffle, you lot, and tell me what's going on," mooed Isabel, now well on the way.

"It's not difficult," said Jonty, slipping into what he took to be a public-school accent, "when you chaps sent me to Coventry, just after I arrived, you were all jawing about Enoch Powell. That's all."

"So?" asked Issy.

"So now you're asking me about paper whatsits."

"That was ages ago. Before you got your beer."

'Didn't think you'd noticed,' thought Jonty.

He said aloud: "I'm not the kind to eavesdrop where I'm not wanted, you know!"

Issy giggled.

"Fool!" said Alexis.

Crehan laughed.

'It's all right,' thought Jonty, 'I can see the way the Wind of Change is blowing, even if Harold Macmillan can't.'

"At a rough guess," said Crehan, "I'd say that THAT has killed THAT topic of discussion stone dead, wouldn't you, Arnold, old son?"

"All right," said Jonty, pointing to Crehan's wide studio windows. "I suggest changing the topic to 'Introducing Our New Louvred Stairex'. THAT ought to suit you, Barry."

"Ah, you like it, do you? Cost me more than a little, did that."

"I believe you," said Jonty. "I suppose this photographic stunt is profitable, eh?"

"I make out, I make out."

Jonty thought of all Crehan's de luxe, melamined and laminated doors, drawers and cheque books, his stainless steel garlic-crushers, his electric meat-choppers, his remote-controlled olive-stoners, his graters and grinders, his flick- switch waste disposal units, and his amiable temperament which was, he claimed, completely safe with children. The commentary in Jonty's mind went on: 'Your remarks are good examples of litotes at their best, are they not, Professor Crehan?' 'Yes, I suppose they are, and that's without including my vibro-electric combined gum-masseur and toothbrush.'

"And all he can say is, I make out! Disbuggerous, isn't it?"

"Yes, Barry, how DID you come to be a studio photographer?" asked Alexis sweetly.

"Ah, well, it isn't easy, you know."

'There he goes,' thought Jonty, 'flashing his meiosis again.'

Crehan picked up his glass and took several large swallows, making his prominent Adam's Apple jiggle in his thin throat. Jonty wondered if he could have done it.

Crehan stood up.

"Come on, people! Let's have another drink, shall we?"

Not any too soon in Jonty's opinion.

9

The time Crehan went over to where Jonty was jammed in the barrel to show him the size and nature of his nostrils, Crehan was collecting in the empties and handing out the fulls. He lingered rather longer than he need have over Alexis, kneeling down to gather in her glass and to facilitate his angle of vision under the hem of her red skirt stretched tight across her shapely thighs about a millimetre below the point of her crotch.

"Same again, Alexis?"

'Not if I can help it,' thought Jonty.

"Please."

'What nice manners she has, hasn't she?' Jonty said to himself.

He got out of the cider barrel with some difficulty and went to sit beside Isabel on Crehan's bed. She was looking very woozy about the eyes now, but she saw him approaching and levered herself upright with care and deliberation, tucking her granny boots up underneath her and patting the nice warm spot she had just vacated next to her. He balanced his drink on something expensive beside the bed, then sat down as close as he could and put his arm round her shoulders.

"Snuggle-uggle up," he said.

She laid her luxuriant head on his unluxuriant shoulder. She smelled of at least £10 000 a year.

"Mmmm! That's nice!" she said

Jonty took the chance of looking across to where Alexis was sitting and she was watching them all right.

'One to me!' he thought.

She crossed her legs purposefully, her eyes glinted at him, and her mouth compressed itself. Jonty thought that this was probably the right time to congratulate her on queering Crehan's pitch and to smile dutifully at her legs. He did so—radiantly.

'I say "Snip!"'

She turned away quickly to watch Crehan at the drinks vault with no answering smile, and uncrossed her legs.

'And you say "Snap!"'

Crehan came over with a full glass of something for Issy.

'Well, he doesn't mind glugging the stuff out, that's one point in his favour,' thought Jonty.

"Come on, ducky! Here's one for you," said Crehan.

Issy snuggled in more closely.

"Not now. This is too nice. Later."

Crehan put her brimming glass beside Jonty's and went back to settle himself in his Bauhaus chair at the angle best calculated to give him maximum visibility in his favourite direction.

"I always think better with a glass in my hand. Where were we?" he said.

'That's right, where are we? Come on, tell us,' thought Jonty.

"How you started up in photography," said Alexis.

Crehan's eyes travelled slowly up to her face, rested there for a moment, and slowly travelled down again.

"Ah, yes!" he said. "Well, you've got to be good at photography, of course. That's the first essential. Whatever else you need, you need to be good at that."

He swallowed some Daquiri and jiggled his larynx a few times, considering what he was going to say next.

'That's another thing he's good at,' thought Jonty. 'But it's probably just practice.'

He picked up his hand-made pot and took a few experimental swallows of beer while stretching and tightening the arm he had round Isabel so that he could put his index finger on his larynx to test the success of imitating Crehan's performance. He wasn't satisfied with it.

"Hey! Don't do that," she said sleepily, "you'll strangle me."

"Sorry! Just scratching."

Crehan was continuing the costive recital of his life's little ironies.

"Well, after I'd spent five or six years at the Birmingham School of Art under Fleetwood Walker, I thought that this is what I wanted to do, so I did it."

'Who'd have guessed he'd been there under him? And doing it.'

"Just like that. Fancy!'

Jonty studied the prune-coloured stripes on Crehan's olive-coloured Rocola shirt and the slight flare of the line of his maroon hand-made slacks. The prune stripes were a good half centimetre wide. Perhaps he fired them in the same kiln as his beer pots to get those colours?

"But HOW did you do it? You can't just DO it, can you? I mean, look at all this stuff," said Alexis, flinging an arm out in a wide sweep, "you've got to have a bit of lolly to start with."

"Ah, well, yes! That IS the difficult bit, I must admit...."

'We're on the litotes again, are we? I thought we'd kicked that, one or two insults ago.'

"As a matter of fact, I borrowed the wherewithal from my father. He runs a little bookie's business. Does very nicely... He's got an office just along from St Stephen's churchyard in Colmore Row. You must have seen it. Says Midland Turf Accountants Limited, over the door."

"Oh, yes! Next to a saddler's, isn't it?" said Alexis.

"That's it."

"Now, the mystery of your opulence is blindingly clear. In my innocence, I thought it must be due to the special configuration of your earholes. Ah, well. That's it."

Crehan looked at him blankly.

"I beg yours," he said.

But Jonty was savouring the softness of Isabel against him, especially that heavy little swelling part resting on his ribs, and the beer was making him feel pretty good, too; so, he took his time before replying to Crehan. Taking all in all, things weren't working out too badly, notwithstanding and in spite of, were they?

"I mean, you had some help from your father."

"Ah, yes! Well, I suppose you could say that."

"That's exactly what I am saying. Didn't you hear me?"

Alexis peeked sharply at Jonty and mouthed "Pig!" at him with an appropriate gesture.

"Okay, okay!" replied Crehan. "I'm agreeing with you."

"That's what I thought you'd say."

"He's getting drunk," said Alexis, turning to Crehan.

"Oh, he's all right, aren't you, Arnold-old-hen? I mean, look at him, wrapped all round Issy."

"Haven't YOU got any vacancies—studio assistant, or something?"

"Not a chance, old hen! Anyway, you're not the sort of assistant I need," laughed Crehan, taking a quick look at Alexis's thighs. "I'm not that big. The old purse just wouldn't run to it."

"What sort of an assistant do you need then, eh?" asked Jonty, belligerently obtuse.

Crehan laughed again, this time showing his forty-eight fluorescent teeth and nodding his head in Alexis's direction.

"Like that!" he said.

"Oh, so you're in the girlie market, are you, Crehan?"

"Aren't we all, dear old hen?"

"THAT'S not the market I had in mind, Crehan. You knew that, didn't you?"

Alexis was looking anxiously at Jonty, recognising his tone.

"Oh, well, here and there, here and there!" replied Crehan, refusing to take offence. "Can't afford to turn it down really. Nothing pornographic, of course. I take care in choosing my models. Real art studies, that kind of stuff."

'Judging by your performance this evening, Mr Crehan, we all know where you'd like to place your zoom lens,' thought Jonty grimly. 'And it's in quite a different area from where I'd place it.'

"The big difficulty is in getting suitable models," Crehan went on, warming to his subject.

Jonty felt he had made a mistake in offering Crehan this opening, as his next remark revealed: "What about posing for me, Alexis? Hey? The money's good."

When Alexis did not reply but simply stared with sudden interest into her gin and orange, Crehan turned towards where Jonty was sitting: "Or you, Issy?"

Issy's answer was a hybrid noise.

"Dear Issy has passed out," said Alexis, looking up from her gin and orange.

'Yes,' thought Jonty, 'it seems safest, under the circs. If I wasn't here, our mutual friend would be getting through one or two of his perks, and his floodlamps would be glowing with avarice and sensuality.'

"No," said Jonty, "I'm serious about needing a job."

"Why?" asked Crehan.

Jonty recounted the story to him.

"It was completely his own fault," Alexis added by way of further explanation.

"Not at all," said Jonty. "Nothing to do with me. It's all in the stars. We're in the Age of Aquarius, you know. I'm Pisces. As a matter of interest, what are you, Barry?"

Crehan laughed aloud.

"Actually—Aquarius."

"We should have known."

Isabel murmured, like a comatose dormouse: "I'm Sagittarius."

"Don't worry about it, darling," said Jonty. "Bows and arrows are fashionable in some parts of the world. You just go back to sleep, there's a good girl."

He patted her bottom and turned to Crehan.

"Got any suggestions?"

"Thought of the Army? Navy?"

"Join the army and see the world. Join the navy and scrub the bleeder. Stop joking!"

"I'm not. The Army is a—okay, okay! Don't wake her up! Something different, hey? Ooh, I don't know. Haven't got a vestige of an idea, really. What do you WANT to do?"

"Nothing!" said Jonty promptly.

"Well—why are you asking?"

"No—I mean—literally. Nothing. That's what I'd like to do—occupy myself with nothing. Doing just what I like."

"Ah, well, yes. That kind of nothing. That's something!"

"That's why I'm working at Burke's, Charles & Long's and Company. It's the nearest thing to nothing I can get."

Crehan laughed yet again.

"But not the something kind of nothing, hey?"

"The only good thing to come out of that factory is Alexis. That's where we met, you know."

Alexis wasn't sure whether to be pleased at the compliment, or displeased with the outcome.

"Yes, I do know," said Crehan.

He sat up suddenly, out of his Bauhaus slump and said: "I've just had a good idea!"

"Going to take a Badedas bath, are you? Things happen after one of them," said Jonty, looking in what he took to be a significant way at Alexis.

"You take the bath! I was thinking of Tommy Wooton."

"How do you mean—Tommy Wooton?"

"That's what he did when he wanted to do nothing—became a student!"

"Good idea! But it's the money. Doing nothing costs money."

"Do what he did! Ask the Local Education Authority for it. Of course, his father WAS in a position to pull one or two wires in the whatchamacallit office. That's true."

Crehan quickly related the story to them of how Tommy Wooton and his father did it.

"Take more than one or two wires, in my case," said Jonty mournfully. "I'd need several octaves of them. Anyway, my old man isn't in a position to pull anything but a few pints."

"Try them!" said Crehan.

"No harm in trying, I suppose."

Maybe he could...? But he didn't really think so, not really, not with HIS ears and old Aquarius wheeling about up there.

"Anyway, cheer up, it's only for life. Have one for the road!"

Alexis shook her head.

"No thanks, Barry. The Sprite's outside and there's probably a breathalyzer parked round the next corner. I feel a bit wavy, as it is."

She put down her glass and stood up.

'That's the last flash of Paisley you'll get tonight, mate,' thought Jonty, meaning Crehan.

She looked around for her Spanish Cape. Crehan was dancing attendance like Harold Wilson at a Commonwealth meeting. He patted her, and smoothed her, and stroked her.

"How's that?" he asked.

Alexis smiled warmly at him, reaching out her hand to rest it on his olive shirt. Jonty noted wryly how they both seemed to like touching, patting and smoothing pieces of fashionable material. Perhaps it was something that came with maturity? If so, he shouldn't despair too easily, should he?

"I'm going to wake up Issy," she said to Crehan, "and take her home."

'One in the eye for me,' thought Jonty, who had other ideas. 'I'm not squeezing into that tiny space behind the driving seat and getting jostled by that trunkful of cosmetics she carries, not to please anybody. No thank you, madam! Not to mention your spare gallon of petrol and the smell of your Airedale.' She knew that, didn't she?

"Ah well," said Jonty more loudly than necessary, "better get the bus tonight, then. If you drink, don't drink, and if you drive, get a lift—as our elders in the Ministry tell us."

But his hint was totally ignored by Alexis, so he shook Issy gently and kissed her under the ear to wake her up. Issy's response was to moan gently and lean more heavily against him. Jonty looked up at Crehan and Alexis standing too close and obvious in the doorway, watching him.

"Have to try something else," said Jonty lightly.

He bent his head to whisper something in her ear. Her reaction was instantaneous. She sat bolt upright and shouted: "Don't you dare! I'll have you locked up if you do."

"Just testing!" said Jonty.

"What's he say, the obscene man?" asked Alexis.

"I was just trying to wake her up, that's all," protested Jonty.

"Well, you've succeeded," said Crehan. "What *did* he say?"

"Never you mind!" said Issy. "Where's my hat?"

Jonty handed her the large floppy orange disc with the tall crown. In a few moments, Issy was as ready as she was going to be for some time to come. Alexis and she were just about to leave when Issy said: "Excuse me!" and rushed off towards Crehan's 'smallest room', as he called it. So they stood about looking at one another, without speaking; at least, Alexis and Barry did, while Jonty looked at the two of them looking at one another. But Jonty felt disinclined to remain silent.

"Let me know if you hear of anything going for me, then," said Jonty.

"Eh?"

Crehan turned to gaze at Jonty without being able to focus on him properly.

'Please adjust your vision before leaving the premises. What's happened to your automatic focussing device, matey? Some photographer!' Jonty said to himself.

But as he watched Crehan's eyes slipping in and out of the images before them, Jonty found that he just had to admit that Crehan was very appetising to women: tall, slim, elegant, cooked to a turn and tastefully garnished. A dish for many a sophisticated palate! Quite a contrast to the plain fare that Jonty offered.

Crehan's eyes suddenly came back into focus and Jonty found him staring fixedly in the region of his sternum. Involuntarily, Jonty became aware of his hand moving slowly up to cover his chest, but long before he could reach the sternum, Crehan's arm and long forefinger shot out and pointed at Jonty's T-shirt.

"What's that?" demanded Crehan.

"What's what?" said Jonty to gain time.

He crossed his eyes and looked down his nose to the place on his chest that Crehan's finger was directed at.

"That!"

'Oh, Christ! Another sodding bedbug!' thought Jonty in a panic.

Jonty found Alexis watching him closely.

"Drop of tomato sauce," said Jonty.

"Looks like blood," said Crehan, doggedly.

"No! Sauce! I'm very fond of a good bottle of Houses of Parliament. Have it every day with my breakfast. In fact, it IS my breakfast."

Jonty pointed at the spot and followed it with a flamboyant flinging away of his fingers.

"Yesterday it was egg. Today, tomato. Tomorrow, caviar. Who knows? The way it crumbles." He laughed.

Under his breath he said: "The little bastard!"

Isabel came back, smoothing down her sack-dress just in time to save Jonty from further embarrassment.

"Thanks for the drinks," she said.

"Yes, it was lovely, Barry."

"Thanks," said Jonty. "I'll invite you round to my roadmender's hut, some time. Ciaou!"

"See you," said Crehan to Jonty, coolly. Then, warmly, to Alexis, "Bye, love."

"Bye!" said Alex.

"Bye!" said Issy.

Jonty didn't wait. He walked briskly towards his late-night bus stop. He heard Alexis's Sprite broom-broomhing off in the opposite direction. Appropriate! He resolved to set up another purge of the bedbugs at the first opportunity, and noticed that he was drunker than he'd thought.

'Dear Mother' he began, 'This will be a short letter because I'm drunk and I've had a girl who was drunker sleeping on my shoulder for the last couple of hours and I didn't do a thing? Is it my genes, do you think? But I did catch sight of a nympho flashing at a photographer. Or was it a photographer flashing at a nympho? Things are bit blurred. What's the best insecticide on the market? Keep in touch.

Yours ever, Jonty.'

10

"Dummock, you bastard! Now you're for it."

Jonty screwed his face into a grotesque parody of one of the grimaces he regularly admired of a Saturday evening on his favourite late-night wrestling programme. He held his trunk poised over his thighs in the authentic wide-footed manner, and then, in a very passable imitation of a lethal back kick, he suddenly whirled on one leg and shot out the other behind him to where Dumniock's scrotum should have been.

Afterwards, he fell over.

"Well," he said comfortably from the floor, "that won't bloody do!"

Jonty was at home—working out the tactics of his 'getting-even-with-Dummock' campaign. He had pushed the white-wood table back against the wall (complete with its covering of the Pink'un), piled up the chairs, stood the folding bed on end because it wouldn't fold, and spread some pillows and cushions in front of the full-sized outline of a man he had sellotaped to the wallpaper. All the nerve-points and other vulnerable spots were marked in vermilion red.

That very morning, Saturday, a large brown envelope had fallen with a heavy and belligerent thud from the letterbox onto the lino in the hall, a long-awaited answer to Jonty's reply to an advertisement in *Tit-Bits*. As he thought of Dummock, Jonty found the recollection of that thud particularly satisfying and smiled grimly. He began work at once.

He was learning Karate.

Starting to square up and try again, Jonty fixed his eye on a nasty-looking vermilion spot just below his adversary's kneecap. This time, what he was about to deliver was going to be fatal. But before he could execute another *pirouette*, a thunderous rapping commenced on the front door, which upset his balance once again. He teetered for a moment, paused, recovered, and once more stood crouched on two feet.

"Oh, Christ, who's that?"

He was badly disappointed. He had been looking forward to perfecting Dummock's deathblow. He straightened up slowly, trying to ignore what sounded like an armed band of Treblitts trying to get in, and walked reluctantly to the front door.

"All right, all right! I'm coming."

The room opened onto a hallway little bigger than a packet of twenty cigarettes, from which the stairs led to the bedrooms. The assault on the front door continued unabated, to which Jonty listened with some attention. There was an interesting clinking component in the racket which he couldn't quite place but which was quite clearly heard now that he was close to it. Jonty took hold of the doorknob, turned it and pulled with great decisiveness. It didn't move.

"Wait a minute! It's stuck! Stop it!"

He pulled again. This time, the door came open with a whump! Jonty found himself spreadeagled and sprawled against the lower steps of the staircase, and beheld his father watching him with great interest from his wheelchair, with two full bottles of beer held at the ready for a further assault on the door of 21 Cheese Grove.

"Oh," said his father scornfully, "just got up, have you? Fine time to be sleeping."

Pyjamas were the nearest things that Jonty had to a Karate set.

"I've not," he said weakly.

His father's eyes settled on Jonty's skinny calves below the rolled-up pyjama trousers, and he lowered the two bottles of beer pointedly onto his knees as if all the strength was going out of him.

"Oh, I see! You must be going paddling then."

Jonty ignored him.

He found he could ignore his father almost at will – almost but not quite – so he was working on ignoring him more efficiently; he felt the effects would be generally beneficial. Jonty's father, in his turn, was good at ignoring Jonty. Very good. Son-and-father ignoring flourished in the Godley household; in fact, it was the basis of their harmonious relationship. The similarity of their neuroses, hates, fantasies and irritations made it not only a luxury that both could enjoy, but a necessity of everyday living. Without this valuable skill, which Jonty had worked hard at acquiring, there might have been a heavy toll on the battlefields of Cheese Grove. As it was, father and son got on mightily and had learned to respect each other, even though it was part of the code to pretend not to notice too carefully each other's feelings, or not to respect them too obviously. But, all the same, each listened very carefully to what the other one said, and even more carefully to what he did not say. That was also part of the code.

"Had a good morning at The Block & Chopper, Dad?" asked his son, considerately.

"Not bad. Lost at dominoes again, o' course."

"Back early, aren't you?"

"When you're on a losing streak—pack it! That's my motto."

"I thought losing at dominoes was part of a bigger strategy?"

"Yes, o' course it is," said his father, with some irritation. "But packing it at judicious times gives it, well, authenticity, you might say."

"I see," replied Jonty.

"What's the good of a strategy if it doesn't convince nobody?"

"Quite right, Dad, quite right!"

Jonty knew the truth of this from his running battle with Dummock.

By this time, Mr Godley had manoeuvred the wheelchair through the little space at the front door and into the living-room which was also his bedroom.

"Damn my neck! What's going on here? And put this beer somewhere."

Jonty took the bottles from his father's outstretched hands and put them on the mantelpiece. One place was as good as another, wasn't it?

"I'm doing a spot of Karate."

"Well, I hope you ain't gooin' to leave that picture of Harold Wilson's nervous system pinned up over my bed. He makes me scream in the daytime when he's got his clothes on. God knows what'll happen at night, displaying 'is physiologgy!'"

Harold Wilson was Mr Godley's *bete noire*. That's why Jonty's father pronounced it 'physiologgy' although he knew the correct pronunciation as well as his son did. He could get more scorn into it that way.

"Okay. I'll roll him up and stand him in the corner."

"Too good for him! Gi'e us one o' them bottles, will you, son? Open it first, though, eh? Bottle-opener's in the drawer."

While his father supped his beer, Arnold went about putting the room to rights, or as near as it would ever get to rights. The bottle was tilted at forty-five degrees to the horizontal as Jonty finished arranging his father's bed against the wall.

"Aaaah! Lovely stuff, this," said Mr Godley.

"Want the telly on?"

"No. Sit down and let's have a chat."

"What about?"

"Haven't seen you much, lately. Out early, in late. Gallivantin' about with some bird, are you?"

"Was!"

"Wassamarrer? Run out of stamina?"

"No. Complications. Looked all right until the last day or two. But there's this bastard, Dummock, you see, he was telling me..."

And he recounted it briefly to his father, making it sound as innocuous for Alexis as he could, not knowing quite why he was trying to protect her. His father listened with attention, sipping his beer from time to time, and looking critically at the label on the bottle after each sip, as if it wasn't quite telling the truth about its contents. When Jonty had finished his story, Mr Godley sighed: "Ah, well, son, a slice off a cut loaf isn't missed. ....Women!" He snorted. "You'll find a nice fresh lass, one of these days. How's the job?"

Jonty looked at his father pensively before answering.

Was the old man being callous, or changing the subject out of a kind of tact? In this case, Jonty wasn't sure, but gave him the benefit of the doubt. What would he have done in the old man's place? Psychologically, there were distinct differences between them, but Jonty couldn't help noticing, yet again, how much like his father, physically, he was: the same slight neatly-made frame, the curly hair (grey on his father), the spectacles, the same pent-up energy, that had, of course, to seek its outlets in different ways, but essentially there in father and son. His father's fingers were rarely still. He watched them, moving continually picking and pulling and twitching at the blankets round his knees. It always distressed his son to see them like that. Obscurely, they reminded him of blind small scuttling animals, disturbing and elusive in their anonymity.

"I'm looking around again," he said, eventually.

"For a job or a lass?"

"Both, I s'pose. But more for a job."

"Get one with no work attached to it! Working for a living's a mug's game. Look at me! Thirty-five years on the railways. Now this!"

He looked down at himself in the wheelchair, pointing with the empty beer bottle.

"What a piss-up to be in! Oh, yes, the pension! Some poor buggers get damn-all."

"Yes, Dad, I know." Jonty sighed.

"All me life, I've been a daft bugger trying to go up on a down line, avoiding a head-on by a joodishious – that's the word – joodishious," the elder Jonty relished the elongation, "by a judicious use of the points and signals. Clackety-ackety-ack! Then, whoof! into a siding, just in time. And here I sit."

"Yes, Dad, I know. You told me before."

"Like the Prime Minister heading for the Trades Union Congress Express. Bam! Result: industry out cold, and British exports in limbo on a stretcher. Then in zooms 'Inflation', its klaxon getting higher and higher. All I got is this bloody wheelchair. Gie us another of them Ansells," said the elder Godley suddenly, indicating the mantelpiece where three full bottles still remained.

'Oh, Christ, here we go again,' thought Jonty wearily, as he handed his father the full bottle of beer, and placed the empty one in the grate. Jonty tried to divert the flow of his father's rhetoric onto a local line. He always stuck to his story that he'd had an accident on the railways, whereas Jonty knew he'd got himself invalided out of the Royal Air Force at the end of World War Two by taking some sort of potion. It had left him with a duodenal ulcer and all the nerves around his pelvis in confusion. The wheelchair was only a device for disguise. When nobody was around, his father got up from the chair and walked about. Slowly! But he walked.

"What do you think I should do, then, Dad?"

"And here I's'll sit for the rest of me natural," his father persisted.

Then his father wheeled himself across to the table where he opened a drawer and took out a bottle opener. A small cloud of froth appeared like a growth on the bottle, and slowly trickled onto his blanketed knees.

"There's more bleedin' froth than beer in the bottles these days," he said, wiping his knees with his handkerchief.

Jonty thought his diversionary tactics had come to naught but he was once again surprised by his father's words:

"Well, son, there are three options, two respectable, and one – well – there's no single word to describe it."

"Oh?"

"One: you can drink yourself to death. Two: you can smoke yourself to death. Three: you can become rich."

"What about drinking AND smoking yourself to death?"

"There's always that. Or you can stay pure and clean and get a job with Alchoholics Anonymous."

"But there's no money in that, is there?"

"You've got to make up your bloody mind in this world, son. You can have money or virtue, not both. Making money's the dirtiest of all."

"Dad, don't be so extreme! Surely you can make money without being dirty?"

"Some! A bit. Not a lot. Never a lot. By definition, making a lot's a dirty game. Think o' Jesus Christ. He knew! That stuff about the camel and the needle. He knew! O'course—"

He took a big swallow of beer, "—There's always wrestling."

"Wrestling!… Look at me!" said Jonty.

"I'm lookin'. Yes, you're right. Better stick to karate with Harold Wilson there. I'd have more chance than you, even in THIS thing. What about football?"

"Football!" said Jonty, scornfully, "I can't even lace up the boots properly."

"I wonder?" said Mr Godley.

"What?" said Jonty.

"Gambling? What about Mr Big-Time Gambler? There's money there, all right. Cleaner way than most."

"Me! A gambler?" Jonty was incredulous. "I don't even know where a gee-gee keeps his crupper! Don't make me laugh, Dad!"

"You only have to know how he runs, that's all."

"You mean the way you do? With your daily losses on the Pink 'Un? No, thanks. And look at the hours you spend reading about the jockeys and the owners and the race courses and the handicaps and God knows what else."

"I'm talking about Big Time Gamblers, son. They don't do it that way. I'm small fry. I do it for aesthetic reasons only."

"Oh, you had me fooled. I thought you did it for the money."

"Only beer money. No! It's the aesthetic appeal that I like."

"How d'yuh mean?"

"Well, it's obvious, ain't it? Life's a lottery, a bleedin' lottery from start to finish. I'm just going along with the inevitable. That's aesthetic, ain't it? I'm just a little bit of the whole piece. I like that. Gives me a sense of purpose in life, gambling. See?"

"I'm not sure," said Jonty. "But I'll take your word for it."

"That's a good boy," said the elder man. "O'course, if I had me time over again there's no doubt about it. I'd be a crook, an' a bleedin' big one."

"Mr Big himself?"

"No doubt about it!"

"You're kidding!"

"I'm bloody not! Business, Big Business and Crookery are twin brothers. They just wear different clothes, that's all. Don't let that take you in! The rich do everything they can to make money, no holds barred, and everything they can to keep it. Dirty deals go on all the way. And me, as Mr Big Big himself, me, Thomas B. Godley, would do everything I could to take it off 'em! There's a very satisfying logic about that, ain't there?"

"The logic is that you'd end up in clink."

"There's always that risk."

"What would be the good o' that? The just society all over again? With bars. Same people running things. Same idea, different gravy. Not for me!"

"Look at the Great Train Robbery! They got a million and a quarter, or summat like it. Pounds sterling. Lovely!"

"Yes! And they caught 'em."

"Not Biggs. Not Ronald Biggs. He boxed clever, yuh see."

"He boxed himself into South America."

"So?"

"So! Another society, another jail."

"How do you ever get out of society, son?" asked Mr Godley, gently.

"I don't know. I'm working on it. Maybe you don't. Maybe you simply beat it. Just at the moment, I'm merely observing. But one thing is certain. The world is full of O'Gradys."

"O' Gradys?"

"O'Gradys. Sometimes they're called Treblitt, or Dummock, or whatever. But they all say the same thing. O'Grady says this. O'Grady says that."

"Son, I'm proud of you. You're a chip off the old block. I can see you've bin thinking. That's a good way of putting it. O'Gradys. You're right, son," said his father, warming to his theme. "They fill the schools, they're all over the place, in the factories, in the Government, the Civil Service, the jails. It's the O'Grady clan that puts up all the little notices telling you what to do and what not to do."

"That's right! 'Opinions not allowed past this point unless on a collar and chain'."

They both laughed. They were beginning to enjoy it. They had reached a fundamental agreement on the universe, they felt. The elder Godley was now into the spirit of it, and added his own piece of hyperbole.

"No original ideas allowed on the grass."

"Thinking allowed on odd dates only," said Jonty.

"No drinking allowed on these premises after all hours," said his Dad with feeling.

"Education sold in three drop lengths: maxi, mini and frayed," said Jonty.

"That's a good one," said his Dad, "how'd you work it out?"

"Haven't worked it out. What about maxi for the rich, mini for the idiots, and frayed for the majority? How does that sound?"

"Sounds right to me. Oh, it's a foine foine world, as me friend Murphy used to say. But, seriously, son, if you want to be rich, you've got to join 'em."

"I know. But I don't like the carrots they expect you to munch before they allow it."

"Well, there's the other!"

"I don't like the sticks, either. To me, if you go for the carrots, it's greed. If you settle for the sticks, well, violence is done. Either way, I don't want it."

"That's a tough spot to be in, son!

"You're not telling me anything I don't know."

"So what's your answer? What DO you want?"

"You mean apart from being happy, and having enough to eat, and all that stuff?"

"That's it."

"I'm not sure, But I s'pose I want to find out who I am and then try to be whoever I turn out to be. If yuh see what I mean? All right! Let's put it this way. What I DO know is that I don't want what the O'Gradys telling me what I've got to look forward to having. That's all."

"All? It ain't much if you say it quick."

"Look! I don't relish what they tell me I've got, and what they tell me to do."

"No more did I. But look at me now," said his Dad.

"At Burke's, Charles & Long's, I'm supposed to jump on the shovel every time Major Knowles says 'shit'. And if I don't, I'm out on my ear. What kinda carrot is that? What's worse is I'm expected to want to BE a Treblitt, or a Knowles, or even a Dummock. That's the way to the top, is it? And the others—fut!"

Jonty made the most disgusting mouth-noise he could at the time.

"What others?"

"The Great Train Robbers. The Biggses. The Sir Thises and the Lord Thats!"

It was the elder man's turn to sigh deeply. He did so. He now felt that the conversation had taken a direction he wasn't quite happy about, despite the basic agreement father and son had reached.

"Son," he said slowly and heavily, "take a tip from your old father, will you? Wait till you come of age before you go in 'thinkin' about things. Rupture your cortex or summat. Stick with Dummock, and your karate. Stick with Alexis and Dummock. They're your men."

"You insulting old bugger," said Jonty, and they both laughed.

"You don't want to end up like me, do you, getting yourself drunk enough to have a go at doing yourself in?"

"That's different, Dad. Nobody blames you for that. Not in that thing." He gestured towards the wheelchair. "My problem's different."

"I know, son. Why don't we have a good stiff cupper, an' ferget it? Drinkin' always makes me thirsty."

"Good idea! An' bacon and eggs for lunch an' the Sports Special on the idiotbox."

"Right."

It was only when Jonty was preparing the lunch, inspired by his culinary endeavours, rehearsing the letter he was going to send to Alexis, that he realized that he had already come of age. He WAS twenty-one, wasn't he?"

Jonty had had a quiet Saturday.

His father had gone out again to the Block & Chopper and Arnold had been able to catch up on his reading of *Vanity*, the young woman's magazine he was very fond of. Jonty felt that, apart from the intrinsic interest of the world it depicted, the magazine kept him in touch with the fads, fashions and failings of the particular range of bint he was interested in.

A close reading of the current week's issue had produced in Jonty a kind of hurt and brooding which he was only partially aware of. On trying to analyse exactly what it was he was feeling, if he was feeling anything (which he wasn't absolutely sure of) he had surprised himself by coming up with an image of himself, Alexis, Crehan and Dummock as a collection of raw ingredients waiting to be served up by circumstances. He must have been more impressed by the cookery section of the magazine than he'd thought.

What Jonty liked particularly about the cookery pages with all their careful instructions and recipes was the concreteness of the writing. Nothing fuzzy. Precise amounts of this and that. No doubt about it, recipes and poetry had the same common qualities: concreteness and precision. Maybe he should write an essay on it and expound the idea to all the eggheads? Maybe cooking and poems had other things in common? Could he, for example, compose a recipe that T.S. Eliot would have fully approved of; you know, modern and concrete, but full of allusion? After all, didn't he write a poem somewhere about a cooking egg?

This idea, together with the gastronomic vision he had had earlier, prompted him to take up a 2B pencil and jot down a few suggestions on a scrap of floral kitchen paper he happened to have hanging about in one of the drawers. A very appropriate medium for a recipe specially composed for his lovely lady, Jonty considered. Floral. Of course, it would depend on Alexis putting two and two together: that was the essence of allusion, wasn't it? Yes, it was, and she had jolly well better be cute enough to see what he was driving at.

Surely she would remember that Crehan was a Scot, for example? And she would certainly know the old saying about the third unwanted member of a party playing the gooseberry. Also, she was certainly aware of Jonty's antipathy to all varieties of cabbage, raw, shredded, boiled, steamed, diced or whole, and she'd make the necessary connection with Dummock, wouldn't she? Yes, it would be all right. The one thing Jonty wasn't certain of was whether her knowledge of colloquial, pornographic idioms was quite up to recognising the significance attached to the fig, especially by the Italians and D.H. Lawrence; but he'd have to risk that. He'd have to remember to recommend some Lawrence to her when he went on a lot about sexual symbolism and Italy. But wait a minute! Wasn't he now mixing up allusion with allegory?

'Oh, what the hell?'

Now that Jonty had persuaded himself by the force of his own arguments, he took up a fresh scrap of his floral kitchen paper and began to write on the back.

Dear Alex,

I came across this recipe the other day in my favourite magazine, 'The Church Times.' It occurred to me that you wouldn't like to miss it. It should go down well at your next party. It's a pity that gooseberries are not in season at the moment, but you might be able to get hold of a few canned ones.

CHILLED CABBAGE MOUSSE

1 large-headed hand-made cabbage

1401b. streaky Ayrshire bacon

1 small hairy gooseberry

1 fresh peeled unsliced fig

2 or 3 sly glances of gelatin

½ bottle of Dacquiri

¼ bottle of gin

3 or 4 oranges

½ pint of sour cream

sharp knife

stock

Measure stock to taste in large pan and bring to boil. Boil thoroughly. Add 1 or 2 sly glances of gelatin and allow to simmer until dissolved. While simmering, strip outer leaves from cabbage, put cabbage into soufflé dish, and pour simmering gelatin over cabbage. Place in deep freeze until required.

Cut Ayrshire bacon into pieces. Soak for several hours in ½ bottle of Dacquiri. Bring the mixture to the boil and allow to simmer for the rest of the night.

Take 1 fresh unpeeled fig, garnish with talcum powder, peel discreetly and pour in ¼ bottle of gin with orange juice to taste. Position in front of simmering Ayrshire bacon and wait for fig to split.

Next, take small hairy gooseberry, smear with sour cream and shave carefully with sharp knife. Take care to nick the skin. Bathe prepared gooseberry in cold water and toss from hand to hand. When finished, throw out of window.

Happy cooking.

Hopefully yours, Jonty.

Jonty read it through, savouring again the idea of Dummock embedded in gelatin, decided it would do, took a stamp from the tobacco tin on the mantelshelf, put the recipe in an envelope and went out to post it. When he returned it was already ten o'clock, so he decided not to wait up for his father to come back from the Block & Chopper. He just had to get at those bed bugs! His chose his weapon: a candle. He lit it and went upstairs muttering:

"Death to all bloodsuckers."

The offending mattress had been obtained by his father from a second-hand shop after he had once sold most of the good furniture in the house to fund his drinking. It was only recently that Jonty had found it to be infested.

11

On a Wednesday, two weeks after his sabbath attack on the bedbugs, the weather turned sunny and bright, and Jonty found himself (with a little surprise and a lot of relief) sitting on the flat parapetted roof of the Works Canteen, reading through the latest edition of the *Weekend Mail* in the fading afternoon sun. He had propped himself up against the parapet on one side so that he could, from time to time, look out over the opposite parapet and see the panorama of Tyseley Junction stretched before him. The static simplicity of the view made a nice contrast with the complex lasciviousness of the articles in the *Weekend Mail*.

But, just at that instant, some movement caught his eye and Jonty turned to watching the toy diesels shunting in and out of the sheds, and darkening and silvering the rails as they moved from empty tracks to black lines of tarpaulin-covered trucks. Why they moved like that was not obvious; basically the picture remained the same. However, it must have mattered to the small figures of uniformed men who kept going into the sheds that the diesels had just left, staying inside for a while, and then coming out again, gesticulating. There were other groups of small men to whom it didn't matter very much, however, as they just sat movelessly and watched those to whom it mattered a lot. But both groups wore British Railways' uniforms. He must remember to write a report on it to the Non-Time-&-No-Motion Committee of British Rail and ask them to explain it to him. Why was it necessary to issue uniforms to BOTH groups, for example?

To Jonty, it was all fascinating. He was struck all over again by the oddness of human behaviour.

Take pollution, as a case in point. Pollution was big news these days. To fulfil the purposes of the Clean Air Act, fumes had to be specially treated before they were allowed to belch out of stacks, as they were doing at the moment from the Smith's Crisp factory. The Act had managed to subtly change the colour of all fumes from a uniform black to a variety of coloured shades that even Warner Brothers would not have been ashamed of. Jonty guessed that the fumes were just as lethal as before, in fact, but now they were less visible and, *ergo*, cleaner. Jonty simply loved lolling against the parapet and watching it all. It satisfied his profound sense of the ridiculous.

Jonty sighed, folded the *Weekend Mail* and put it in his pocket. He considered he had read enough, enough, that is, to convince Treblitt that he'd been away for a reasonable length of time chasing up the prints from the Progress Office. Jonty supposed he had better take the precaution of making a detour through the Progress Office and carrying a few blank sheets of rolled tracing paper on his way back to his drawing board, in case the nosy sod followed his wont of believing the worst about Jonty on the minimum of provocation. Of course, Jonty had to admit to himself that Treblitt's worst was rarely as bad as the facts. Anyway, best to get back; there were only twenty minutes to go before the five o'clock hooter.

Jonty stood up and took a last lingering look at the sun putting out a long shaky yellow fingernail to the red roof of the crisp factory across the road, thinking that it looked a little sore where the sun was scratching it. Reluctantly, he turned away and climbed down the fire-escape to the Canteen below. In the Canteen, which at that time of day was empty, Jonty retrieved the hammer and screwdriver that he had secreted behind the heavy drawn curtains of the stage. He had borrowed them earlier from Jimmy Harris and he wanted to take them back to Jimmy in the Toolroom before reaching the Drawing Office. Jimmy was away for a few moments when Jonty arrived, so, when no-one was looking, he laid them quietly on Jimmy's bench, where Jimmy could not help but see them when he returned, and quietly withdrew. If anyone connected Jonty with those particular implements, it could be embarrassing later on.

Jonty reached the door of the D.O. and opened it as slowly and surreptitiously as he could, but Treblitt, who was slumped over one of his technical magazines improving his lordosis and his mind, nevertheless raised a frowsty grey brow and eyed Jonty with distaste as he entered.

'He doesn't seem to be humming, either. Bad sign,' thought Jonty.

However, Treblitt returned to his magazine and Jonty breathed a sigh of relief. He didn't even mind the derisive mutterings and quizzical looks thrown in his direction from various quarters of the drawing office. He reached his drawing board unscathed.

He noticed that Dummock's stool was empty. That made him feel better. Happily, Jonty went into a vigorous routine of lifting up and putting down and turning over and turning round all the drawings on the table beside his board, for all the world as though he'd mislaid a sheet of calculations. He probably fooled no-one. But it made Jonty feel better. Now, he'd managed to feel better twice in less than five minutes. Surely that was enough to offset the effects of Treblitt's frowsty grey eyebrow? Jonty was beginning to think so, and the palpitations in his chest had certainly lessened, when – dammit – Alexis came into the office. Why, at this particular moment, did she have to be wearing another of her sex-kitten outfits, one of her skinny-rib sweaters and a skimpy flowered mini-skirt, besides all the other things she couldn't help wearing, and carrying that irrelevant sheaf of papers? Why? He pretended not to see her and bent with tremendous concentration over his drawing board.

'I hope she isn't coming to me,' thought Jonty in some exasperation.

But she was. It could send Treblitt off the deep end! Jonty heard her granny boots coming up behind him and, as she got closer, the faint brushing of her nylon tights on the insides of her thighs. Jonty felt a vague surge of desire, then panic as he remembered the letter he had posted to her over a week ago. He had not seen her since.

"Arnold! I want to see you for a few minutes. By the clocks. Five. Okay?"

Jonty turned his head enough to catch sight of Treblitt trying to get his neck into the vertical so that he could peer over the intervening drafting boards.

"Go away, for God's sake!" he hissed. "Treblitt's got his peelers on me."

"All right, all right! I'm going. But DON'T FORGET."

Jonty worked on, not even turning round to watch her taking it all with her.

It was now very close to five o'clock. Stools began to scrape on the office lino. Feet shuffled, paper rustled, instruments clicked, drawers squeaked, matches flared, lungs sucked. But Jonty sat unmoving at his desk. He had resolved to stay like that until he heard Treblitt's Cherry Blossomed boots clumping their uncertain rhythm across the floor, homeward bound. Then he'd feel safe.

He waited in trepidation for the cherished sounds, straining his ears in the general disturbance made by the draughtsmen preparing to depart. At last, he heard the scrape of Treblitt's office door. He must be going!

"Jonty! Come here a minute. I want you."

Jonty shut his eyes. Instantly, the darkness was lit up by coloured stars, streaks and clouds from the explosive cursings that formed themselves spontaneously in Jonty's mind. He fancied that a smell of cordite trickled from his ears. He began to cough and splutter in his efforts to prevent his feelings from reaching audible configurations. He'd better get over to the old bugger.

Jonty knocked and went in. Treblitt was standing in his characteristic S-shape, looking out of his window at all the departing workers in the street. The wodges of turnups on his heavy serge trousers were manacled above his spotless boots with the kind of bicycle clips, now years out of date and unobtainable, that fasten all round the ankle by means of a device at the rear. Jonty reckoned that the bicycle clips in place were a good sign. Putting those on was no easy matter. What on earth could he want? Probably some kind of a routine reminder about something utterly trivial to Jonty but enormously important to Treblitt. Treblitt seemed to fill his life with matters of that kind. His rugby scarf and merde-coloured trilby lay on his faultlessly neat desk.

"Oh, so you decided to return to us in time for the knocking-off hooter, hey, Godley?"

"How d'you mean, sir?"

"That's all right, Godley. I think we understand each other, don't we?"

Jonty said nothing. Using his surname was a bad sign. So the bicycle clips had been a psychological ploy to lull him into a false sense of security? Well, well! Didn't think he had it in him! Treblitt chewed the threadbare ends of his moustaches for a while, and then moved to stand behind his desk to study his desk-blotter with such absorption that Jonty began to think he'd gone into another of his Yogi-like contemplations on the rate of consumption of office pencils. But he recovered and said to the blotter:

"Heard any news of that interview of yours yet?"

Jonty was taken aback, having assumed Treblitt had forgotten about that. He should have known better.

"Er—no, not yet. I think they're still considering the short list."

"Humph!"

Treblitt clumped about his office, once up and once down.

"Do I know these people, Jonty?"

"Which people, sir?"

"These people who're considering employing you."

Jonty shook his head vigorously. He didn't like the way Treblitt had said 'considering.'

"Shouldn't think so, sir. A very tiny firm, they are. Make wire products."

"What's the name?"

"Can't remember for the moment. They make wire frames—for bras."

"Bras!"

Treblitt's eyes flickered onto Jonty's face for a moment before dropping again.

'Guessed that would stop him cold,' thought Jonty.

Treblitt suddenly jabbed out a forefinger, pointing to his desk. "Do you know what that is, Godley?"

Jonty was about to reply, "A desk," when he noticed something on it that wasn't usually there.

"What – what is,—sir?"

"That card!"

A long narrow buff-coloured card jumped into focus for Jonty. Oh, my God, he knew only too well what it was.

"No sir!"

"Thought you wouldn't, Godley. I'll tell you. It's your clocking-in card, that's what it is."

Treblitt pretended to study his desk-blotter again and waited. Perhaps it helped him to concentrate? Treblitt's silences were much more interesting than his conversations but Jonty was anxious to leave the office before Dummock got back from his assignment and Jonty especially wanted to be not available when Dummock arrived this evening. So Jonty thought he'd better say something:

"Oh, is it, sir?"

Treblitt looked up, startled. "Is WHAT it, Jonty?"

"My card, sir."

'Surely the old breadfruit couldn't have forgotten, could he? Nearing the end of the season, perhaps?'

"Yes. That's what it is, Jonty. A record of your arrivals so far this week. And these others – " said Treblitt, taking a pack of similar cards from one of his drawers, "—are the cards you've punched during your present six-month – er – sojourn with us." Dummock's return couldn't be far off,

'So that's why he stationed himself behind the desk! The cunning old fruit!'

"So far, there are twenty-nine or thirty. I've been scrutinizing them."

'You've also been counting them,' thought Jonty.

There was another funereal silence in which Treblitt bowed his head, fixed his myopic stare on the blotter and chewed his moustaches. 'Make friends with the Great British Sausage,' intoned Jonty silently, and only just managed to choke back a snort of laughter. Why doesn't the silly old sausage get on with whatever it is he's trying to get on with? Treblitt slowly tilted his head a little towards the vertical and gazed suspiciously at Jonty for an instant.

"Did you say something, Jonty?"

"No, sir. Just clearing my throat."

"Humph...Major Knowles asked me..."

Treblitt shot another fast glance at Jonty.

" You know who major Knowles IS, I suppose? He asked me to have a word with you, Jonty, about them. If, he says, your time-keeping doesn't improve – er – drastically, there can be only one end to things. And you know what THAT will be, don't you, Jonty? As it is, he's asked me to tell you that beginning tomorrow your wages will be docked according to the rate of one quarter hour's pay for every minute of lateness up to fifteen minutes. For every minute lost of the next fifteen minutes, you will lose ANOTHER quarter hour's pay. And so on. Do you understand me, Jonty? We realize fully that for office personnel this is a very unusual step. But, in your case, we have agreed to make an exception. Further, Major Knowles would like to know, Godley, how, out of something like one hundred and twenty or so – er – er – attendances at this factory, you've managed to get here ON TIME FOR ONLY FIFTY PER CENT of the – er – time?"

Jonty just gazed. Despite that little mix-up with the repetitions of the word 'time' at the end of his peroration, Treblitt's eloquence had stunned him. Until now, Jonty had not realized that Treblitt knew so many words, or could even put sentences together that had subordinate clauses in them. But he'd subordinated a lot of them in a very effective way. Obviously, a slight reassessment was necessary, at least, of Treblitt's grasp of English grammar. Normally, Jonty would have cottoned on to the fact that he might as well be fourteen minutes late as one, which would give him more latitude about getting up in the mornings. But his mind was, at this juncture, only subliminally aware of it, so deeply had Treblitt's display of consecutive thinking disturbed him. What was worse was that Treblitt didn't seem, yet, to have finished saying his say.

"That's HIS question, Jonty. My question is rather different. I'd like to know how – or even why – you manage to come at all?"

12

'When is that bloody hooter going to sound?' thought Jonty.

Treblitt had certainly got on with what he was trying to get on with that time! Jonty regarded him with a new respect. The old breadfruit had hidden juices, that's what he had.

The hooter shattered Treblitt's deliberately heavy ironic silence and dropped it clanking and clattering at Jonty's feet.

"Well, Godley?"

"As a matter of fact, I'm not in the best of health, sir. I've had some rather nasty bouts of sciatica lately and—"

Jonty petered out because Treblitt had begun to shake his head slowly and emphatically at his first words and gone on shaking it throughout. It unnerved him.

'And, furthermore, if you go on doing that to your head you could do yourself a mischief. It might come out of its joints, fall and roll over the oilcloth, under the desk or the hat stand, or somewhere,' thought Jonty, looking round the office for other possible hiding places, 'and then I'd have to scramble about on all fours and—"

"It's no good, Godley," Treblitt shot out at him: "That one's dead!"

"Oh, is it?"

"As a doornail."

Jonty was vaguely aware of the draughtsmen filing out of the office on their way home, but far more aware of Treblitt's use of cliché, and that Dummock might return at any moment.

"And so far we haven't even mentioned these anonymous letters, supposed to be written by the Management and others, that keep appearing all over the factory. Have we, Godley? NOW THAT'S ALL GOT TO STOP, GODLEY."

Treblitt had almost shouted the last injunction at him, but he seemed somewhat shaken by the half-rhyme and faltered before recovering his step and continuing.

"I had hoped, when I took you on, that you'd show some – er – promise. But no! I'd LIKE to recommend you – LIKE to – for a pay rise, in due course, and a somewhat better position in our Jig and Tool Drawing Office later on. But in all conscience, I can't. I'm afraid I just can't. I don't dislike you personally, Jonty, but—"

He lifted both arms ataxically.

"Don't you WANT to get on, Jonty?" he asked, rather plaintively.

"Oh, God!"

It was out before he could stop it. Jonty had spotted Dummock coming jauntily into the office, carrying a large roll of drawings and looking very pleased with himself.

"Well, if that's how you feel about it, Jonty, I can't, of course—"

"I don't!"

"You don't! But you've just—"

"Oh no, sir. I—I—that—I suddenly remembered something—something—I—er—should have done. You see, sir?"

Even as he said it, Jonty knew that it was something he shouldn't have said. But now it was too late. It had been done.

"No, I don't see! But never mind. I think that just about winds up what we've got to say to each other, hey, Godley?"

There was a pause.

"Good evening," said Treblitt, reaching for his rugby scarf and his excremental trilby. "BE EARLY TOMORROW, JONTY."

Jonty realized there was nothing he could do but go, even though he was sure it hadn't wound up what HE had to say to each other. However, the presence of Dummock in the office induced Jonty to say nothing but "Good night!" and leave Treblitt to stew in his own breadfruit juices for the meantime.

Dummock was opening and shutting his table drawer, putting things away, tidying up his table and preparing to place the cover over his board, as Jonty, keeping as many desks between Dummock and himself as he could, made his way back to his corner. Jonty caught the hybrid scuffling-cum-clumping sounds behind him that indicated Treblitt was on his way home. The departing strains of 'Colonel Bogey' wafted towards him. 'Treblitt-situation normal?'

Dummock was watching Jonty sidelong and smirked at him all the way back to his board. As Treblitt left through the office door, Dummock said: "So the old bugger's caught up with you at last has he, Arnold boy, me old lad?"

Jonty was not feeling in any mood for Dumnmock's pleasantries. A short rude word rose effortlessly to his lips, but, in his own interests, he suppressed it before it blossomed. It wouldn't do to antagonise Dummock at this exact instant. Something milder was called for.

"I suppose you think there's only one God in the universe, hey, Dummock? Well, you're wrong! The other one's just come out of that bloody office in his rugby scarf."

Dummmock laughed. "Bad as that, is it?"

Jonty covered his desk in overdrive. He had very little margin left. Jonty had already wished Dummock happy dreams and he was well on his way to the door when it happened. A weird strangulated scream pierced the tranquillity of the Drawing Office. It made Jonty think of the frenzied mating call of an orang-outang that had caught its throat in the fork of a tree. It chilled Jonty's scalp. It didn't sound like Dummock at all. Jonty accelerated. He thought he'd made it, but just as he was about to touch the knob of the door, Dummock called out: "Jonty, you bleeder! I'll swing on your gonads for this!"

So Dummock had taken over the role of an orang-outang in a big way, had he? Jonty hurriedly began to open the door.

"You go out of that door, Jonty, and I'll tear you into little bits."

Dumnmock seemed obsessed with his simian role.

'Not with my mastery of karate, you won't,' thought Jonty.

But as he was beginning to vividly picture Dummnock covered in hair, Jonty revised the thought, and it now went like this: 'Not with my mastery of karate, you will.'

Jonty reasoned that perhaps, for the moment, discretion might be the better part of valour; but he wasn't thoroughly convinced. However, he turned slowly about and looked at Dummock. No, he wasn't covered in hair at all, but he had gone subtly puce: his cheeks, his jaw, his eye-sockets, all varying in subtlety.

"Come—here—Jonty."

Jonty walked slowly and carefully nearer, taking care to make sure stools or desks were placed strategically between them. As he approached, Dummock's teutonic head was magically getting squarer, and there was a horrible grimace forming itself on his now puce and puffy face. Jonty began to fancy that, after all, Dummnock perhaps had a few millilitres of orang-outang blood somewhere; or at least an aunt who was decidedly *homo pithecanthropus.* He moved at little closer to Dumnmock, extremely cautious.

"Ooooh! Your eyes have gone all pink, Dumnmock!"

"Gone all pink have they? That's nothing to the colour you're going to go when I've finished with you. LOOK—AT—MY—— SHOES!"

They were in their usual position by Dummock's stool, elegant and bright.

"Look all right to me."

"So they look all right to you, do they?"

Dummock's usual conversational flow seemed to have lost its sparkle and dash.

"Yes."

Dummock took a huge breath, darkening the puce. "You—you—you bleeder, you! I'll—"

"Now look here, Dummock, I'm not staying about simply to listen to your Orson Welles' voice giving an impersonation of Charles Laughton giving an impersonation of Captain Bligh of the Bounty."

"Come back!" screamed Dummock. Jonty paused in his tracks.

"Pick those bleeding shoes UP!"

"They're not my size. I don't want your shoes Dummock, even though they are wine-coloured and hand-sewn."

Dummock began to look homicidal. He made a quick snatch at his table drawer and took out a long iron file that he used to point up his pencils.

'Oh, so it's like that, is it?' thought Jonty.

"Your size or not — PICK THE BASTARDS UP!"

Jonty moved gingerly towards them, making sure that he had a clear run to the office door should Dummock turn nastier than he already was. Jonty descended slowly towards the floor, watching Dummock. He took hold of the shoes and straightened his knees.

"I can't!" he said.

"Of course you bloody can't, as if you didn't know! Because a weedy malicious four-eyed—" he spluttered.

His new-found fluency deserted him again.

Eventually, he said: "Some—some—wanker—has—has— SCREWED THEM TO THE FLOOR. My beautiful fifty quid's worth of hand-made—Jonty, I'm going to kill you."

He made a sudden lunge at Jonty with the file, but Jonty had been expecting some such attack and he skipped agilely round the table, where Dummock couldn't reach him.

'Oh, Treblitt, you damned old idiot, you had to pick today to tell me all that bullshit about – Whoops! Nearly had me that time.'

Jonty was working out the odds on him getting to Treblitt's office before Dummock, and locking himself in. Luckily, the chances were with Jonty at the minute. Dummock had taken off his working shoes before donning his claret-coloured footwear, so he was still in his plum-coloured nylon-and-wool socks and wouldn't find it easy to keep his feet on the lino. At least, that was what Jonty was banking on. If he was really nippy, he could reach Treblitt's office while Dummock was correcting his oversteer, and jam a chair under the doorknob, and then crouch on top of the filing cabinet and taunt Dummock through the window. Dumnmock wouldn't dare trying to force Treblitt's door, would he? But he was certainly going to try doing something. He had climbed on top of his table, and was now preparing to leap onto Jonty from above and maybe plunge the file straight through his T-shirt. Jonty backed away, drew in breath, and made a dash for it.

Jonty had a lead of two drawing boards on Dummock, and was more than halfway to his sanctuary, when Alexis rushed into the office.

"Arnold! Why haven't you – ?"

She stopped stockstill, staring in bewilderment.

Dummock put on his anchors, his socks screeching to a standstill, and turned back neatly into a parking slot about a yard in front of Alexis. You had to admire the speed of the man's reactions in the presence of bint, that was certain! Dummock was attempting to put the file nonchalantly into his top pocket together with his murderous face, and turn himself into a man women went crazy about.

"Oh, hello Alex! Did you want to speak to me?"

She was staring at his socks. Jonty, meanwhile, kept steadily on course. He wanted very much to make the first manned landing in Treblitt's office.

Alex glared into Dummock's face.

"What's going on here? Why aren't you wearing shoes? What's Arnold trying to get into Treblitt's office for? Why have I had to wait for—?"

"Whoa! Hold your horses, Alex. Nothing much to worry about. Just a—just a—point of difference between me—and that—specimen, there!"

It cost Dummock a lot to confine himself to the use of that epithet alone, but he won the struggle after a while. It was a marker of how much he wanted to impress Alexis, despite his derogatory words about her to Jonty earlier. She frowned at him and walked over to where Jonty stood glued to Treblitt's doorknob. She removed his hand and tried the door. He submitted quietly. It was locked. Jonty was stunned into silence, finding the consequences of his miscalculation too awful to contemplate. He should have remembered that the old whatsit never missed on things like door locking and counting rubbers. The clockwork breadfruit!

"Arnold, we had a date—remember? Come! I want to speak to you."

Jonty shook his head, grimacing and pointing at Dummock. "Not while he's got no shoes on."

Alex looked over at Dummock. He was doing his best to smile at her.

"What have shoes got to do with it? Don't be silly! Come!"

"Tell him to get into his shoes first."

"Why, you bloody little—!" Then, he remembered how irresistible to women he was and changed his tone.

"Look, let's just call it *pax* for the time being, shall we?" said Dummock.

"Okay, you're on."

Jonty moved slowly away from Treblitt's office, and edged himself towards freedom, taking the precaution of putting Alexis between himself and Dummock *en route*; but why did she have to stop in front of him again? Jonty also stopped. He needed his shield. Alexis looked from one to the other. When she was looking at Dummock, Dummock was smiling at Jonty and Jonty was glaring at Dummock. When she was looking at Jonty, Jonty was smiling at Dumrnock and Dummock was glaring at Jonty. As she turned to scrutinize them in turn, she was accompanied by this pantomime of smiling and unsmiling, glaring and unglaring.

"Just like a couple of kids," she said.

They both began to protest. She held up her hand, like a schoolma'am. They were silent.

"I don't want to hear a word from either of you. Look at the time! I've been waiting downstairs! Fifteen minutes. If you don't want to see me again, Arnold, just say so. Are you or are you not—coming?"

"I'm coming."

Originally, Jonty had had no intention of keeping the date by the clocks, not after the trouble he had taken to write a goodbye recipe of Chilled Cabbage Mousse. But in the circumstances precipitated by Dummnock wearing no socks and Alexis wearing a skinny rib sweater (that seemed even skinnier now than earlier in the afternoon), Jonty considered that the better prospect was certainly Alexis. On the one hand, he could be faced with the loss of his chastity; on the other, with the loss of an arm. The former was a possibility, the latter a certainty, and he wasn't ready to join the unpensionable disabled just yet.

"Well, good night, Dummock. Mind you don't tread in any puddles on the way home!"

Dummock said nothing, but he gave Jonty the distinct impression of trying to form himself into pieces of shrapnel before exploding lethally all over the office. Alexis turned and walked off without bidding him good night. Jonty was no more than in inch behind her mini-skirt when she reached the door, but he couldn't resist the urge to contrive two fingers round the door's edge and waggle them at Dummock obscenely, before he disappeared down the stairs to the clocks with Alexis.

Jonty was very pleased with himself. He felt that he'd come out of that little encounter pretty well, considering. Of course, he wasn't overly analytical in considering what that 'considering' was really considering or not considering. No. He stopped short of that. Just in case. In case what?

'Oh, what the hell!'

"Let's go for a coffee, shall we? I feel like drinking mine out of one o' them skulls," he said.

Alexis looked at him strangely, but assented:

"Okay."

Jonty grinned to himself with satisfaction. Not bad! Walking off with Alexis right under Dummock's nose like that. That'll teach him to buy hand-made shoes and socks of exotic colours. Let him wear Bata shoes-and-no-socks, like any normal individual.

He hid his chuckle by clocking out, so that Alexis wouldn't see his amusement.

Three hours later, after a coffee in The Old Victorian Cellar, Jonty and Alexis were sitting in The Woodman, supping draught Bass with Barry Crehan and Isabel. Alexis had wanted to make amends to Jonty for the night of Crehan's party when she had zoomed off in her red Sprite and left him high but not dry. So she had thought up this little surprise gathering just to show Jonty it was Isabel that Crehan fancied and not her. But he reserved judgment on that.

They were all sitting in one of The Woodman's Victorian cubicles, quite silent, absentmindedly sipping their beer, while they concentrated on trying to eavesdrop on the conversation of a fat tarty-looking woman on the telephone in the corridor next door.

"Shh!" shushed Alexis. "Listen! She's finished all that shopping list."

Isabel giggled loudly. Alexis glowered and she stopped.

"Dear old hens, we oughtn't to be doing this, you know."

"What ought we to be doing then? It would be worse if she listened to our conversation, wouldn't it? That could be very traumatic for her. She might be struck by *anorexia nervosa* and shrink to nothing."

"Her! Oh, what a vision!" shrieked Isabel.

"Shut up, the lot of you! She's starting again."

"How's Bertie?… Yes, dear... Really?… In the gas oven?' It must have been agony for the poor dear... He's where? No, he CAN'T BE.... I say!... My dear, it needs a very SMALL deposit... Yes, fully automatic... Yes, all right, dear. 'Bye!"

The fat woman came to the end of her marathon phone call and began to put the small pile of silver balanced on the call box back into her handbag. Jonty noticed that the bag was as plump and padded as its owner. She felt Jonty watching her and turned to stare directly at him, stoney-faced. Jonty stared back, raising his glass in a mock toast.

"To gas ovens," he said.

"Gas ovens!" screeched Isabel.

The fat woman turned away, muttering, and waddled off.

13

When the fat woman had gone, Alexis said: "There's no need to be rude."

"There was no need to eavesdrop," said Jonty turning to Barry for support. "Hey, Crehan?"

Crehan ignored him and continued his peroration.

"I was in the middle of telling you all about this new non-drip paint. I have it on the best authority that...."

Jonty let his mind wander. His eyes rested for a moment on Crehan's animated face and then noted, in surprise, that Alexis and Isabel were actually listening to him. It just went to show, didn't it? You couldn't help meeting human nature everywhere. What was it that Crehan had that allowed him to hold the interest of two attractive girls with a disquisition on household paint? Was it his up-to-the-minute gear?

Look at it! Tonight was obviously tweed-night: waistcoat, bell-bottom slacks, and a jacket that just missed becoming an overcoat. Was his polo jersey knitted out of tweed as well? And his lingerie? But why all those clashing colours? It was very puzzling. Jonty couldn't help conceding that Crehan himself must have something to do with the answer, because if Treblitt had been made of solid tweed and here in Crehan's place tonight he'd have lost them on household paint in no time at all. Not even a solid tweed Dummock would have been as good. Per chance, being Scotch had something to do with it, the appeal of the exotic, and all that? Jonty gave it up, and let his eyes wander all round the pub, while Crehan burred and brogued on.

The pub was full, mostly of students from the University and Art College nearby. Funny, the way they all liked to jam themselves together so that they could scarcely lift their elbows up to drink! He was struck again by the O'Grady nature of British Society; and the pub was one of the few institutions that wouldn't take it seriously. This one was a world of mickey-taking notices!

There were text notices, posters, pokerboard mottoes, photographs, line drawings, and even a sprinkling of engravings from the Band of Hope era. One of these was a favourite of Jonty's. It showed nine moustachioed bobbies sitting in a row smoking pipes with tankards beside them, and said, wittily: 'Nine pints of the law.' The love and care with which the artist had drawn those policemen, with their homely faces and little potbellies, pleased Jonty immensely. It reminded him of Archie Casbolt.

Just after the long conversation Jonty had had with his father on the subject, he had tried out a classification of notices along the lines of those that told you what you must **not** do (Group One), those that told you what you **must** do (Group Two), those that were meant to **amuse** (Group Three), and those that were meant to truly **inform** you (Group Four). The last group, which contained 'Ladies' or 'Gentlemen' or 'Frying Tonite', was the smallest. The biggest, by far, was Group One. Group Two came second. Conclusion: the British Democratic System was based on the fact that the *hoi poloi* elected people who liked giving orders to people who liked taking orders, which, if true, might suggest the advisability of exchanging the present system for government by junta. On the whole, pubs served a very useful function by selling a lot of beer and catering for Group Three, which most people slid into when they'd taken a drop or two. How else could you account for the plethora of debunking injunctions that appeared there, except as a counterbalance to the millions of O'Grady type notices nailed, stuck, painted, welded, printed, erected, or hung up across the length and breadth of Britain?

"We won't take cheques and the banks have agreed not to sell beer," murmured Jonty into his Bass.

"I beg yours?"

"Aren't you feeling well, dear?" asked Isabel. "Jonty!!"

"What did you say?" asked Jonty, vaguely.

"No! What did YOU say?" said Issy.

"Me? I didn't say anything," said Jonty.

"We all heard you, old hen, Didn't we?"

"Oh, THAT! Just thinking aloud."

"From wherever you've been, dear, welcome home. All is forgiven," said Isabel.

Alexis stared at Isabel before saying to Jonty: "I've been telling them about you and Dummock."

'More to the point,' thought Jonty, 'tell 'em about YOU and Dummock.'

"Didn't you hear me?" asked Alexis.

"I heard."

"Come on! Tell us," said Isabel. "What were you and Durnmock fighting about?"

"Okay. Come closer." Jonty leaned forward and started whispering like a conspirator. Four heads drew together over the table. "You see, he's not well. It's in the family. He's got – " Jonty looked around as if there were spies everywhere, —*Dementia Praecox!"* He finished in a dramatic stage whisper.

"You fool, Jonty!"

"He has! Why do you think he went running round the office in his psychedelic socks?"

Alexis looked pityingly at the others.

"He just can't help it, you know!" she said, inclining her head slightly towards Jonty.

"That's what I'm telling you," said Jonty. "He's a compulsive."

"Not him! YOU!"

"A compulsive what, old hen?"

"Ask Alex! She knows all about the *Praecox* bit, don't you?"

Under the table, she kicked him hard on the shin.

"Ooooh! That hurt!"

"That's what happens to pigs! Now give us the truth. I know for a fact that Dummock didn't come in until five and – "

Jonty turned and looked at her very deliberately, a little smirk on his lips. Alexis faltered and stopped, realizing that she had already said too much.

"Now, just how did you happen to know that, I wonder?" he said gently. "Telepathy? Or something more—shall we say—tangible?"

Alexis set her mouth in a straight line and kept silent.

"It just so happens that that old idiot, Treblitt, called me into his office at the last minute, or I'd have been away before your friend Dummock got there."

"What did Treblitt want?" asked Isabel.

"I'm not sure. He kept talking in grammatical sentences and I was so surprised I couldn't follow his drift. At first, I thought it was Tamil, or Walloon, or something."

"Stop fooling about and tell us," said Isabel. "We're your friends. You can trust us! Can't he?" she asked the others.

"Of course," said Crehan.

"Well, in that case, you're entitled to know," said Jonty, looking hard at Alexis.

He told them about the afternoon's events as briefly and quickly as he could.

"It doesn't look good, old hen. Think about the advice I gave you the other night. Anyway, let's not dwell on it, shall we? Drink up! What about another wee snort? Same again?"

"Same again."

Alexis was looking daggers at him.

At that precise moment, Jonty decided he was going to get drunk.

When, some time later, they got outside it was raining.

Crehan, of course, had brought an umbrella. Issy and Alex huddled underneath it, with Crehan in the middle. They tripped and tottered along the wet pavements like a black scalloped mushroom with six legs.

Jonty danced in the rain.

"Gene Kelly has nothing on me," he sang, stamping in the gutters and pirouetting round the lamp standards.

"Look everybody, 'Singing in the Rain'," he said to the passers-by.

Nobody looked. They huddled under their hats and dripping Macintoshes and passed by.

"Thank God I brought the old umbrella."

"Thank God for granny boots."

"Thank God for trouser suits."

"Thank God for God," sang Jonty, and a very wet clergyman peered through his holy streaming glasses at the soaked and godless Jonty.

"I mean it," shouted Jonty.

The prelate hurried away.

"So should you. HE found you a job."

When they reached the Birmingham Public Library, a building of red-brick Victorian Gothic that Jonty loved more than any other in the city, Jonty made an elaborate bow before it.

"Good old Waterhouse," he shouted. "You're a bloody genius."

Then he turned and made a sudden dash.

"Stop him! He's heading for the fountain!"

They tried, but he broke loose and reached the parapet, where he stood teetering for a moment, before he fell with a sploosh into the basin. The trio stopped mid-chase, turned and retired in a rush to the shelter of the arched entrance of the Waterhouse library, to watch and to wait. There was no stopping him in this mood. Jonty broke surface, laughing.

"Come on in, the water's lovely," he carolled, and hit it with the flat of his palms.

The light from the carbon streetlamps desiccated into a thousand jigging flakes, appearing, growing, melting, breaking, and vanishing, while the soaked and darkened Jonty projected out of the dancing surface, his arms stretched heavenward.

"It rains on the just and the unjust, the ripe and the rotting on the bough," he intoned.

"We'll have to get him out," said Isabel. "He'll catch pneumonia."

"Or a policeman," said Barry.

"Three cheers for Samuel Becket!"

"Oh, God, yes! A night in Steelhouse Lane Station, going bail for Jonty and drinking stewed tea out of tin mugs is more than I can bear right now. Barry, you've got to do something!"

"Me! Why me? Isn't he your boy-friend, old hen?"

"Oh, really!"

"But, you've got an umbrella," said Issy irrelevantly.

Barry was indignant.

"I can't go in and fetch him just because I've got an umbrella, can I?"

"Well, you could hook him round the neck with it," said Isabel.

"Ach! lassie, what a splendid idea!" said Barry, jumping at the chance of preserving the pristine condition of his tweeds.

"Let's try."

They rushed out to the basin of the exotic Birmingham fountain. Jonty had no head, only legs and shiny smooth suedes. He was trying to do handstands in the basin.

"As soon as he comes up for air, get it round his neck!"

"Okay, I'll stand up here, and you give me your hand... Right! Now, you hold Issy's hand, and as soon as I've hooked him, pull and pull for all you're worth. If you let go – ! There he blows!"

Crehan made a lunge with the handle of the umbrella.

"You got him first time!" rhapsodised Isabel. "Barry, you clever man!"

"Don't let him get away."

Jonty, feeling the talon of Crehan's umbrella round his neck, immediately countered by putting one leg in the air, his spine rigid, and leaned his weight backwards against the handle. He threw both hands in the air, like a vaudeville act.

"No poaching allowed in the fountain," chanted Jonty.

"Reel him in!"

"My arm's nearly out of its socket. Pull! Pull!"

"That's it!"

The fresh leverage brought Jonty upright. He was forced to put his leg down. He stood there a-straddle, upright for a moment, and then, in slow motion, he began to keel forward to the point where gravity got hold of him and, in a rush, fell flat on his face in the water, just short of the stone parapet.

"That was a close shave!"

"Now, grab him!"

"Don't let him get away!"

"Whew! He's freezing."

They managed to haul Jonty into a sitting position on the parapet, where he streamed and gurgled and smiled in great good humour.

"I'm going to climb up that statue," he said, pointing to Queen Victoria, "and dive in off her head."

He swung his feet back into the water.

"You most certainly are not, old hen."

"She won't mind."

"OUT you COME! That's it!"

"Thank God, for that!" said Issy.

"AND me!" said Crehan.

"You were marvellous, Barry, wasn't he, Alex?"

"Lucky for you lot you got him out," rumbled a deep blue voice behind them.

Three heads turned round. Jonty still had his eye on Queen Victoria. A young policeman made like a bull in a shiny black waterproof was watching them from one of the lower steps of the square. Jonty became aware of another centre of interest.

"What's that?" asked Jonty, pointing at the constable.

"It's a policeman," said Issy. "What d'you think it is?"

"One arm of the law," said Jonty, drunkenly. Then: "Are you the left or the right? Do you like my uniform?"

Jonty indicated his soaking wet clothes, which had changed to a deep dark blue under the lights and the water.

"Another comic, hey? You'd better get him orf the streets and quick before he turns the same colour as his clo'es," said the bobby. "We lock up people who turn blue in public. In cells. To cool orf!"

He laughed energetically at his own joke. The others, dutifully.

"Laughing in public is not allowed on even dates," said Jonty. "Lock 'em up!"

"You wouldn't, would you, officer?"

"Not right now."

"Oh, what a lovely policeman! Come on, before he changes his mind and Jonty turns blue."

"I'm not blue. I'm happy! He's blue! Lock him up, lock him up!" Jonty chanted, and began to hop and circle, Red Indian fashion, round the fountain.

"You just take him orf, smartish. Now! The sergeant'll be round in a minute."

They marched him off smartish. Crehan took one arm, Alexis the other, and Isabel pushed him from behind. Jonty began to sing 'Land of Hope and Glory', but his words were different.

"*Land of Soap and Water*," he wailed. "*Mother of the Clean...*"

"Let's get him on the next bus. He'll be all right, then."

"Sure?"

"I'll manage him. My flat's right on the bus route," said Alexis. "He'll be all right."

"Well, we'll wait to see you on it, lassie! He might break out again."

"He seems quiet enough, now," said Issy.

Jonty was skewed sideways, mechanically walking, his head resting on Alexis's shoulder, his eyes closed.

"There's one coming! A 29A. Is that okay?"

"That's the one. Wait for us!"

They manhandled Jonty across the road to the waiting bus. The conductor was hanging from the platform at the rear, beckoning them on. When they reached the platform, they all bundled Jonty onto the nearest seat, and Crehan and Isabel got off again.

"Thanks for waiting," said Alexis, to the conductor.

"That's all right! Orf we goo, then." And he rang the bell.

When he came to, in Alexis's flat, Jonty's head was full of the soft flutterings of pigeons' wings, but hard little beaks were attacking the soft places at his temples with a rain of tiny blows. He felt stiff as stone, except for his feet, which were brimming with ice-cold water. Liquid was spurting from a small hole in the top of his head like a plume and falling about him in a fine spray, trickling down his face, his trunk, his arms, his fingers, falling and forming this pool of icy coldness at his feet.

Then, very slowly, he began to turn right over. His feet rose gracefully into the air and the water trickled out of them only to be replaced by the flutterings perched on his toes, claws piercing the skin, while his head slowly submerged itself in icy water. It tasted of urine and fresh yeast. Then bird-droppings. Then wet tweed. Then shampoo. Then his head floated on the top of the water. Finally, the smell of coffee stole inwards to the sound of a voice and something spidery on his face.

"Up you get. Come on. Drink this."

It was a woman's voice, so he swallowed the liquid to find out what would happen. A thin hot wire streaked from his throat to his stomach and stretched tight, but it wasn't unpleasant.

"Measured out his life in coffee spoons," he said. "Lock him up."

"That's right! Drink some more. You'll be all right."

He wiped his hand across his face.

"Nasty 'piders!

He could feel their webs clinging to his eyelashes. Then, there was more coffee in his mouth, changing the world.

"Wet clergymen shouldn't be allowed," he said. "That's right. Drink up."

Two hot heavy feelings sheathed in silk were on his chest.

"Somebody's loving me and I want to die under the water, water, water, water…"

"It's not water, it's coffee. Come on, there's a good boy."

He began to move vertically upward, gathering speed. There was mist all around him.

"Four, three, two, one, zero," he said. "Boom!"

"Boom to you."

Now he was a parachute, drifting through immense silences. There was a weight swinging on him, below, pulling on his strings. A wind was breathing in his ear.

"Cirrus, cumulus, stratus, nimbus, tumulus, murmurous, thunderous—come and have your dinner."

Somebody laughed.

Then he was down with a little bump, to find himself sprawling all limp on something smooth and billowy. He found that Alexis had an arm round his shoulders lifting him slightly, administering coffee, in a coloured silk kimono, with her hair over her face, breathing scent, the softness of her breasts on his chest, and he was lolling in a black leather armchair with a high back and wings, wearing a woman's dressing gown with his bare feet protruding below it.

"Hello," he said. "I'm Arnold Jonathan Godley. Although wouldn't think it. Spelt with an 'e' for 'evil'. The Man-Up-There has an ironic sense of humour."

He looked down at himself, ruefully.

14

"Hello. I'm Alexis Treadgold. How'd you feel now?"

"Who knows? Why am I dressed in this pink shroud?"

"That's not a shroud! It's my best gown. Nun's veiling. Silk edging. Look at it. You should be thankful."

"I knew a nun once. She was young and beautiful. 'A Bride of Christ,' I says. 'Oh, no!' she says. 'I wouldn't say we're married. We're just going steady. I'm an initiate.' And two weeks later, I saw her in Corporation Street wearing a mini-skirt. What a pair of legs! 'I've broken it off,' she says. 'We never really clicked, you know.' So I took her for a frothy coffee to the Old Victorian Cellar. She was some sexy acolyte, she was!"

"Don't be profane! Getting better, are you?"

"Don't be so bloody Roman Catholic!"

"Condition normal! I don't really know why I like you. I **am** a Catholic!"

"You mean besides my obvious attractions of being a recipe-writer, a Dummock-hater, a Treblitt-baiter, and a recoveree from a hangover?"

"My God, you were high! High as a kite. They nearly threw you off the bus."

"What for?"

"You kept trying to climb into the driver's seat."

"What happened?"

"They let you wear the conductor's hat and you quietened down."

"Conductor's hat! If I'd been sober, I'd have demanded his entire uniform." Jonty gave an abrupt groan. "Ooooh!"

"What's up? Feeling sick? Shall I get you a bowl?"

"No, thanks! I'll be all right. Except for my eyelids. They feel like British Railways sandwiches. And my heartbeats. Which have turned into ultra-sonic booms."

"Poor dear! You must feel ill; you actually said thanks. Like some more coffee?"

"All right," he said, grudgingly.

"Don't force yourself. Making up for saying 'thanks', are you?" she said over her shoulder, on her way to the kitchen.

Jonty looked over Alexis's flat from his vantage point of the billowing chair while he attempted to bring himself fully back to whatever it was he'd got to get back to. He didn't feel strong enough for more – just yet. He'd accompanied Alexis once before to pick up a book she wanted to return to the Public Library, just an in-and-out affair. On that occasion, he had had time to be struck by the overwhelming expensiveness of it all, but not time to find out why he was so struck. Now, he had time to find out (a) why it seemed expensive, and (b) why its expensiveness seemed overwhelming at the time. He pushed his elbows into the soft black leather of the chair and bounced his naked feet up and down on the footstool.

"This is some bloody chair, this is!" he shouted to Alexis, and immediately wished he hadn't. "Ooh! My head."

"Oh, THE chair?" Alexis called from the kitchen. "Yes, isn't it? A Parker Knoll Statesman. Present from Daddy. Glad you like it."

"Like it! Daddy must have a profitable stall in the Rag Market to give you this sort of rubbish."

"Yes, he has."

"The footstool's more comfortable than my bed." In an undertone he added: "And no bedbugs either..."

Then, more loudly: "What's the griff on all this other stuff? That long bulbous bed with elephantiasis, for instance, at the end of the room?"

"That's not a bed! It's an environmental sofa: An Ambrose Lloyd, to be exact."

"Don't you mean a HAROLD Lloyd?"

"No, I don't."

"Look at the size of it! Shouldn't it come under the Town and Country Planning Act? Or, maybe the Health Department. What's it full of? Wheat germ with rich natural protein?"

"Some foamy stuff! I'm doing a poached egg and toast. All right?"

"Tell you later."

The wallpaper was grey with terracotta weals and bumps on. Beside the Harold Lloyd sofa stood a Buster Keaton table: small, funny and expressionless. It seemed to be made out of a black morgue slab, with stubby overweight dachshund legs under it. But then he saw that they were hollow. Mmm! Make good ashtrays, those would. There were tiny white statues standing on it, made out of icing-sugar. Against the wall, gooning blankly at the room, was a new 400-line idiot-box. Jonty's eyes went back to the statues.

"Alex! Why have you put cake-decorations on this dachshund table?"

"They're not! They are Stubbingses' moquettes and models, darling!"

"Stap me! I should have known."

"Of course."

The carpet seemed to be made out of the same stuff as the wallpaper; or, alternatively, the wallpaper was made out of the same stuff as the carpet. He couldn't really tell in his present condition. And there was a small perspex table with an olive-coloured Remington typewriter on it, and, scattered about the room, two or three see-through perspex cubes, with shelves in for no good reason that Jonty could see. They were transparent, it was true, but where on the shelves would you put anything worth putting?

Just then, Axis brought her head round the door of the kitchen and caught him grimacing.

"And the carpet is Chlidema and the desk is made out of glass," she said.

"Oh, that's a desk, is it? Pleased to meet you!"

"And the pictures are Stubbingses."

"Those? You're kidding. They're stains on the wallpaper that have been framed."

He paused, while they gazed at each other for a moment or two, he defiantly, she quizzically. Then, added: "You know, Alex, I've decided **not** to marry you, after all."

She seemed more amused than put out, but she went back to the kitchen without a word. An instant later, her voice floated in clearly: "Haven't asked you, sir," she said. "What brought that on?"

"Don't know," said Jonty truthfully. "I feel hemmed-in by all this poverty. Crehan's place has the same effect."

"Oh, Barry's place is lovely. You'd soon learn to ignore it."

"But would it learn to ignore me? Every piece looks out at you with a built-in sneer. Anyway," he said, putting his feet on the open novel lying on the leather footstool, "I could never live with anyone who reads Barbara Cartland."

"What's wrong with her?"

"At least, not unless you sneaked for a sly chapter into the john."

"She's not as bad as that."

He picked up the book and read a few words at random.

"It's worse! ... And I suppose you're an enthusiastic follower of Godfrey Winn, as well?"

"What's wrong with Godfrey Winn?"

"Difficult to put into words. You might think I'm trying to insult you."

"Well, aren't you? One or two eggs?"

"One! Yes, I suppose I am, really. Look here, Alexis. Exactly why do you bother with me? I mean, there's Dummock. And Crehan. Crehan's more your style than me."

"You're on that again, are you?"

'That's what I'm on,' thought Jonty.

."Why don't you just relax? Enjoy yourself for a change! Instead of all this – all this – oh, I don't know," she ended in a wistful tone.

Jonty weakened

'Yes, why don't I?' he thought. He said aloud: "Okay. But I really would like to know what it's all about."

"What what's all about?" she asked, as she came back into the room with a tray of coffee, fried eggs and toast. "Move your feet!"

He did so, and she placed the tray on the pneumatic footstool.

"Christ! you're infuriating, Alex. For once in my life I try to be serious and you just won't play."

"Have an egg, she said. "Why do you want to be serious? Sugar?"

"I don't know. Must be the hangover. P'raps it's bringing back my TB."

"Sugar?"

"Two. But just look at all this – this – camping equipment. Lavished on you by a doting father, who is dying romantically of South African Brandy and a passion for Airedales."

"He isn't!"

"Isn't what?"

"Doting. He loves me."

"Not to mention a free year at the University and a brand new Austin Sprite for failing your exams."

"It isn't like that!"

"Look at me! Wages, irregular. Worldly goods: four T-shirts, three pairs of thin jeans, one cord jacket. Occupation: unknown. Hobbies: growing moustaches. Parents: unlikely. I mean! You can't expect me to take kindly to—"

"—Oh, shut up! Possessions don't make the man."

"They make some men. Look at Crehan!"

"Yes, but—. Hey! Watch out! You're dropping egg down my nun's veiling."

"They make some women, too. Another thing, how do I come to have nothing on under this length of pink piety?"

"I couldn't let you freeze to death, could I? Even *my* clothes were soaked where you'd leaned on me."

"That psychedelic trouser-suit! Made me wish I was like my Dad – colour-blind."

"Pig! How's your coffee? Feel better, now?"

"Yes, I do thanks!"

Jonty was melting under Alexis's determined good humour and concern.

"But what's the score? I'll probably get another attack of TB after all that water. So be good to me! Flatter my mood. I may not be with you for long."

"You and your hypochondria. You're as healthy as I am."

"Be careful! My hypochondria is sensitive.... But you're much prettier."

"Thank you, sir," she said.

She put down her coffee cup, and squatting, sat down close to Jonty's chair, and putting her head in his lap, smoothed his loins with her long fingers. He looked at her thick black hair. It shone like a raven's wing. He touched it.

"Minmm! That's lovely," she said. "Such a sensitive hypochondria." She was stroking the inside of his thigh.

"You want to watch out, doing that. I'm liable to lose control over my coffee cups in these situations. You could get an earful of best Kenya."

"But you won't, will you?"

"God knows what I shall do! I've been known to go right off even a steaming cup of Nescaff at times like these."

"Empty boasts will get you nowhere."

She pushed the footstool with the tray on with her feet, and moved in front of him, easing his knees apart to rest her head on the inside of his thighs. Her hand slid up the soft inner skin under his gown.

"And if I just loosen the knot like this—"

Her fingers were fumbling with the waist cord.

"There! I warned you. You've made me put my coffee down, and..." He stopped in wonder as he felt her mouth on him. He could do nothing but submit.

'Christ, Mother of God, Mother of mine, you'll never guess what's happening now! It's all because I drank fourteen draught Basses without stopping and then swallowed the Public Fountain in Stephenson Place to quench my thirst and flew here in a conductor's hat and I'm naked under a nun's habit in a nymphomaniac's flat full of foam rubber and perspex furniture and my genitals have disappeared in a fallout of ravens' wings and something that has never happened before in the history of the world is happening to me now and never going to stop and even if it is and has I never knew girls did things like this for real except in 'Ulysses' and her breasts are full of fire and sorry it's all coming out without a breath but I can't stop now and — oh —oh — Mother of mine, I'll write later when I can find the commas and whatsits love love love love Arnold or Jonty...'

He lay back on the voluptuous leather chair, exhausted. Alexis was watching him intently. Her mouth was red and moist as a burst fig. Her brown eyes smouldered.

"You want to watch you don't catch fire," he said. "I'm too weak to put you out."

"Then, I'll burn you up."

"You can't! I'm only ash now."

Her brown eyes continued to watch him, still smouldering. He took a breath.

"Where's me steaming cup of Nescaff?" he asked, hoping to distract her. "I can't even raise fresh hope, at the moment."

"That's all right," she said relaxing. Then, matter-of-factly, she said: "I'll just put the pot on."

She rose easily, fastening her gown over her naked body and went into the kitchen. Jonty allowed everything in him to fade until there was only some tiny spot of awareness glowing deep inside him, and waited for his strength to return.

When she came back, she said: "Like a cig?"

Jonty shook his head. It felt hollow and empty like his legs. Her gown had fallen open again, revealing her breasts.

"They're Markovitch," she said.

"What? Your boobs?"

"Idiot! The cigarettes."

"I couldn't even raise the strength to smoke a bloater with all that peeping out of your kimono."

Alexis looked down at herself, laughed, and fastened the gown yet again over her body. She lowered herself to recline near the small humourless table on a large white fluffy rug straight out of that advertisement with the two Persian cats where there was a shell for an ashtray, and lit a Markovitch, drew in a heavy lungful and let it trickle from her lips and nostrils, wreathing her face in smoke. The gown had somehow contrived to reveal most of the lower half of her body, and Jonty enjoyed it while he could.

'My! You're a cool dolly, and no mistake. If that's what they teach 'em in convents, maybe I should convert to RC?' mused Jonty.

"Minm! That was lovely, wasn't it? And it doesn't leave you with a hangover, either."

"No, I suppose not. Just this feeling of general debility, thirst, a tendency to anorexia, and a strong resolution to do it again sometime."

"What's anorexia?"

"Not fit for the ears of a young maiden like you. But it's not contagious!"

"Fool!"

He could hear the coffee beginning to bubble on the stove iii the kitchen.

"See what you've done to me? I'm starting to percolate."

Alexis balanced carefully her cigarette inside the shell, rose (now with decorum), went out, and returned at once holding aloft the coffee pot.

"Voila!" she said.

15

"Voila!" still kimonoed, she said.

She poured out two cups, and then said, casually, much too casually to convince Jonty: "By the way, I've been meaning to ask you, why did you send me that recipe? It was rather beastly."

"How did I know you wouldn't like a spot of Chilled Cabbage Mousse?"

"You know what I mean."

"Beastly's going a bit far, isn't it?"

"Does it mean you're just a weeny bit fond of me, then?"

"Well, it's either love for you or hatred for Dummock. I'm not sure which."

"You really are a pig! You won't say anything nice to me, will you? Why not?"

"I've never been in favour of rights for women."

She picked up the coffee pot and slapped it down again forcibly on the black-slabbed table, so that a little hot coffee jumped under the lid and spilled.

"Oh, for God's sake, Arnold! Can't you see I've been trying to make it up to you? I'm doing the best I can. Why do you keep running away?"

"That's not good for the Buster Keaton table, that hot pot on it."

"To hell with the table! And you too!"

"Let's drink to that," said Jonty, raising his coffee cup.

Alexis began to cry, quietly, with little drawn-in sobs of breath, her head turned away, her shoulders sagging. Her posture was one of defeat. Jonty felt a pang of compassion and, a little chastened, he said: "We all get feelings, sometimes, you know."

"Go to hell!"

Jonty put down his cup, got off the Parker Knoll Statesman and went over to where she was sitting hunched up on the huge dropsical Ambrose Lloyd. He put his arm round her with tenderness. She heaved away from him, stiffly. Her kimono had come loose and he could see her cleavage and the brown tunnelled swelling of her breasts. He slipped his hand inside the kimono. Her breasts and nipples were so firm in the palm of his hand he almost shouted with the joy of it. Alexis shuddered and leaned her weight against him.

"I'm sorry!" said Jonty. "It's this – this – nympho thing that's got under my skin."

Alexis leaned away and looked at him in sorrow and indignation. Her face was wet with crying.

"It's just that sod, Dummock!" she said. "Honest, it is. He's wild because I'm going round with you. You know what a liar he is, Arnold."

'Yes,' thought Jonty, 'and I seem to remember a little white fib you nearly brought out at Crehan's the other night, not to mention "Sensational Confessions in an Old Victorian Cellar". Maybe it's all a rumour put about by people who know you can't get enough of it? I don't know what you – ! Okay, okay, drop it, Arny! Let's give this other kind of stuff a go for a while, shall we?'

During this interior monolgue of Jonty's, Alexis had watched him intently, trying to read his thoughts. Although it was only a matter of seconds, Jonty judged that he'd better say something conciliatory, and say it rather promptly. "Dummock's that, all right."

Alexis perceptibly relaxed.

"I don't know why I want you, but I do."

She paused, looked at him, and called his name softly but imperatively: "Arnold! Jonty! Whoever you are."

"Yes?"

He looked at her as non-committedly as he could, not being able to go all the way yet with his recent resolution. She had two red spots high up on her cheekbones.

"Do it to me!" she said, excitedly. "I want you to do it NOW!"

Jonty knew that he was going to have to give some kind of assurance to her, even if it was no more than an open recognition of the physical desire she was stirring up in him. He hadn't gone in for having actual desires for Alexis until now, only ideas about desires. But on being forced to consider the matter, he was realizing more clearly as the seconds ticked by that he strongly approved of the general direction he seemed to be going in. However, after her earlier performance, with all its indications of the range and accomplishment of her armoury, he had to admit, apprentice that he was, he couldn't be sure what it was she wanted him to do.

"What shall we do for openers?" he asked, playfully.

"Anything you like," she said, just as playfully.

'Well, she couldn't say fairer than that, could she?' he asked in his mind. Aloud, he said: "What about this, then?"

Tentatively, he opened her kimono and removed it. Her compliance encouraged him to go on; so, gently, he pushed her backwards onto the Ambrose Lloyd couch. With some diffidence, he began to kiss her breasts and run his hands over her body.

'Maybe that will do for a start,' he thought.

She moaned and pulled him fiercely down on to her. He tried moving his tongue on her and found her teats hardening under its tip. Her thighs went round him, tight, squeezing the breath from his body.

'That seemed to work all right. Or a bit more than all right. Look at her! How brown she is! Her nipples are sweet as aniseed balls and the aureoles like russet apples in Autumn, ready to fall, – and the scents, the odours! Oh, my God she's fierce! A circus lion. Listen to it roar! And I've only got a few scraps to feed through the bars. And— wheeh!...'

Jonty stopped observing. He stopped thinking. He stopped feeling. He stopped being Jonty. He became somebody else he'd never been before. He became part of something that someone else was being part of. If he was anywhere, he was in a region where all his attitudes, his prejudices, his ignorance and his knowledge had not visited hitherto and did not know what to do there. In this new place, he began to feel things, mysterious unexplored guesses that seemed to supersede all his old feelings and set them in a different rank order. Jonty was no longer in charge. What was in charge must have been lurking about inside some hideaway all these years, just waiting for a chance to emerge and take over, and God! here it was, 'here it is, here it bloody well is!....'

He became aware that she was calling out his name under him. He found himself saying words he had only seen on paper and expressing feelings he had previously fought shy of.

"Darling!" he said. "Oh, my darling! Christ, what a thing!"

"Yes, my love, it was, it was, it was," she whispered.

And she kissed him all over his head and his face and his neck. She moaned noises into the pores of his skin whose meaning went straight through to the something in him that didn't need words, that short-circuited all the normal channels of communication and by-passed his intelligence. For once, he had been divested of his mind and, to a certain extent, his consciousness. He felt naked, physically and mentally. He had been unfastened. He would have to find out how he felt about it. Maybe he'd never zip himself up again? The thought unnerved him, so he distracted himself by saying to Alex: "Oh, what a beautifully superb pair of incredibly sensual earlobes you've got. I told you, didn't I?"

Alexis laughed.

"Oh, you did, you did! Wasn't it just something? What a climax I had! All melting and gooey and formless and — oooh! – let's lie here forever, shall we?"

"Okay! At least, that little bit of forever that goes as far as nine o'clock tomorrow at Burke's, Charles & Long's."

"You clown! Now you've bloody well spoilt it." Alexis sat up abruptly.

"No!" he said. He pulled her down beside him again and kissed her. "There's still quite a bit of that forever left yet."

She snuggled up close to him, crooning softly to his chest. After a while, he said: "You know, I'm sure about two things now."

"Oh?" she asked, dreamily.

"Yes," he said, decisively. "When I came to your flat the first time, all this stuff," he swept an arm through the air, "seemed overwhelmingly expensive." He paused, thinking.

"And now?"

"After making love on Harold Lloyd – "

"Ambrose!" she interrupted.

"All right, Ambrose – I KNOW it's expensive. And that's why it SEEMED expensive. Q.E.D!"

"Fool!" she said affectionately, and kissed him under the ear.

"And are you still overwhelmed by it?"

"No! Only by you."

Jonty was beginning to feel very tired. All that he had recently experienced (and he wasn't quite sure yet what it was he had experienced) was going to be enough for him for some time to come. As marvellous as it had been with Alexis, Jonty felt that too much of that sort of thing would necessitate a thorough servicing and respraying job on his current beliefs and attitudes to the world. He wasn't at all sure that Alexis was the woman he wanted, or that she was worth the initial deposit. When you laid out that kind of money, you had to be sure you were on to a good thing. Taking everything he had learned about her into consideration, he felt tentative, decidedly tentative. He recollected the joke about the clergyman, who, on his honeymoon night made love to his wife for the first time and, when she asked him how he felt, said: "Now that it's over, I'm giving a prayer of thanks to God. I wouldn't like to go through that again."

Jonty lay back and prepared himself for what he hoped would be a deep sound sleep. Alexis leaned over him. He sighed.

"Hold still!" she said.

She fluttered her eyelids against his cheek.

"What's it like? Butterflies?"

"If you like."

"Now, you do it to me. Go on. Not there! Here! Yes, yes, like that."

Jonty breathed deeply.

'God,' he thought, 'why is there so bloody much of the night left?'

Jonty closed his copy of *The Weekend Mail* with a sigh. He had managed, by careful scheming in the D.O. and a continual surveillance of Treblitt's office, to catch half an hour of late afternoon sunlight on the roof. It was cold but fine. He had huddled down comfortably behind one of the warm-air ventilators. There was a moderate wind and rain was threatening.

He was not alone. A pimply hobbledehoy in a dirty blue boiler-suit had slunk up a few minutes after Jonty had arrived. They did not acknowledge each other. Like Jonty, he had settled himself behind a ventilator and had been listening to his minute transistor ever since. Jonty caught snatches on the wind. A DJ (grossly overpaid) was interviewing a young pop star (criminally overpaid) who seemed bent on revealing to his fans (indecently underpaid) that not only did he have no voice, and that his success was all due to wiring, but that he was also mentally subnormal and found great difficulty in using the English Language.

"Yeah! thass right. Right! I mean, I had to... you know... er... succeed. Yeah! thass what I had to do. You know?"

Question from DJ.

Reply from Young Pop Star, "Oh, well, I mean... I – I — I — just kinda...

Jonty decided to go; he'd had the best of the sun, anyway. The hobbledehoy seemed to be trying to get right inside his tiny radio set. Jonty left with no feelings of regret.

When he reached the D.O., he scrutinised the notice on the door to see if any further judicious depredations were necessary, decided he was satisfied with its present condition – D.O… BY… RD – pushed the door ajar an inch or two, and then peered through the gap. He saw numerous heads bent over boards and heard the click-click of the set squares and drafting machines. Dummock was not at his desk and Treblitt wasn't in his office. Jonty strained and squinted to try to cover his survey of the entire office, but certain areas remained un-surveyed. Where was the family breadfruit? He pondered opening the door a little wider, but decided he was probably safe, so he pushed it open jauntily and went to his board, whistling. No-one challenged him.

Jonty had already decided how he was going to spend what was left of the afternoon. He intended taking up the suggestion Barry Crehan had made a week or two ago at his party. The idea had slowly taken root in his mind and he was now about to give it a go. He had already worked out the contents and shape of the letter in his head. All he had to do was write it. Why shouldn't he qualify for some kind of an educational grant as well as the next? He had heard of assistance to promising candidates before whose parents were in straitened circumstances. Circumstances didn't come much straiter than his Dad's, did they? Jonty's expectations were great.

Maybe a beginning like this would fill the bill?

> *Dear Sirs, I am writing to you from conditions of dire financial hardship. The danger my academic career is running has prompted me.*

Something of the sort!

He took the sheet of paper that he had specially stolen for the purpose from the Stationery Stores out of his drawer and arranged it carefully under his T-square. He placed an old print of a gap gauge handy in case he had to disguise his activities urgently. Then, on the brand new watermarked quality sheet he wrote Alexis's address in his best printing style, and under that, in the exactly correct place, 'Dear

Sirs,' in his cursive *scritto numero uno.* Pretty good! He sat back, sucked the end of his pencil and admired his handiwork with great sincerity.

The stealthy squeak of rubber-soled boots behind his stool disturbed his homage and he turned. The sneaky old bastard! Creeping up on him like that!

"Ah, good afternoon, Jonty! Eating pencils again, I see. Have you had a good nap?"

The round shapeless shape that Treblitt tried to pass off as a face glowered at him unequivocally. Jonty looked down and wondered how Treblitt had managed to get so near without the usual rolling tympany accompaniment, or falling over the clearly unmanageable weight of his boots.

"I see. Got nothing to say for yourself, hey?"

Treblitt peered over Jonty's shoulder.

"What's that? A letter?"

"Y-yes. That's what it is. A letter."

"Personal or business?"

"Well, it's a bit of both, really."

"What's that you say?... Jonty, you sadden me. I am not an unintelligent man, Jonty, whatever you may think. I do wish you'd remember that! Either it's for the firm. Or it's for you. Which?"

"Well, it isn't for the firm, and it isn't for me, either, not directly, anyway. There's this charity, and I thought—"

"What charity?"

Treblitt let one shoulder sag to show his extreme and sudden fatigue, screwed up his eyes, put out his chin, and regarded Jonty with all the suspicion he could muster.

"Eh? Well—it's—it's a society for paraplegics and I was just going..."

"All right, all right! I see, Jonty, I see. This is yet another of your schemes. You're a very busy man, Jonty, aren't you? You haven't really got time to earn a living, have you? To learn to — "

"—I thought the firm wouldn't mind so much seeing it was on behalf of — "

"—A charity! Yes, yes, I know. Well, don't worry about it! I've got it all in hand, Jonty. As a matter of fact, I thought I'd better pass on the message to you while you were actually in the office."

"Message?"

"Yes, Jonty. From Major Knowles. He'd very much like you to meet him in ten minutes time. We'll go together, shall we?"

Treblitt dropped his bombshell and waited for the explosion. Jonty refused to react. But, as Treblitt did his comic walk away, even his boots were smiling.

Jonty was flabbergasted. Treblitt had caught him with his jeans down this time. Jonty felt that a hiatus was called for, some kind of an embargo on consciousness to allow him to convalesce for a while, and he did his best to extinguish himself by following in his head all the instructions for the exercises given by Yogi Ramacharaka in his book *Hatha Yoga*. Consequently, he was not fully aware that Treblitt and he had walked together to the office of the Works Manager, and he looked round wondering if he'd arrived by some kind of levitation.

Major Knowles was saying: "So this is the chap, eh? Wants a recommendation for a rise, what?"

"No, sir! That is another one. This is the one we were talking about on – "

"Oh, that one! I see."

16

Major Knowles was a short stump of a man, very well fed, thinning hair, expensive clothes, and an ambience of unremitting distractedness and undirected goodwill. His eyes kept skipping to the telephone, or to the in-tray, or to one of the piles of letters on his desk, as if he couldn't make up his mind what to do first. Then, he would look again in the general direction of Jonty without actually looking AT him. Obviously, he had scarcely heard a word of the tale Treblitt had been telling him for the last few minutes, or registered who Jonty was, or even what he looked like. Jonty stood quiet and still, listening, weighing up his chances of getting the sack.

"And then there are all these notices that keep appearing on the noticeboards," Treblitt was saying.

"That's what they're for, isn't it?"

"What?"

"Noticeboards. Show things are going on."

"Yessir. But not this kind of notice. I found this one in the men's lavatory – in one particular cubicle to be exact."

Treblitt handed a small oblong of green cartridge paper to Major Knowles, who took it and read aloud:

OPERATION THRIFT

Please use both sides of the paiper. Thank you very mush. Now wash yore hands.

Knowles laughed aloud. "I say, that's going a bit far. Both sides. Ha, ha! General idea's good, though. Economics. Hey?"

"And the other one is even more offensive. I found this in my – the same cubicle."

This time Treblitt chose himself to read it aloud. He wasn't taking any chances on quirky interpretations by his superior:

NOTICE

This company is sick and tired of purchasing several tons of best quality medicated toilet rolls each week for the MEN'S conveniences. In future, only lined foolscap of a sturdy make (which we buy in bulk at economic rates) will be provided.

Jonty noticed Major Knowles nodding his head, as if in appreciation of the notice, while Treblitt droned heedlessly on.

It should be specially noted that the company of Burke's, Charles & Long's will take no responsibility for cuts and abrasions sustained in the use of this product...

For the first time since Jonty had been in the Works Manager's office, he saw Major Knowles give his full attention to Treblitt, who was now finishing his performance with a flourish.

Please return the quire to the nail in the corner when you have finished with it.

Signed

Major H.B. Knowles, D.S.O.,

Works Manager.

Treblitt looked up in anticipation at Major Knowles, throwing up his hands in mock despair as he did so. Knowles was rubbing his chin, thoughtfully.

"Foolscap, mm? Yes, foolscap! Funny! Don't remember writing that! Dated when, Treblitt?"

But Major Knowles's concentration had waned again, and he was now fingering the cover of a file on his desk with something like vainlonging in his eyes. Treblitt was aghast.

"No, sir! YOU didn't write it. Godley did."

"Who?"

"Jonathan Godley! This man here, sir."

Major Knowles stopped fiddling with the manila cover of the file of papers for a moment and allowed his clear blue eyes to wander to Jonty's impassive face. A rapid very affable smile flicked on and off. Jonty guessed he must be developing a nervous twitch, or maybe going in for some kind of subliminal advertising. Jonty stared back at him, pugnaciously, refusing to respond to either.

"I see, I see," said Major Knowles, installed fully once more in his habitual distractedness. "Always like to see initiative. Bit unorthodox. But sound idea, sound idea! A rise, you say, Treblitt?"

Knowles raised his eyebrows vaguely towards Treblitt. Treblitt let the air out of his mouth in a suppressed sigh. 'The old breadfruit is looking a bit over-ripe,' thought Jonty, who was beginning to think that he'd discovered an unintentional ally in Major Knowles, and was considering a radical re-assessment of him.

"No, sir, I didn't say. What I had in mind was – "

"—Well, consider it, man! Young chap. Initiative."

"No, sir. I'm afraid we're not communicating. Let me try to…"

Treblitt explained all over again what it was that had brought him to Major Knowles's office. During his account, Jonty figured that Treblitt must be trying to demonstrate some kind of chorea to the Major: his arms and legs jerked spasmodically, emphatically, or ataxically, according to his meaning and his feelings. Jonty noticed that he used the word 'Jonty' rather a lot. Major Knowles's eyes searched restlessly for a means of escape.

Jonty began to feel unreal. Perhaps it wasn't happening? Maybe it was all an act? Or rather, they were all posing for a photograph in a surrealist collection of Salvador Dali's; or a scene in an allegorical film directed by some neurotic Swede, called 'Amnesia Meets Schizophrenia While Anarchy Looks On.' It was the first time he had actually come face-to-face, if that was the expression, with Major H.B.Knowles.

As Jonty mused on the quirks and crotchets of the Works Manager, things that Dummock had told him when he first arrived at Burke's, Charles & Long's began to return to him. What was it he had said?

"Watch out for Knowles. He's got M.B.D."

"What's that?"

"Maximum Brain Damage!"

But the name of the Major had meant little at the time. It seemed that Knowles was notorious throughout the area for his distractedness. Apart from the fact that he was a wizard on cost analysis and, contrary to expectations, a very good organiser, he was a man of quiet and invincible obsessions. You had to approach him gingerly and watch for the signs if you hoped to reach him. Unless you happened to hit on the particular obsession he was working with at the time, he would regard you as an intruder trying to break into his private affairs, and humour you with flashes of bogus attention and phatic conversation, hoping to get rid of you. Treblitt seemed to have hit upon an affair marked PRIVATE with his customary eptitude, and was getting the full Knowles treatment as a consequence.

"Are you, Jonty?"

Jonty was plucked roughly back from his reveries.

"What's that, sir?"

"Late! Several times a week," interjected Treblitt, "And besides this persistent lateness, he is missing from his board for hours at a time. I have been told he spends his time on the roof."

During the period of Jonty's meditations, Treblitt seemed to have penetrated Major Knowles's defences, as there was no doubt now about his attentiveness to Treblitt's remarks. Wonder how he did that?

"On the roof! Extraordinary!"

"Yes, sir. With copies of magazines. Only a short time since, Mr Dumnock was telling me...."

'Oh, so Dummock had been round Treblitt's earlobes, had he?'

"Screwed to the floor! Not still there, I hope?"

"No, Mr Dummock did manage to remove them after a great deal of trouble, quite ruined."

"A rise for this man is quite out of the question, Treblitt. Thought it would have been obvious."

"And it has been rumoured to me, Major Knowles, that Jonty has been going round the works from time to time trying to extort money for—er—charities. He has been seen with a number of tins—"

"—What kind?"

"The tall slotted kind with long loops fastened at the sides and hand-made labels stuck round," said Jonty. It was out before he could prevent it.

They both looked at him in severe surprise. It was the first time he had offered an unprompted contribution since his arrival in the office. Treblitt recovered himself quickly.

"Oh, so you admit it, do you, Jonty?" he asked, simmeringly.

"Admit what, sir?"

"About these charities! Getting money on false pretences."

Jonty realized that he had made a serious error of judgment in drawing attention to himself. He began to fabricate some kind of a defence.

"I kinda... just sorta... described... the kinda tins... you – er..."

"All right, Jonty. Thank you for that cogent explanation.... So, you see, Major Knowles, I thought you might consider that a dismissal was not too—"

"Dismissal! Mmm. Must be careful. Trouble with unions, what?"

"In this case, sir, I think the grounds are more than sufficient."

"Quite so, quite so! Still, not altogether happy. What's the man himself got to say, eh? These—these—notices stuck about the place, and the letters, eh? What?"

Major Knowles flicked up his clear eyes *tout de suite* to Jonty's brown ones, and as quickly flicked them away, two blue minnows seeking the shadows. Jonty took it as a signal to start explaining himself. But, this time, his inventiveness seemed to have deserted him.

"The notices! Yes—er—the letters!"

"That's right!" said Treblitt, scenting the kill. "Well, Jonty?"

It looked as if Jonty could not any longer avoid speaking. But what? He searched for something un-incriminating to say, and, at the same time, a way to avoid saying it. The jolting starts and stops that he made flipped a switch in his memory and he found himself falling into the bah-bah lingo he had heard only a short while ago.

"You mean the letters, kind of, I kind of pin up?"

"That's what we mean, Jonty."

"Yeah, well, I mean, I just kinda started... and as I started kinda.... to do that, you know... I mean, I just had to, you know... do it... a kinda compulsion.... sort of... you know?"

"We know, Jonty!"

"You just couldn't help it, eh?"

"Right! Right!"

He turned to the Major. "For God's sake, thass — thass just what I mean, Major Knowles. Yeah, yeah!"

Jonty's remark addressed directly to the Major had produced a kind of horror in him, and he visibly pressed himself against the back of his swivel chair; but recovered well enough to say to Jonty: "Why?"

"Ugh?"

"Why?"

"Aah!... Why?... Well... ah... ah... you know, suddenly... kinda... something hit me... ah... right there." Jonty clutched his stomach. "And I kinda realized... if you wanna be happy in this world... you just gotta —"

"If you want to be WHAT, Jonty?"

Jonty looked at Treblitt. Was it his fancy, or had that shapeless shape of a face begun to take on some form and feature? Was it actually in the process of transformation?

"Ah.... well.... happy kinda."

"Go on, Jonty. This is very interesting."

Jonty asked himself how it was possible for something so much a part of the vegetable world as a breadfruit was able to show an expression of decisiveness. But it certainly seemed to be doing it. And how, at the same time, it could transmogrify itself into some kind of a physiognomy. But it seemed to be doing that as well. Intriguing!

"Yeah... well.... you just gotta be yourself.... that's it... I felt in such a damn' hurry... to get to be... myself.... kinda... kinda... forgot myself.... and started pinning up... ah.... them letters... I just let go, man...."

"Tell me, Jonty, why—being the kind of person you obviously are—why do you want to be yourself? Why not try and be somebody else for a change?"

"Like who?... Ugh?... Like who?... ah... Mr Treblitt?"

Major Knowles had clearly misheard Jonty's intonation and took the name as a suggestion.

"Yes, exactly, like Treblitt! Hey, Treblitt? Or, even, like me!"

"Right! Right! I get your drift... ah... Major... and for God's sake Major... ah... you got me there... you sure got me... there... if you wanna be a big star, Major... you just gotta give it your best shot... you gotta play it straight... honest, see... sure as hell... I... ah... ain't got nothin' to damn' well answer to that."

"Well – " Treblitt began, but Jonty cut him off. He wanted to halt the transmogrification in its tracks. Enough was enough.

" – If you see what I mean, Major?"

The Major looked up at Jonty, startled to the depths of his blue eyes.

"Yes, of course!"

"Should we ask Jonty to leave us now, sir, and we can....? All right, Jonty. You may go. I'll talk to YOU later."

There was no doubt about it. Treblitt was evidently set on completing the transformation. He must have finally realized that growing a moustache on a breadfruit was, in essence, quite ridiculous – although he had managed to prove that it was feasible. He had also managed to get people to accept it as normal. A good P.R. job, you had to admit.

As Jonty left the office of the Works Manager, he heard Major Knowles sorrowfully saying: "Extraordinary lingo! I'll never keep up. Young people! Never. Was he—was he quite right in his upper storey, Treblitt? What did you say his name was?"

"Jonty!" Jonty said. "His name is Jonty. Yeah.... we're juss good friends... kinda. Okay, okay! Don't crowd me," he said to the imaginary reporters. The gang of newsmen shrank back and disappeared.

Jonty went down the wooden staircase to the D.O. His ordeal was over. It was the worst so far. He had a feeling that, this time, he would never manage to finish his census on the horse-hairs stuck in the varnish of that other wall. Another unanswered question in the enormous succession of unanswered questions that his life was made up of.

'Why is it that things I find important and worth doing, other people find absurd? And why is it that things other people find important and worth doing, I find absurd?'

'Why is it all going on?' he sighed, and went back to finishing his letter.

17

S ome time after his interview with Major Knowles, Jonty was having a cup of tea in a British Railway buffet. Treblitt had wanted to talk to Jonty, but only very briefly: a week's notice and a month's pay. Treblitt had succumbed to the temptation, naturally, of adding a few more germane comments, but they may as well have been in Tamil, as Jonty had no recollection of them at all. It was the bit he'd said in English that had held news-value for Jonty.

"Goodbye, Godley, and good luck. You are going to need it!"

"What, me? I'm an Aquarian!" he lied defiantly.

Treblitt didn't waste time staring at his blotter, or sucking his moustache, but said at once: "Then I'm afraid your water-jar's leaking."

"Pisces must be in the descendant again."

"Oh, I see, Godley. You mean drowned in all that leaking water! Good-bye, Jonty. Call in at the Wages Office on your way out."

It was curious how, in the last few hours, Treblitt had somehow produced features for his face, complete with expressions, and managed to get his mind into synch with his mouth. The speed with which Treblitt had come back at Jonty had been quite bewildering. Where had he been hiding it all these months?

Several hours later, still bemused, but now for somewhat different reasons, Jonty surveyed the large, bleak, high-ceilinged Buffet under the fluorescent strips, and observed his companions. Funny, how grey and shagged-out and hopeless people in British Railway Restaurants appeared! Only the odd Aquarian here and there smiled happily into his instant coffee. Tonight, he couldn't see any literary johnnies or arty-crafty types about. Couldn't stand the British Railway prices, perhaps? No—wait a minute! That little knotted-up black chap in the corner with the big eyes and the mobile mouth, surely that was James Baldwin? Must be fresh over from the States judging by the eager expression he displayed. Maybe working on the British Race Problem for a new book called 'Go Tell It to the Stationmaster'?

'And much good THAT will do him,' thought Jonty. 'Good luck to James Baldwin! With the exchange rate of the pound as it is, the prices wouldn't worry him too much, anyway.'

Jonty now felt satisfied, He usually managed to locate one of the literary crowd pottering, lounging, or sniffing about. He was pleased it hadn't been T.S.Eliot; he wasn't feeling in the pious mood required for an audience with the Pope tonight. Nor was he feeling amiably disposed towards the half-finished dry bread roll on his plate. He regarded it with distaste.

"You don't look much like the Staff of Life to me!"

A plump middle-aged middle-class middle-browed woman at the next table, wearing a floppy felt hat, and a heavy tweed check skirt stretched tight over a rump that projected well over each side of her plastic seat, looked up at Jonty with great suddenness and astonishment.

"What did you say, Young Man?" she asked in an expensive voice.

"Oh, not YOU, madam!" answered Jonty cheerfully. "I was talking to my bread roll."

"Yes, of course, of course!"

She did her best to look as if she hadn't understood but she couldn't carry it off. So she closed, very quickly, the novel she was reading, picked up her case, and began to waddle away. Jonty called after her, blowing her cover completely:

"All these British Rail bread-rolls have got too much to say for themselves. Try the custards. They're much quieter. When you've tasted them, you'll know why!"

She gave an apprehensive glance over her thick tweed shoulder and made for the most distant corner of the restaurant, where she put down her case and sat staring at Jonty with great intentness. Jonty picked up his cup and held it out to her in a toast. She turned sideways on her chair and stared out of the window.

'Another poor soul not strong enough for the world,' thought Jonty.

James Baldwin had watched the whole performance with interest and amusement, looking for copy. Jonty extended his cup to him, also, but he merely grinned. Jonty put down his cup without drinking.

He had been pondering what he would do if he did not hear very soon from the Education Office (Grants Section). It was more than a week ago that he'd left Burke's, Charles & Long's and he was getting anxious. His letter must have reached there long before. Jonty wondered if he'd forgotten hearing that the GPO was on strike again. But he hadn't missed any newscasts just lately, had he, or seen any mention in *The Weekend Mail*? Just part of the general malaise, maybe? Things had altered a lot since Anthony Trollope's time.

Then Jonty had a hunch that made him sit bolt upright in his chair.

"Has that sod Dummock put the poison down for me in some way? I wonder!"

After Treblitt had good-byed him out of his office, Dummock had smirked him back to his drawing board—triumphantly, every step of the way. Dummock had known that it was going to happen all right. Still, who hadn't? It was common knowledge that Jonty would be given the elbow, sooner or later. Jonty knew it better than anybody. But, come to think of it, Dummock seemed to have known exactly WHEN it was going to happen, and he'd been the first to commiserate, too. The next morning, Dummock, wearing his greasy work shoes and Orson Welles voice, had crooned:

"Sorry about that, Arnold lad! Unlucky in war, lucky in love, eh?"

Arnold lad stared at Dummock's aubergine-shirt with the almost invisible stripe, willing it to disappear spontaneously for ever. He beheld the thin handsomeness of Dummock's face, wishing he could change it, radically; marvelled at the way Dummock managed to cause

154

his white coat to look more like a surgeon's than a housepainter's; inspected Dummock's smile, gauging exactly what he meant by that love bit; and, knowing what he knew, asked with great deliberateness:

"Would you like me to stuff the *Daily Telegraph* crossword down that smile, Dummock? You wouldn't win a book-token with THAT one!"

Dummock looked aft. Treblitt was still in his office: he felt safe. He smiled on. He turned round completely. "You couldn't," he said.

Jonty got off his high stool. Dummock moved back a pace or two, still smiling. Dummock was genuinely enjoying the situation.

"Oh, yes, I could Dummock. Together with your favourite set of Alexander Dumas."

To reinforce his boast, Jonty took up one of his recently-learned Karate stances, investing it with as much menace as he knew how. He held his thirty centimetre ebony-edged ruler in his right hand.

Dummock didn't budge. He reared up perfectly straight in front of Jonty, extending his left hand towards him, palm upward, and waggled his fingers, calling him on.

"Come and see what I've got for you, Arnold boy. Don't be so unfriendly!" His smile widened. "It might prove very useful to you," he added.

Dummock took a folded sheet of paper from one of the side pockets of his surgeon's coat and held it out to Jonty, confidently. Jonty stiffened, and then began very slowly to straighten up. He was aware that several of the draughtsmen in the office were watching them curiously, and he felt relieved that Dummock and he had kept their voices low. Jonty, now erect, leaned back on his high-stool, letting his feet trail in front of him.

"Nice pair of pumps, those, Arnie boy!" said Dummock with heavy sarcasm, looking at Jonty's footwear.

Jonty had known at once what the paper was: Dummock had him by the pubics.

"Give me that letter, Dummock."

"Oh, no, Arnold boy! Wouldn't be good for you. It's a safeguard, an insurance I've taken out to protect our friendship. It's very good, very good indeed! One of the best begging letters I've seen."

"Glad you like it!"

"Oh, I do, I do! As an attempt to extort money from the British Taxpayer, it's very interesting."

"You're dramatising, Dummock. There's no extortion. You know that, don't you? It's an application, only."

"Do I? Well, I'm hanging on to it for a while, in any case. I might add a codicil and send it on to the Chief Education Officer myself. And Treblitt hasn't seen it, yet."

Dummock shook his forefinger at Jonty.

"Naughty, naughty! You shouldn't leave things like that about. Very careless."

Jonty had wondered what had happened to that first draft. It should have been on his board when he got back; but Dummock had not wasted his opportunity while Jonty had been with Knowles and Treblitt. Oh, dear, no, not Humphrey Smedley!

"And so?" asked Jonty.

"So this, Arnold boy!" On the instant, Dummock stopped smiling, and began to show signs of the simian ancestry Jonty had detected earlier. "KEEP AWAY FROM ALEX! Understand? If I see you've been hanging around her—well—I leave the consequences to your imagination. Okay?"

"Not okay, Dummock. Alexis wants me to hang around her, Dummock? Or hadn't you noticed?"

"There's your lack of experience talking, Arnie lad. Women are easily put off. Give them a little—buttering-up—you know the sort of thing I mean—and you can make them think they didn't want what they thought they wanted, but something different. They're just like poodles. A rough word here, a soft word there. I'm sure you understand, hey, Arnold old lad?"

Jonty picked up what was left of his bread roll and crumbled it into little bits.

"And you too, Dummock!" he said aloud, but this time nobody listened.

His mind went back to that night at her flat. Yes, that night! The entire experience had been a kind of epiphany for him. He'd seen things he hadn't seen before. Some he wouldn't have minded seeing again; others he wasn't so keen on. On the one hand, he was delighted he wouldn't see his virginity moping around any longer. He'd got rather ashamed of dragging that about in public, trying to make believe it had nothing to do with him, and then trying to smooth it down and reassure it in private. But, on the other hand, there were things he would assuredly not mind having another peep at, much too obvious to be for instanced. Jonty found himself smiling at the crumbled bread-roll on his plate.

"You heap of aphrodisiac, you!"

Alexis had not been as difficult to put off as he had expected. He was, in a way, grateful to Dummock for crystallizing his feelings about her, as well as crystallizing them about Dummock. No doubt, Dummock was going to get nastier than he normally was; he was going to work at it, that much was clear. And Jonty had found out in the process that Alexis wasn't worth him getting free treatment on the National Health service for injuries sustained in battle. Of course, she'd taunted him.

"So you got what you wanted and now you're off! Men! All the same!" she said.

"Yes, I know, and it's that particular kind of sameness you like so much, isn't it?"

"Pig!"

"Anyway, just ask yourself—who wanted what? I sent you a goodbye recipe. It's as plain as a pikelet. I'm mad about Chilled Whatsit Mousse and you can't stand it. That's no firm basis for marriage, is it?"

"Who wanted marriage?"

"Then there's your passion for Barbara Cartland in the lavatory, Harold Lloyd in the sitting room, Dummock in the Works Stores, and a pinch of Crehan in his studio. That's some goulash!"

"You know, you've got a delicate talent for making everything sound obscene."

"Not everything, only—"

"—any vows. I just wanted us to be—"

"—Good friends. I know!"

"Well, what's wrong with that?"

"Nothing! I come from an earlier form of man—that's all. I break out in a neanderthal rage when I see my woman dragged off by the hair to somebody else's cave. Can't help it! It's regressive genes, or ingrown hormones, or something."

"Never mind the oratory! You want to own me body and soul and I'm not—"

"—I'll ignore the latter for now! That's not the bit you give to Dummock, is it? I just don't like having shares in a public body."

"Why you—you—insulting sod!"

She had picked up the pieces and placed them in the palm of her hand, sadly, and oh! so sadly, had said to Jonty:

"Will you do me a favour, Jonty?"

'Oh, so it's Jonty now, is it?' he thought.

Aloud, he said: "If I can."

"You can. Just go. Just bugger off. You are a nowhere man, Jonty! Just leave me alone."

That was two weeks ago. Now, here he was, keeping company with the most brazen bread-and-butter roll that British Rail could offer him. Two weeks! The phrase jogged his memory. Hadn't he written Alexis's address at the top of his application for a bursary? She had picked up a handy volume of Barbara Cartland and threw it at him, hard. Unluckily for her, it had missed Jonty and ruined one of her moquettes. An Anthony Newley moquette, though!

"A knock-out from good, clean, romantic stuff like that could have brought me to my senses, I suppose?"

Of course! The reply from the Education Office could be waiting for him there. However—problem!—how to get the letter? Would she burn it? Would she tell Dummock? Would Dummock tell her? Mmm, it required deliberation.

At that moment, Jonty's attention was caught by the arm gestures of the tweed-bottomed woman standing at the counter with her case, talking volubly to a small harassed man in the regulation grey of British Rail uniforms. From time to time, they turned to stare at Jonty. He stared back. He soon stared the woman out, but the little man just kept looking. After a while, he would turn and peer steadfastly at the kitchen ventilators. Could they possibly be discussing the removal of cooking odours, steam arid condensation from the restaurant kitchens, and have Jonty in mind as contractor? If so, he'd willingly give them advice, but they'd have to hurry because his time was valuable, and getting more valuable by the minute, and he couldn't hang about giving free advice to strangers who looked at him so suspiciously, and...

Jonty stood up awkwardly and limped on the pinned joint to the double glass doors. They watched him in disbelief, their eyes moving from feet to head, up and down. When he reached the doors he joggled round on his gimpy leg to wave them good-bye. Tweedy lowered her floppy hat tactically over her eyes and the official representative of British Rail continued to look glumly at Jonty, notably unmoved. Jonty knew in his bones that if one of the Horsemen of the Apocalypse had been standing in his place, the little man's expression would have remained awfully unchanged. British Rail seemed to favour a policy that selected employees of that kind.

"Good night," he called, and limped away.

Outside the buffet, a soldier sat on a bench engrossed in reading a newspaper. Two Post Office employees were stacking mailbags on a trolley at the end of the platform, too busy to notice Jonty.

'Ha! So they're not on strike, after all!'

The station emptiness soared enormously up to the sooty glass roof, curving its Gothic arches across the glinting tracks. Conditions were exactly right!

Looking about him, Jonty walked over to one of the chocolate-vending machines. He stopped in front of it and surveyed the platform once more, just to make sure. No one! He skipped in smartly to one side of the machine and gave it a jolt with the heel of his hand. Lo and behold! A drawer flew open. A block of Fruit and Nut. Jonty turned his back on the machine and surreptitiously removed the chocolate. Then, he leaned backwards to close the drawer. His routine was impeccable: it had taken a lot of practice.

Jonty knew that there was another machine on the platform that sometimes responded to the same kind of treatment—a cigarette vendor. Jonty preferred this appliance because inside each packet of ten was sixpence change. He knew exactly where to thump each machine. He was about to administer the next K.O. when the doleful uniformed man came through the doors of the restaurant. He spotted Jonty at once and inspected him glumly. Jonty re-assumed his gimpy leg and limped sadly along the platform and up the steps to the bridge. At mid-span, he risked a reccy through the girders. Woeful Willie stood watching him! Jonty took to his toes, not wanting to explain anything to anyone.

Puffing, he arrived in the booking hall, and went across to the row of telephone cubicles at one side. Four of them were occupied. He went into the vacant cubicle and closed the concertina doors behind him. He took the sleeper from its cradle and dialled a number and spoke into the mouthpiece:

"Think of a number," he said, "two, double it, four, take away the number you first thought of, three, and the answer is—number engaged."

It was a diversionary tactic he employed in case someone happened to be watching him. He put the sleeper back in its cradle and pressed the money-back button. There was no responsive clanging of rejected coins. Disappointed, he left the cubicle.

Meanwhile, someone had vacated one, so Jonty tried it, with the same result. As he was about to leave, a small globose man with a long fleshy nose and pendulous cheeks tried to push past him into the cubicle. He was agitated. The inevitable happened. His rolled umbrella jammed sideways across the entrance, preventing him from going in and Jonty from coming out.

"Get out of the way, can't you? Urgent call!"

"Look, Mr Hitchcock! You push on your end, and I'll push on mine, hey?"

"You're mistaken. My name isn't Hitchcock. Be careful! You'll break it."

"I saw your last film, Mr Hitchcock. Allow me to congratulate you on—"

"—For God's sake, move, man! Can't you see—Oops!"

The umbrella came free. Mr Hitchcock shot forward. His embonpoint met the apparatus inside, the glass windows rattled, and a clinking and clattering noise began. It was music to the ears. Jonty, jammed hard up against the framework, goggled hard at the coins tinkling and clattering freely onto the concrete floor. He struggled to free himself from the imprisoning bulge, managed it, and bent swiftly to the floor.

"Silly me!"

He smiled up at the suffused face of the breathless Mr Hitchcock.

"Forgot to get my money back."

He pocketed the coins speedily and left. Mr Hitchcock was still recovering his wind. Jonty spotted a policeman, some way off, looking curiously in the direction of the cubicle. He seemed familiar. Could it be the same blue policeman from the fountain, by any chance? Probably not. Most policemen looked just as blue. But Jonty wasn't taking any chances; he left quickly, entering the bustle of New Street, and got lost in the Birmingham night. But consolation was near at hand. Jonty turned abruptly into the entrance of it, climbing the steps of The Queen's, as it was popularly known, and ordered himself a pint of draught Bass. While waiting, he counted his haul.

'Three and six!'

He was feeling elated: another guerrilla skirmish, successfully fought.

'Pisces is on the way up again!'

He took a long, long pull at his beer. The clock on the wall of the bar said ten-thirty. Closing time! But the night was still young; young enough to visit Barry Crehan, at least.

18

"Well, I'll ask her, Arnold, old hen, but if it's the way you say between you and Alex, I can't make any promises, can I?"

"Appeal to her better nature. Tell her it's important for my future."

"She might turn completely Bolshie, then!"

"She wouldn't! She's Roman Catholic!"

Crehan laughed. "Anyway, I'll keep the letter here, if I get it. How's that?"

Jonty nodded agreement. Crehan swallowed some of his malt whisky in satisfaction, and jiggled his Adam's apple once or twice to show he still had the knack. His long gleaming hair fell back into the shadows as he drank. 'The shampoo with the nature inside, hey?'

"Have the other half," said Crehan, rising from his Bauhaus chair.

"Don't mind if I do. Thanks!"

Crehan was as elegant as ever. Every time Jonty saw him, he'd got something different on. Tonight, he was wearing some kind of beige-

and-brown cross-breed, the lucky outcome of an encounter between a singlet and a waistcoat, which he had donned over a sweater that Jonty could have bought only on hire-purchase over forty eight months, provided the deposit was low. It had three huge buttons and two large pockets and purred quietly to itself. His bell-bottomed woven trousers weren't even creased around the crotch. Crehan was probably in a straight bloodline from Narcissus and—who was the tailor of the gods? Jonty sighed. Money!—Nice just to look at the things you could waste it on!

"Here you are, old thing."

Jonty took the handmade pot, noting appreciatively that Crehan had poured his bitter without a bubble of froth.

"To you!" He raised it aloft.

"So what are you doing now?" asked Crehan, sinking back into the pneumatic leather.

"If you mean money-wise—nothing."

"All right—otherwise?"

Jonty hesitated. He didn't entirely trust Crehan, but he didn't know why he didn't. Crehan had always been pretty decent to him personally: open house, beer, chat. He couldn't have been better, could he, short of offering him full board and lodging? Yet, Jonty's instinct was to hide as much as he could from Crehan. He knew Crehan wasn't keen on him. Maybe he wasn't quite fair to Crehan? Wouldn't Jonty himself have ogled Alexis's paisley-flashing, if he'd been in the same position, wouldn't he? Well, yes, but he wouldn't have taken so much trouble to get into that position, would he? No, he wouldn't. Anyhow, Jonty had no claim on Alexis now, none at all, so – 'what the hell, Archie, what the hell?'

"I'm working in the Reference Library, most of the time. It's warm. It's free. It's open till eight. It's all right."

"Aye, I'm sure it is. Doing what?"

"If you must know, I'm working on an essay."

Crehan laughed. "'An Apology for Idleness', eh, by Robert Louis Godley."

Jonty smiled, reluctantly: there was no malice in Crehan's pleasantry. Jonty had to admit it sounded bloody silly, even to him.

"I know! Me—writing essays!"

"No job in the offing, then?"

"Hundreds in the offing, but not in the offering. Employers and me don't see eye to eye about things. I prefer to start at the top and work my way down to the level of my own incompetence: it's called the Jonty Principle. Might as well do what I'm doing, as what they want me to do."

"Aye, I see," he said, slowly. He gazed speculatively into his neat malt, and twirled the pure crystal whisky glass in his fingers, as if he could read something there. "Yes, it's nice to have the filthy stuff! If you can get it clean, so much the better. But it's verra difficult, verra difficult!"

For once, Jonty had no idea of what was passing through Crehan's mind. Suddenly, he looked up at Jonty. There was a new decisiveness in his eyes as he spoke, and a new seriousness.

"You know, I've never thought of myself as a crook, but the older I get, the less surprised I am to see how far I can bend in the interests of lucre."

"I've never caught you bending."

"Well, you wouldn't, would you, old hen?" He was back to his usual tone. "It isn't part of the game to be caught doing that. But I do it—in a small way—nothing big, you understand."

He paused, as if still making up his mind about something. Then, with the note of seriousness in his voice again, he said: "I'm actually looking for a bit of help, at the moment?"

"What—selling dirty postcards to the tourists?"

"Whatever makes you think I sell those? Of course not! My photographic markets are nicely sewn up, thank you! Touting is for the Trogs, old hen."

"I see."

Jonty couldn't help wondering whether or not he had qualified, in Crehan's vocabulary, as a "trog". He had a pretty good idea what Crehan meant by it: lack of money, status, bloodline; the evidence was all around him, in Crehan's studio. Well, he didn't FEEL like a "Trog", but he probably looked like one; and as far as his origins went, which wasn't very far, he was a front-runner for the title. The trick lay in persuading people who thought you were one to act as if they thought you weren't, when you kept behaving as if you were. It wasn't easy!

"So, you're offering me a job as a tout, hey?"

"Look here, Arnold, old hen, I didn't say that. Don't be so touchy. Have the other half."

"I've had it!"

"Well, this is a new one!"

"Okay! Thanks."

'It's true; he doesn't treat me like trog. He's bloody decent. But me reacting like that probably manifests the authentic logo of the species, hey? Rub it out! Try an apology; you might like it.'

Jonty tried it: "That WAS a bit hormonal...! Sorry! Why don't you make things a dab clearer, then?"

Jonty found himself being tactful, and was very surprised to find that he rather enjoyed the sensation, and even more surprised to discover that watching Crehan once again seating himself in the best that Germany could design for his posteriors, comfortably sipping his 'Water of Life', actually intensified the sensation. Was he getting drunk?

"I'll try, old hen! But I wouldn't like to offend you, and I need safeguards selfwise, naturally."

"How d'you mean—offend me?"

"Och! well, Alexis tells me you're a mickle Puritan, really, and you spend your time trying to hide it."

"Oh, does she? Well, if you don't fall into an area marked out by Oscar Wilde, Al Capone and Edward Heath, she thinks you're hopelessly perverted by virtue."

"Oh, c'mon, she's no' as bad as that."

Jonty noted how Crehan's Scots accent was growing as he felt more at home with him. Wasn't that a commendation of some kind?

"Well, I might agree to include Sappho and Casanova, if you insist."

"No wonder you and Alexis didn't hit it off! You weren't exactly made for each other, were you? Anyway, let's not get off the point. Are you interested?"

"What am I supposed to be interested in?... I might be."

"Well," said Crehan, putting down his glass, and leaning quite a long way into the discussion, "as far you're concerned, it could mean a trip to the South Coast once or twice a week – not more."

Jonty inhaled audibly.

"I'd pay your Exes, of course," put in Crehan quickly, "and a retainer, besides."

He leaned back and waited for the effect.

"Sounds nice! I fancy a couple o' trips a week to the seaside. What's the catch?"

"The catch is, old ducky, you'd bring something back. A wee something, fits into a pocket. And that would be the end of it."

"A mickle something?" Jonty couldn't resist the banter.

"If you've got absolutely nothing else to do, of course?"

"If it's as easy as that, why not do it yourself?"

"Have been doing, ducky, but it takes me away from my business, here. Not good! Better if you'd do this little thing for me."

"And safer, eh?"

"Naturally, for everybody!"

"And what is it I shall be bringing back with me, then?"

"Arnold, old love, we don't have to name names, do we?"

"Fits into a pocket, eh? Shouldn't be too hard to open."

"Ah, but we'd agree that you didn't, see? Part of the bargain. What's inside is my concern; yours is just to get it here."

"How much do you pay?"

"Ten pounds a trip and expenses."

"Two trips, twenty quid. Christ! sounds too easy."

"There's a slight risk! It comes across the Channel. You just meet our contact and—Bingo!—you're in the moolah, as they say."

"Or the cart! Where do you sell it?"

"About, about! The world's full of—customers—Hippies, Drop-outs, Sikhs, Indians, Pakistanis, West Indians, Executives, Brits, Conservatives, Voters, Housewives, Brummies... Call them what you will. To me, they're just consumers. There's got to be a supplier. That's the logic of life, old hen!"

"It might be the logic of yours, it isn't the logic of mine."

"What's yours?"

"I'm still working on it."

Crehan laughed, genuinely amused. If Jonty didn't want to go along with him, that was his affair. Live and let live was Crehan's motto. He probably had it embroidered on his blankets. Or somewhere.

Jonty added: "I always took you for a Pillar of the Establishment, Crehan."

"Oh, I am, I am, but here and there, I fill in a little rococco detail, you know."

"Dog eat dog, eh?"

"I wouldn't say that. I prefer a different vocabulary: Initiative; Free enterprise; Profit and Loss. You know, words like that, beginning with capital letters. What do you say, Arnold, old chick, in or out?"

"Out! I've seen some of these junkies."

"Oh, come, come, harsh words! Who said that's what it is, anyhow?"

"Well, isn't it? Besides, skillet and mailbags and one bath a week wouldn't be good for my health. I'm trying to avoid that on the outside, never mind going inside to get it! Let's drop the topic! I'll go back to essay writing."

"Suit yourself! One thing, Arnold, old hen."

"Yes?"

"Our secret, hey?"

"I'm no clipe!"

"Guid! That's settled, then. What about another wee snort?"

Crehan wanted to know all about the essay Jonty was working on, in earnest, this time: its subject, the reading it required, why he was doing it, et cetera. When Jonty told him, Crehan wished him luck, and once more offered to help him by his contact in the Local Education Authority Office. Jonty was struck by the contrast between Crehan's reaction and Dummock's. Dummock wouldn't have done what Crehan was doing; but, then, Dummock wouldn't offer what Crehan was offering, would he? And did what Crehan was offering make up for what Crehan was doing? And did what Dummock wouldn't do make up for what he did do? When it came to people, personal people, Jonty preferred Crehan, any day. But what did that prove? It was all one big bloody conundrum, wasn't it?

"It was your idea in the first place," said Jonty.

"So it was! Well, here's to it!"

"Skol!"

♣

Ten minutes ago, Jonty had thought he was preparing to go to bed, but he had discovered he wasn't. He gave one final blast of pyrethrum and let the mattress fall back on the springs.

"Twenty at one blow," he said aloud to himself.

All the selvages of his flock mattress had been systematically sprayed and cursed, and he had fired salvoes under all the serrated leather rosettes where colonisers had landed from the mainland situated at one corner of the bed. There was even a phalanx under the iron angles of the bed-frame, and he saw them stagger when the spray hit them. Jonty smiled at that.

Jonty opened his window to the chilly night air.

It was a mystery where they all came from. Their breeding-rate was prodigious – a real copulation explosion, you might say. Jonty had thought, at one time, of researching into the sex-life of bedbugs; but he'd had rather a nasty shock when he realized that he was their sole source of food. Scholarship could be carried too far. Unless, of course, they practised cannibalism? Maybe he could research into that? But

Crehan's remark about the blood-spot on his shirt had put an end to all disinterested speculation on the matter. War had been declared!

Jonty's mattress had quite a history attached to it. He had acquired it just after the last Grand National. Ever since his father had won two hundred pounds, a decade or so ago, on a fifty-to-one outsider called Airborne, he'd been trying to repeat his success and became gradually more reckless with each successive loss. He would bet on almost anything, which was fully in accord with his belief that the universe was run as a lottery. He lost and won consistently. During the football season, some small household article or possession would spend a brief period in Uncle's, to provide the stake money; and, then, one day, it would be back in its place. Neither Albert nor Jonty ever mentioned these events: that was part of the pact between them.

But flat-racing seasons could be extremely hairy. Jonty didn't know from one day to the next whether or not he would go home to a house that had been stripped of its decencies and essentials during his absence. But day-by-day, little by little, a small win here, a small win there, he might find things returning. More often than not, a large piece of furniture, such as a wardrobe, disappeared for ever, only to be replaced by another if the gee-gees came up with a sizeable win. One day Jonty returned to find that his mattress had disappeared and that his bed had been made up with one or two under-nourished pillows. He had spent a fretful night on the springs and, for once, registered his protest.

"I'm thinking of putting an ad in the Personal Column: Indian Fakir Wanted Urgently," said Jonty over a cup of tea.

His father looked at him above the Sports Page. "Why the hurry?"

"I'm thinking of changing that spring for a bed of nails and buying a rope-trick," he said nonchalantly.

His father had totally ignored the remark and gone back to the day's runners; but the Sunday morning following the Grand National, without a word being spoken, he had handed Jonty a couple of pounds to buy another mattress. It wasn't much, but after a long search he'd found one in a second-hand shop in the district of Small Heath, an area favoured by far-flung bits of the old Empire. He had obviously purchased the livestock as well, but there had been no mention of this at the time of the transaction, and they discovered him before he them.

As the man had promised them, wafted along on the Winds of Change, they had never had it so good!

Now, the winds had changed again; it carried destruction on its breath and the windows were wide open. Jonty finished making his bed and went downstairs to wait for the fumes to clear. There was a hot tingling sensation in his lungs as if he'd put the little plastic nozzle in his mouth and pressed it. The damn' stuff wouldn't do his TB any good! He opened the front door and stepped out onto the small square of compressed dirt the Council called a garden. Jonty had once shewn an interest in gardening, but he had decided to concrete it all over and do his gardening with a broom! It was a lot easier than messing about with forks and rakes, but the cost of the cement had put him off. He inhaled several times, hard, and felt dizzy.

"Heady stuff, this fresh air! Nearly as good as beer," he said to his neighbour, a hunchback, who had just come out of his house flourishing a bicycle pump.

"Give me the beer, any day," said the man, who came back loaded from the Block and Chopper every Saturday night, singing dirty songs right up to his front door and into his sitting-room, and then accompanied himself on a wooden spoon and enamel jerry into the bedroom, until he fell asleep with the spoon in his mouth and his feet in the pot. His wife said he slept like a baby and had never had a headache or foot cramp in his life.

"Going to get a bit of frost tonight, eh?" he said, peering upwards awkwardly.

Jonty looked at the sky. It was the colour of a Chow's tongue with sprinklings of salt here and there. It wasn't really dark, but Jonty couldn't see a moon anywhere.

"Don't know. It's bloody cold, though."

"It is that."

The light from the open door fell thick and yellow, slantwise, in an angular wedge, onto the bicycle that leaned on the fence between the two houses. The hunchback took a step towards it and began to pump up its tyres.

"Every night I blow it up," he said mournfully, "and every bleedin' day it goes down. A new tube, too. It's the air, yuh know. Tain't what it used to be." A whiff of pyrethrum drifted down from Jonty's open bedroom window.

"Christ!" said the hunchback, "you can even smell it."

"No, Roley," said Jonty, "that's my bedroom!"

His name was, unfortunately, Horace Balls, but everybody called him Roley rather than face up to the fact. They addressed his wife as Mrs Roley.

"Oh, is it?" said Mr Balls in a queer voice, and abruptly changed the subject. "I see'd your Dad down at the Block and Chopper again tonight. Celebrating Christmas a bit early, ain't he? There's a good month, yet."

"No, it's not the festive spirit, it's a little windfall."

"Wonder what the pick-up was?" mused Mr Balls.

He went back to his pumping and afterwards to his house. "Goo' night, then. And you want to look under them planks!" he said, mysteriously, closing the door. The golden wedge of light dwindled with it.

"Good night, Roley."

Jonty walked down the path at the side of the house to the back garden. A small wooden ramp was leaning against the wall near the kitchen steps. He placed it so that his father could wheel himself in when he arrived. No matter how drunk he was, it was a point of pride to manage his chair. He had not overturned it yet, even on a fast bend. He closed the door, leaving it on the latch.

"Brrr!"

It was a cold night. Jonty sat down at the living-room table and gazed at the sheets of paper and open books scattered about on it. He picked up one of the sheets, half-full of his handwriting, scowled at it, and put it down again without reading it. What exactly was he playing at, and especially on a night as cold as this?

He looked at the fire. A grey epidermis was beginning to form over the red layers below. The room had been beautifully warm all night. Now, a chill began to be noticed. But coal was not something the Jonty household was short of, thanks to the allowance his father got from Social Security: 'the reg'lar lick of the lickorish stick', as his Dad called it. He stood up, moved over to the coal bucket standing on the hearth, and self-indulgently placed a large lump of free coal on the free fire, watching the free grey ash fall inwards and the free flames lick round its free black heart.

19

He went back with fresh resolution to his papers. He picked up a sheet and read aloud:

'The theme of <u>29 and a half Poems</u> continues the theme of <u>6</u> <u>and</u> <u>a</u> <u>half Poems</u>, but with less hysteria. He is calmer in his acceptance of life and its processes. In his search for permanence on this earth, he is harassed continually by man's loss of innocence.'

He put the paper down in disgust.

"Man's loss of bullshit!" he said. "And if he wants permanence, there's always the Leicester. Their premiums are reasonable enough. God! They'll never fall for it."

Jonty was working on a critical study of a Welsh poet who'd been a legend in his own lifetime. 'Aren't they all?' he thought.

However, not only did Jonty fail to understand what the Welsh poet was writing about most of the time, but he failed to understand what he, Jonty, wrote about what the Welsh poet was supposed to be writing about, most of the time. This was his third attempt to start the essay and he felt he knew less about the Welsh poet now, after a couple of months' work, than he did when he'd only read what the reviewers had to say. Sometimes, he had felt the reviews were better than the poems; and, sometimes, the poems had seemed better than the reviews. The most that Jonty felt he could commit himself to, with any certitude of truthfulness, was that the reviews, as poems, were only partially successful, and the poems, as reviews, were less so. It was difficult to say at the moment just how much better as poems the reviews were than the poems as reviews were. He could work on it. However, he felt he was much nearer to the position when he would be able to say with the utmost frankness that even the poetry as poetry was awful; and that the reviews as reviews were worse, but if you submitted them to a bullshit test they were marvellous. It really was most disappointing! The fact is, if he wanted to enter for this scholarship, he had to write the essay, whatever conclusions he reached, and that was bloody that!

He sighed and picked up another sheet of paper, looking for a nugget in the paydirt. In large printed letters, it said: DON'T FORGET DUMMOCK. DON'T FORGET DUMMOCK.

Well, he hadn't, and any time now Dummock would be made aware of the fact. He scruntled up the memorandum, wishing it was Dummock he was scruntling, and threw it into the fire, which would have been appropriate for Dummock, also. Then, he looked listlessly at a sheet of notes with some quotations on it. They were taken from a poem about a hunchback. Jonty wondered vaguely if the one next door spent all day in the park dreaming about young women with no clothes on; but he knew from long observation that Horace Balls preferred his beer, his dirty songs on Saturday, his bicycle, and his wife, in that order. And then again, if he didn't write about this Welsh poet, who would he write about? Another Welsh poet? Although he couldn't understand much of this Welsh poet, he liked him better than other Welsh poets he could understand, and better than most poets of any kind, understandable or not.

Take Eliot, for instance, and all his claptrap about an escape from personality being essential to the poetic act. Now, who, just who sodding who, had a more obnoxious personality than Pope Tom? All gin and sin and incense. No wonder he wanted to escape from it! Who wouldn't? Of course, you couldn't say outright that you disagreed with Eliot's opinions, as expressed in his poetry; oh, dear no! Because if you did, all the critics shot you down in flames, shouting loudly that he hadn't put any in his poetry, as Pope Tom himself had been telling them for years, and, mostly, they believed him. Nevertheless, if you could not actually take issue with Tom's opinions, which were allegedly absent from his poetry, YOU could at least disagree with what opinions the poetry implied, and the feelings Tom had about the opinions he didn't express. Couldn't you? Jonty wasn't sure. Which all went to prove that Tom Eliot wasn't a suitable substitute for a Welsh poet, anyway.

True, there were other possibilities. Jonty liked some of the brand new poets very much. But you had to watch it; some of those Oxbridge dons were not too keen on modernity. His essay might get itself read by somebody like Sir John Shrike; or worse, not somebody like him, but him, the great bird himself, who not only disliked David Herbert Lawrence but also believed that all modern poets, since and including Wystan Hugh Auden, dispensed with meaning on principle. The only thing he claimed to understand was their names. This eminent eagle shot arrows into the air from the fastness of his Oxbridge eyrie not much caring where they fell—and Jonty didn't mind whether he would have objected to the mixed metaphor or not. Well, if somebody like him read his submission on one of the newer luminaries, he wouldn't have a Doberman Pincher's chance of getting into an Oxbridge college, even if the Master was mad about dogs. He could imagine what Sir John, or his like, would say:

"Do you think he's the kind of chap we want up here? Look at his assumption: that this feller's worth reading and writing on. He could be rather uncomfortable to have about, don't you think? I sincerely hope that no-one sitting around this table would – er –. Gentlemen, are we agreed?"

Jonty had no difficulty in imagining just how unanimously agreed they would be. On consideration, perhaps he should burn all his papers and forget a bursary altogether? If only the Local Education Office would come up with a reply! Was Crehan's friend on leave, flown the country, or dead? The fire was getting low, anyhow. It needed more fuel. No! Better sleep on the Welsh poet. He didn't want to end up gainfully employed again, did he? What about a quick shifty at *The Weekend Mail* before a spot of bye-byes?

'That sounds good.'

He took the newspaper to bed with him, and was soon fast asleep.

Jonty was dreaming that a tousel-headed legendary hunchbacked poet, stark naked, was riding, as drunk as a Jonty, through a silent Welsh-speaking village in Welsh Wales, on a boneshaker old as the hills with six of the slowest slow punctures ever known, watching the smoke-growing chimneys of the roofs bobbing like corks, and firing a sawn-off shotgun at the cowardly moon that would not stand still in salvo after salvo. Bits fell off the moon and tinkled like glass. The smoke thickened and thickened and the light of the broken moon danced on the crazy walls and the crazy poet fired shot after crazy shot at the crazed moon, and a man in academic dress stood up in the square, crying, 'Gentlemen, I move that the name of Arnold Jonathan Godley be struck from the tablets of the Oxbridge Bibliography of English Literature, for ever and ever, Amen. Now, let us join together to sing For He's a Jolly Bad Fellow.'

And it was then that Jonty awoke. At least, he believed he had awakened. He almost opened what he imagined was an eye, but closed whatever he had opened very quickly because he seemed to be floating about on a bed enveloped in an orange-red cloud, though he knew for sure that he'd gone to sleep in his own room on a mattress that reeked of pyrethrum. And who on earth was firing a gun? What time was it? He tried extending an arm towards his alarm clock; if it was where he had put it, on the chair beside the bed, he must be at home.

His fingers touched the cold blue metal of the clock. That settled it! He opened his eyes: the clock said one-thirty. But why was it so light, and the light that funny colour? And where was the shooting?

Jonty sat bolt upright with a jerk, fully awake. There WAS smoke in the air and an orange glow was located somewhere outside his bedroom window. It was still open. He jumped up and put his head through the curtains. He heard another loud crack, like rifle fire.

Suddenly, smoke billowed upwards into his face and lungs, making him splutter. The windows below him began exploding in bursts.

The house was on fire!

The realization sluiced his brain clear of sleep, but froze the skin on his bones. He managed to pull on trousers and jacket over his pyjamas and rush to the head of the stairs. He crept down. An orange glow came through the small frosted windows of the front door from outside. Smoke was seeping under the living room into the tiny hallway from inside, like swamp-mist. It was lucky that both doors were firmly shut, or the stairs could have been alight. What to do? Go back upstairs and jump from the bedroom window? Or —? He could hear the sound of burning in the living room clearly now, and the crack!—crack!—crack! of the windows. Where was his father? He took a deep breath, and plunged through the door into the room.

Hot reeking air hit him full tilt, solid as a rugby forward. Searing fingers went down his throat and into his lungs, probing his tissues bitterly. He felt sick and started to retch. The fierceness of the heat mauled him. He staggered back into the little hallway and fell onto the stairs, his blind eyes streaming.

'Foul, foul,' he said in his mind.

He struggled to his feet, closed the door of the living room, opened the front door and staggered into the air. He dragged in lungfuls of it and, when his head had unblurred, went by the little path to the back. He opened the kitchen door. It was clear of smoke. The adjoining door must be shut. He went in. He fumbled about for a hand towel, found one, soaked it under the tap, tied it over his nose and mouth, and returned to the front of the house.

His senses were lucid now. Flames were spurting out of the flat front windows of the house, sporadically leaping and trying to reach the bedroom curtains. There was a lot of smoke but not much fire; at least, not as much as he'd expected. He opened the front door of the house and entered the living room. The window frames were still smouldering in stretches red as fresh paint, but parts between were black and furred, bristling with smoke. The curtains had gone, the windows were jagged. The table near the window where Jonty had been working was a smoking charcoal square. The tablecloth and all his papers had disappeared.

He turned. The middle area and rear of the room seemed to be untouched by the flames, but reeked with the bitter smoke. Was that his father's chair at the back, against his bed, next to the kitchen? Oh, God, yes! His arms hung down over the two-railed wheels, his head lolled backwards, his eyes were shut and his mouth was open. He was breathing in with great snoring scoops, and the shredded air was hissing out again as if through an empty honeycomb. He seemed to be untouched. Jonty felt a lurch of relief in his chest. Why hadn't he heard the old bugger before now? Funny how the brain acts in an emergency; just like Archie Casbolt at the entrance of Burke's, Charles & Long's, deciding what's to be let in and what isn't. Jonty wheeled the chair into the yard behind the house and waited for the air to revive him. It could have been worse!

Jonty returned to the kitchen and flipped the switch. Darkness! He felt under the sink for a bucket, found one and filled it with water from the tap. He hurried into the living room. Places all over the room were alight. Little flames jumped from the floorboards, scattered about like brilliant spiky weeds. Chair backs, table legs, anything wooden, burst into flame, died, smoked, burned again impulsively. He began spilling, throwing, emptying water wherever anything ignited. Then he soaked the floorboards and table, rushing back several times to fill his bucket.

The transom windows, which were open, still flared, and the lintel was reddening, urged by the breeze. He threw half a bucket of water upwards, soaking the walls and windows. Blackened plaster, like huge pieces of charred toast, fell off, shattering to crumbs on the floor and table. He went back again and again to fill the bucket, and the toasted plaster kept slamming to the floor. At last, the flames were nearly out, but while the woodwork smoked, the wet depressing odour of soaked ash kept filling his head, and he worked until he was sure that nothing could erupt again. This time, the fire was really out. He sat on his father's bed, in darkness, except for the livid glow of the sky, gasping.

When he had recovered, he went to examine his father in his wheelchair outside, but the sky-glow was insufficient for him to see details. He was in the position he had left him, but his breathing was nearly normal. Jonty peered more closely at him. God, he was ripe! And it smelled fresh, but the Block and Chopper had been closed hours ago. How come? His father still wore his overcoat, having been too drunk to remove it, evidently. Jonty felt in the pockets and came up with a metal hip-flask. The odour of whisky wrinkled his nostrils.

There was about one small nip of it remaining. So after drinking his quota of beer at the pub, he'd chased it up with a good half bottle of whisky, too, the crazy bugger! Jonty put his hand under the coat; he could feel his father's heart beating steadily.

Well, that was a relief!

But if he didn't come round in ten or fifteen minutes, he'd have to get help. Jonty was relieved, also, that no-one had had been awakened by the fire, not even Mr and Mrs Roley, next door. The wee small hours and the wee small dram had worked their spells! What had happened? An inquest on the whole matter, at the moment, would have been painful; and Jonty was too exhausted to even care very much.

He sat down on the kitchen step, under the wintry sky, to watch and to wait, and he tried not to think of anything at all.

♣

When Jonty came out of the hospital, it was snowing.

He hunched himself against the cold and shrugged himself deeper into his Army Surplus greatcoat. The air was full of large swirling flakes making it impossible to see more than a yard or two all round, despite the filtered violet light from the tall carbon lamps that lined the driveways. During the visiting hour the snow had fallen steadily, spreading its wadding to the depth of a ping-pong ball over everything. The ground lay like a patient, swathed and quiet and white, nursing its hurts, while Jonty, a vertical dark lentil of loneliness, walked through the centre of hurrying flurrying whitenessess that gyrated and eddied in a cup of half-darkness. He strode in a muffling silence that moved where he moved, as if it belonged to him.

'Perhaps it does,' he thought.

The orderly sound of the crisp snow under his feet, and the small musical noise it made, was comforting; although wordless, it gave a voice to his loneliness.

He stopped at the end of the driveway. Behind him, the huge rectangular blocks of the lighted hospital, with its hundreds of windows that stared blankly inwards at death and disease and pain and convalescence and cures, were utterly invisible. It would be useless to go for a bus; they would have given up, the beams of their headlamps turned back on their drivers, dazzling them. He decided to walk from the hospital through the tangle of University roads and buildings to the Bristol Road. It wasn't so far to Crehan's, maybe a mile at the most. Though it might take him the best part of an hour in this snow.

He looked to the right and to the left for the road that he knew was there: only silence and the countless innumerableness of the flakes and the weird owl-light of the invisible lamps. An almost obliterated kerbstone was the only detail that indicated his whereabouts. Two figures loomed out of the reeling amethyst light behind him, already uniformed in white, and disappeared away to his left. Whichever direction you took, it was going to be an act of faith. He turned to the right and began to walk tenaciously.

Jonty was struck, once again, by the contradictoriness of things: how contradictory could they get? Inside the hospital was warmth, movement, voices, light – the blooming, buzzing confusion of purpose. Outside, we are all anonymously and invisibly alive; right now, the realities are altered and reversed by the thickening of appearances. At what point did the realities merge with their seemings and with what seemed to be their seemings? Perhaps, sometimes, things were what they seemed to be, and appearances non-illusory after all? If I wanted to baulk these questions, those questions, any questions, and heave-off into I didn't know what and go where I didn't know where, why shouldn't I? My confusions, my doubts, my joys, my decisions, were all my own, weren't they, and I could do what I liked with them, couldn't I? So why did They persist in trying to make out that there was something wrong with you if you did what THEY didn't want you to do with what you were and what you had? What bloody right had THEY got to stick labels on people?

What kind of a conspiracy was it that said you had to conform; conform to something? A mystique, that's all, a mystique they tried to turn into rules and regulations—about living and not living, living together and not living together. Everywhere you went you came across train-lines, guidelines, notices, uniforms, pigeonholes: no thinking allowed on the grass; dying on odd dates only; et cetera. The sudden recollection of the conversation he had had with his father along these lines caught him by surprise and he felt it in his throat, and he had to make an effort to stop it taking his entire body in its grip.

And then there are all the labels they put upon you. What's she do, dear? I think he's something in the city. You mean, like a public convenience. No, I mean like an executive. Or a park attendant. Or a dustman. Or a politician. Or a failure. Or a corpse. All labels. What happens to the persons who make up the people, and the individuals serving apprenticeships to become persons? Can't they let us make up our own bloody minds about bloody anything? Can't they just bloody leave you bloody well a-bloody-lone, can't they? No, they can't; how could they? That's what they're bloody for, isn't it?

One day, simultaneously, all over the world, in every country, on every building, in every public vehicle on land, sea or in the air, we shall see that they have miraculously sprouted notices, millions of them, in all the different languages of the planet, and they will all be all saying the same thing: IT IS FORBIDDEN TO READ THIS NOTICE. And soon, there will come the final notice, the ultimate order, the last hoarse instruction of the greatest O'Grady of them all, and it will say: FORBIDDEN. Just like that, no punctuation, no fuss, no explanations, nothing more, one word – one is one and all alone and evermore shall be so. That is when they will have GOT us. We shall see thousands of millions of individuals looking fearfully over their shoulders, knowing what is forbidden is them, what they are, what they were, with all the ingredients that make up the recipe – forbidden. There we'll be, the spineless troglodytes of the world, one huge united prohibition. Forbidden. You are all forbidden. Arnold Jonathan Godley is forbidden.

"Am I? Are we? I'll bloody show 'em!"

Jonty had been angered, and he found himself shouting into the hush of the swaddling snow. His cogitations had made him feel as faceless and temporary as the flakes about him. He took a hand out of a pocket and made a grab in the air. He opened his palm and watched the ones he had caught melting and trickling away over his hand.

"What's wrong with that, eh? A big hand catching you out of the dark and dissolving you up? It's allowed; you're only snowflakes. Well, I'm a snowflake, my father's a snowflake, we're all snowflakes. And if we want to fall into a big dark hand and vanish, why not?"

He bent down and began scooping up handfuls of them. He rolled and patted them into snowballs and hurled them one by one into the night.

"Why—NOT? Why—NOT?"

Each time, the snowball and the question vanished soundlessly into the vortex of flakes. He did it over and over, until he was breathless. Afterwards, he did not stand up but stayed crouched over the shrouding snow, balanced on his toes, elbows on his knees, his head bowed, a lonely bent figure in the soundless ward of the night. His shoulders began to shake, as noiseless as the snow....

20

In a little while, Jonty had gathered himself together and stood up and strode off into the millionfolded streets. The buildings of the University, the lecture halls, the laboratories, the students' hostels empty during the vacation, were all around him, obscured by the storm. He knew his way through them by instinct: this is where he had wanted to come when he had left school. But that is not the way it had been. The way it had been was the way it was now, with Jonty walking like a ghost through an unrealized world; or rather, an unrealized Jonty walking through a world he only partially realized.

He now had to admit to himself that it had been more of a shock to visit his father than he had anticipated. He had reached his father's ward along a number of corridors locked at both ends, where every entrance and exit was attended by an orderly with a lot of keys and the doors were unlocked and re-locked as you passed through, and there were bars at every window.

"Ah, they've let you through, have they? Watch it, they mightn't let you out again!"

His father's bed was near a door. Inside, the ward looked like those you find in any hospital—except for the window bars, and the orderlies at the locked doors; even the patients looked normal. It was bright. There were flowers on the bedside cabinets, grapes, magazines, headphones, visitors by the beds, patients in the beds, hygiene under the beds, and an idiot box in one corner showing nothing but its tuning card on the screen.

His father was pale and pinched, but his eyes were clear and his hair brushed. He'd tried again! They shook hands and Jonty sat on the hard chair that encouraged you not to overstay the visiting hours. The man in the next bed had a face like a saucer with a button nose in its centre; he kept nodding and smiling and twitching at Jonty, as if he knew him. When Jonty smiled back, the man took no notice. 'Well,' thought Jonty, 'he must be a friend of Treblitt's'; but he had no visitors while Jonty was there.

"How're you feeling then?"

"Fine! Except for the burns, and no booze, and the doctors, and being cooped up in here. How're you?"

"All right! How're the burns?"

"Burning!"

Thomas Jonty rolled back the bedclothes and pointed through the frame to his blistered leg.

"See!"

"I see. Bad!"

"Not so bad."

Jonty hadn't noticed at the time that the blanket his father wore under the overcoat in his wheelchair was smouldering over one leg.

"I s'pose it could 'a' been worse."

"Or better."

Jonty knew what he meant.

When his father had refused to come round after the fifteen minute deadline he'd given himself, Jonty had awakened Roley to ask him to get on his bike to a public telephone and call an ambulance. After they had taken him away, Jonty and Roley had started to clean up the mess.

"Why didn't you go with him?"

"What can I do? I'd be in the way."

"I s'pose you would. We can give you a place to kip, if you want it."

"Thanks. I'd be glad."

Father and son looked at each other, embarrassed by the constraints of a situation neither had chosen; Jonty couldn't remember a single instance when either had felt he HAD to talk to the other, still less when they had had to talk ABOUT each other. It wasn't part of the code that had been worked out to protect so efficiently the sensibilities of both, a code that had no hint of manners or gentility about it, but that had its own delicacies, and that few would understand. Jonty wondered how many. millions of people had been forced to confront each other across a hospital bed, caught in a mesh of polite expectations, wishing they could avoid it. But that was typical of society, with all its elaborate formulas for not coming to grips with what Jonty and Jontyers tried to examine, wasn't it? Yes, it was. Thus:

"Good morning."

"Morning."

"How're things?"

"Fine. How're things with you?"

"Not too bad."

"Good. Pass the salt!"

The tuneless phatic rhapsodies the world sings! It was only when you were off guard—not looking, or caught in a crisis, or cut off in an experience where you forgot yourself—that you revealed who you were: making love, shouting through the window of a departing train, dying; or, maybe, locked up in a special ward.

"Son, have you got another job yet?"

The question startled him out of his speculations.

"What? Oh, yes. Sort of."

"Sort of what?"

"Sort of—part-time. Car park attendant. Evenings. In a car park."

"Go on! In a car park! You must be joking. That's a bloody funny place to look after cars in, ain't it?"

Jonty laughed. "You know what I mean."

"Buggered if I do! I know what you said, and I know that you're sitting there with a face as long as a wet weekend, but what you mean by it, I'm buggered if I know. That is, if you mean anything—which I bloody doubt."

'Of course, he's right. What the hell do I mean? What the hell does ANYTHING mean? What the hell DOES anything mean? What the hell does anything MEAN? Oh, Mother, help me!'

"I suppose you're worrying about what they told you?"

"Eh?"

"Said I'd got some of my slates missing, I suppose?"

"Well, they didn't say that exactly."

"No? They don't often say things exactly, but that's what they mean exactly."

"If you're off your nut, Dad, so am I!" Jonty exclaimed.

"I know that! But d'you think we could convince them? If we talk nice to the matron, maybe she'll give you a bed, son, right next to your old Dad, hey, how's that?"

Jonty laughed again. He began to feel a little better.

"You don't sound worried."

"I'm not! Why should I? Waited on hand and foot, three square meals a day, nothing to do but swallow pills, answer questions, make a ballsup of their tests. No! Money for old rope!"

"Don't you want to get out?"

"What for?"

"Well, that's a daft bloody question if you like! Maybe they're right about you!"

"Maybe. But what's the daft bloody answer? You don't know, do you? Look at it! The experts don't know the answers, do they?"

He began to tick off on his fingers.

"The copulation explosion, pollution, diseases of deprivation and diseases of affluence, inflation, deflation, demos for race, demos against it, drugs, sex, South East Asia, Palestine and Israel, South America, Africa, the ionosphere, madness!"

He pointed out of one of the Windows.

"But, in here, peace an' tranquillity! I reckon I'm on to a good thing in here."

Godley Senior looked round the ward and smiled generally and fondly over its length and breadth. Godley Junior wasn't sure that he was kidding.

"But there's one thing missing in here!"

"What's that?"

"Beer!"

"You've got me there, son! THAT is an unanswerable argument. You've convinced me: out's better than in!"

"Now you're talking!"

They both laughed, relishing the joke. Suddenly, a shattering clangour started up near at hand, scattering the peace and tranquillity in all directions, and echoing distantly in other parts of the hospital.

"Cripes!" exclaimed Jonty. "What's that?"

And his thoughts answered: 'Sixty-five alarm clocks confined in a bedpan.'

"It's Matron! She's dropped a syringe."

But the visitors knew: they began to lean over beds, put on hats, coats, gloves, get up, push back chairs, and walk to the doors, where they waited for an orderly to let them out. Jonty stood up, too.

"I suppose it's time. See you, Dad."

"Okay, son. Oh, yes!" His father fumbled under his pillow and drew out an envelope. "Get a five bob Postal Order for this, will you, and don't forget to put a stamp on it."

Jonty looked at the characteristic envelope.

"Winning another forty thousand on the Treble Chance, are you?"

"Naturally! It's sickening! Every week, I win a fortune."

Jonty put it in his pocket, shook hands with his father (a disturbingly new experience), and joined the queue at the door. The orderly waited impatiently for everyone to arrive: a few stragglers held them up with their last-minute goodbyes. When they had all congregated, the orderly let them out without a word into the dim aseptic corridors with the barred transomed windows. More orderlies were posted at the doors of the lavatories, and they stood there without embarrassment in their white Dummock-like coats, and their keys dangling from huge key rings attached to their belts.

They went through the same shilly-shallying ritual with the doors at the end of every corridor. Jonty felt that there were parallels with employment at Burke's, Charles & Long's, and some differences. For example, you weren't required to clock-in-and-out of the loony bin, nor compulsorily have to belong to a union of idiots; but, on the whole, the resemblances seemed strong.

When Jonty saw a half-open door called MATRON, he knocked on it and went in. It was a square room with no windows, painted from floor to ceiling in a pale beige colour. Maybe the Matron was colour blind, very rare in females? A beer-coloured desk was planted diagonally across the room like a barrier, and a grey filing cabinet stood to attention in one corner behind it, kept company by two or three white-painted chairs. There was nowhere to sit as you entered.

A woman in a blue uniform sat writing at the desk in front of Jonty; she looked up at the interruption, in the manner of a someone detecting a bad smell. Rimless spectacles rested on a thin nose, but not too confidently, and no wonder: her face was the same shape and colour as a brand of well-known throat lozenge. Jonty glimpsed the white flash of a hand-basin through another door over her shoulder. She saw him looking at it, swivelled round on her chair, got up, closed the door, came back, sat down, swivelled forward, picked up her pen, went on writing and, eventually, said "Well?" to the end of her ballpoint, in a deep contralto voice: it sounded like Edith Evans playing Lady Bracknell, a mixture of derision, outrage, astonishment, disbelief and outright impeachment.

"I'd like to talk to somebody about my father," said Jonty.

"Have you made an appointment?"

"No!"

"Then it's out of the question. I'm very busy. I can't see you, now."

"That's because you're not looking! I'm standing right in front of you."

"I'm sorry."

"Now that I'm here, so am I! But let's keep our personal feelings out of this, shall we?"

She lifted her head very deliberately and stared at Jonty. He noticed that her irises were full of tiny flecks, as if they'd been sprinkled with black pepper.

"I suppose you're Mr Godley's son?" she said, accusingly.

"Any law against it?" asked Jonty, contentiously.

"You look like him."

"Should I be sorry?"

"These things happen. Except for the clothes, of course. Members of the public aren't allowed in here, Mr Godley."

"I know, only if you're balmy. But it's just the same outside. I passed a notice as I was coming along here, on the Bristol Road. It said, in very large letters: MEMBERS OF THE PUBLIC ARE NOT ALLOWED."

The Matron's eyes began to twinkle.

"Surely, it said something else as well? Weren't some of the letters hidden b—?"

"—Perhaps. What about my father?"

She got up and came round to where Jonty stood. She took him by his biceps and tried to manoeuvre him to the door. Jonty shook himself free and went round her desk and sat down on one of the white chairs. She was nonplussed. She wasn't used to disobedience, small as she was—not much taller standing up than she was sitting down, which surprised Jonty, because she FELT so much bigger. Her body was the same shape as the familiar throat lozenge, as well.

Unexpectedly, the Matron broke into a smile, and then broke out of it, just as unexpectedly. This also surprised Jonty, and seemed to bewilder the Matron herself for a moment.

"I see," she said, and Jonty wondered what it was she saw.

"What do you want to talk about, Mr Godley?"

"I want him out."

She remained standing.

"Out? That's impossible, quite impossible!"

"How quite is quite? You don't have a warrant for his arrest, do you?"

"It would be against his own interest to—"

"How do you know what his interests are, Matron? It isn't as if—"

"—I think I'd better fetch the doctor."

She turned away on the instant and waddled out of her office. Jonty took the opportunity of using her lavatory. When she came back with the doctor, Jonty was sitting placidly on the lavatory seat, cleaning his nails, with the door slightly ajar, but not unshut enough to make his performance public. He heard her say: "Oh, I'm sorry, doctor. He seems to have gone!" He caught a swift intake of breath and the sharp clip-clop of her shoes across the parqueted office to the lavatory door. It closed with a firm click, but not before Jonty heard her muttering to herself:

"I was sure it was shut!" And then her muffled dramatic voice said: "Sorry to have got you here for nothing, doctor."

Jonty got up, re-arranged himself, looked in the mirror, wondered why, crossed the tiny floor to open the door, and stood under the frame as if he was posing for a picture. The Matron stepped back in alarm, with an expression on her face that could not have better expressed her feelings if Jonty had tried to put his hand up her skirt. Disgust was the predominant ingredient but indignation, too. The doctor looked vaguely amused, watching him interestedly through half-asleep eyes.

"Sorry!" said Jonty. "Got caught short. Hope you don't mind!"

"I don't mind," said the doctor. "It's natural. Sit down, Mr Godley."

The Matron stared at the doctor as if she disbelieved her ears and closed her face up with a clang like a metal gin.

"Not there!" she said. "Take it to the other side."

Jonty picked up the chair and moved into the space in front of the desk, where she and the doctor stood. The Matron promptly went back behind her dissolute-coloured desk and indicated to the doctor one of the two white chairs beside hers. Jonty placed his own chair right in the centre of the space before her desk and sat down on it with unmistakeable firmness. The doctor then sat down on his own chair and began flicking through a number of file cards he carried with him. Nobody spoke. Matron had started writing again, as if she had been alone. Jonty studied the doctor.

He was a well-made middle-sized man, about forty, with curly brown hair and a sand-coloured face that had wrinkles going in unexpected directions like the map of a river delta. He had a white surgeon's coat on that was quite un-Dummock-like. He spoke in a light tenor voice that ran the words into each other in a kind of blur. Jonty guessed he was from the West Country, somewhere.

"Are yooaware yourfather hasaweakh — eart?"

Well, there be nothing blurred about the meaning of that, be there? A straight left to the point.

"No, I didn't know."

"Has he complained about it sometimes?"

"Not to me, he hasn't. Is it dangerous?"

"Heart conditions are always potentially dangerous."

"I mean—is he likely to pop off?"

"Not if he looks after himself. Or rather, if somebody else looks after him. I understand you are his only close relative, is that right?"

"Unless he's been holding out on me."

"And your mother is....? Yes, I see. There are, of course, his burns—which have been—which we need to watch carefully. He has unfortunately picked up a strain of bacteria that is—has developed a resistance to—er—the usual antibiotics..."

The doctor then muttered something that sounded like 'Pseudo Motors Ready Toaster'. Or was it 'pseudo monas oronginosa'?

"Pseudo what?" asked Jonty.

Matron looked up and smiled radiantly at Jonty. The doctor said:

"Just a name! Not important. The important thing for us, Mr Godley, is that I see from your father's—er—medical history that he's—there is some evidence for believing he's—er—"

"I know. He told me. You think he's got some of his marbles missing."

The doctor smiled: he had crooked teeth. But he didn't want to look at Jonty.

"That is hardly the way I would have expressed— er—his symptoms, and—"

"I think the news has rather upset the younger Mr Godley, doctor."

"Yes. He would seem to rather overstate the case. However, he has shown certain—er—chizophrenic tendencies in the past, and there is one instance on record, I believe—"

The doctor riffled through the file cards in his hand and studied one intently.

"Ah, yes, when—well, let's talk to the point, shall we? He tried to take his own life, and that is something we can hardly ignore, under the circumstances."

"What circumstances?"

"Well, the circumstances that brought him to us – the—er—fire. His inebriation at the time—"

"Kismet! That's what he says it was! Friday is his night for getting paralytic, doctor. It was an accident. He left his cigarette burning, it caught the curtains, and Whoosh! it went up…"

"Mr Godley, I'm trying to give you the medical side of the picture. In all cases of schizophrenia, there is a dissociation between the rational faculties and the—er—affective side of – er—"

"You mean his feelings pull him one way and his grey matter another?"

"Well—in a manner of speaking—yes, I suppose that would cover it."

"It's okay, doctor, you can speak in words of more than one syllable. Anyway, who isn't like that?"

"Like what?"

"Schizophrenic—give a bit there, take a bit here. You'll know all the old stuff—repressions, unconscious wishes, syndromes of this and that, Mummy frightened by Sigmund Freud when she was five,

Daddy's toy Oedipus hanging in the clothes cupboard. Who isn't a bit shredded, doctor? Or are you two—exceptions?

"Ah, I see you are not ignorant of psychological terminology!"

"I've read a few Penguins, in my time! But let's get to the point. I don't know whether he tried to kick the bucket, or not. But you don't know, either. We've just heard a clang. Anyway, if he did—so what?"

"Mr Godley!"

"Yes, Matron?"

"That's a terrible thing to say!"

"Is it? What about Japan, hey? Popular there for hundreds of years, a nation of schizoes, is that what they are? Ever hear of Yukio Mishima? Or Virginia Woolf? Or Ernest Hemingway? Wasn't much wrong with them, was there? If there was, they soon cured it. So—my dad doesn't like the life he's living! Well, why should he? It's bloody awful!"

The doctor took a big breath and shut his eyes. When he opened them, one was still partially closed, drooping in a delayed kind of wink.

'Ah, a touch of ptosis, eh, a crack in the ramparts?'

"Yes, I know, Mr Godley. There may be something in what you say. Unfortunately, I haven't the time to discuss the ethics of the matter with you now. My job is to act, and the important thing is—"

He hesitated.

"Yes?" queried Jonty.

The doctor appeared to make a decision and went on, hurriedly.

"I believe your father's paralysis might be curable. I'm not promising anything, you understand. I'm saying that there's just a chance that we may—may—you understand, be able to do something about it."

Jonty was halted in his tracks. He gazed at them both. He had lived with his father's paralysis for so long that the doctor seemed to be talking of an impossible concept; though Jonty had less trouble with impossible notions than most people, all he could say was: "Christ!"

The Matron was clearly affronted. "Are you, by any chance, a Christian, Mr Godley?"

Jonty meekly shook his head.

"I thought not. I ask you to moderate your language out of consideration for those who are!"

"Quite so!" said the doctor.

"Sorry!" said Jonty.

Jonty had to admit that this feller was no amateur: he'd started gently, shuffling in a bit flatfooted, hunched over his cards, putting out a feint here and a short jab there. But now, he had opened up—a right hook zooming in from the shoulder that had made him blink. Jonty was conscious of a feeling of admiration for the chap; wonder what kind of ear lobes he's got? Maybe they're?—He leaned to one side to get a better look at the doctor's aural equipment.

"So you see, if there's a chance that— What's the matter, Mr Godley, are you feeling unwell?"

"Oh. no, I'm all right thanks."

He straightened his posture in the chair.

'So he hasn't got a cauliflower! Insignificant little lobes! Well, well!'

"Mr Godley – ?"

"Oh, yes, you think you can do something, doctor?"

"Well, we must try, that's all. If, as I explained, my diagnosis is correct and its origin is psychogenic—well—it is essential for your father to remain under care and supervision. You do see that, don't you, Mr Godley?"

Bam! the KO! Jonty had a feeling that he'd fought himself into a corner and at some secret sign from the second—in this case, the squat matron—his opponent had let him have it, the twistsock! Just as he was starting to get to his feet, the man said:

"So, we're agreed, Mr Godley. Your father stays."

Jonty kicked a shower of snow up into the air.

"Damn and blast the bloody man!"

The flakes were a dusky gold under the orange sodium lamps.

"Anybody'd think I WANTED him to do himself in. It's the bloody principle of the thing. They tell you when to die and what to die for, when to live and what to live for. Don't we ever get to choose for ourselves?" he shouted aloud to the golden whirling of the flakes.

Where the snow drove, in front of him, he was a leaning blur of whiteness. Crehan's place couldn't be far off now. If he was lucky, Crehan would offer him a dram and maybe he could touch Crehan for a couple of quid to see him through to his first pay. Car-parking! And no gloves! How do you direct cars with your hands in your pockets? And, just think, fourteen years of nail-biting beaten by the winter. Wouldn't Aunty Jessie in *Titbits* like to know about that? But try as he would, it came back to haunt him like the snatch of an old song— giving in like that, what had he betrayed, who had he betrayed? Had he betrayed anything or anyone?

21

Jonty held the phone at arms length.

Last night at Crehan's had been a bit of a bender and the effects had not entirely worn off, although the sound of bells ringing upset him at any time: they reminded him of getting up in the morning.

He flicked through the advertisements in *The Weekend Mail* and wondered idly if Dummock's wife had started divorce proceedings against Herbert Smedley yet. Jonty smiled radiantly at the idea.

The telephone kiosk smelled. Somebody had clearly used it at one time or another to breed rabbits in; after that, it had been hired out as a dog kennel. It must have been at this point that the General Post Office had hit upon the idea of turning it into a phone booth and had taken it over for the use of the The Great British Public, which had shown its appreciation by kicking in one or two windows, bending the coin-box with a battering ram, tearing the plank-like Directory in half, and scratching obscene mottoes in the paintwork. Also, it seemed to be in general use by people with full bladders and distressed souls who smoked Woodbines down to nub-ends of four or five millimetre thickness. How else could you explain the pools of nicotine-coloured stale nestling in the lower corners? True, he WAS using one of the remoter field-posts near the Salvation Army Hostel in the hinterland of Deritend. However —.

His observations were broken into by the signal that told him that somebody had picked up the receiver: a rapid one-toned succession of brain-paralyzing quavers, worse than the bells. This morning, it made him feel as if somebody was pushing a kilo of ripe cherries into his middle ear where they exploded one by one, followed by the disturbing sensation that his eustachian tubes were filling up with cherry stones and juice. In desperation, he pushed a coin into the slot. It stuck.

Jonty gave vent to an oath that mixed cursing, crudity and blasphemy in fairly equal proportions and thumped away at the box until the coin fell out. It rolled into one of the puddles. Before he had decided to take another coin from his pocket, his copy of *The Weekend Mail* had slipped from under his arm and was now demonstrating its absorbent properties on the concrete floor. Then his client rang off.

A bead of sympathy for The Great British Public was distilling in his heart: he began looking frenziedly about for something to wreck; but concern for his own physical safety got the better of him, and he decided, instead, to write a strong letter of recommendation that the Postmaster General turn the kiosk back into a urinal for the nearby Salvation Army Hostellers, ASAP.

In the meantime, he tried the number again: the same sequence of shudder-producing noises ensued, but this time he could not distract himself with his favoured journal. He held an unbent coin poised at the ready. Luckily, the onslaught on his ear drums was short: a thin nasal voice said: "Hello, yes, hello." Jonty pushed the coin swiftly into the slot, and spoke into the receiver.

"Hello! Is that Mr Lacestone?"

A sound came through the earpiece like a seventy-five c.c. gnat changing gear on Mount Snowdon. Jonty was convinced by now that nearly all his experience was this morning going to be surrealistic. A short backfire exploded in his ear. Then he remembered: wasn't this the way Lacestone cleared his throat? It may be three years ago, but he'd never forget it.

"Yes, Lacestone speaking."

Jonty had a vivid recollection of Lacestone's ashtray piled high with tiny butts. Should he recommend a reliable garage to him? You'd have thought he'd have had his throat serviced by now, wouldn't you?

"Oh, good morning, Mr Lacestone. You may not remember me, but—"

"—What? Hello, hello? Are you still there?"

He sounded very faint, as if speaking from the end of the Mersey Tunnel. Suddenly, his voice got loud but muffled.

"Hello, hello! Are you there?" Lacestone repeated.

Then he spoke through a megaphone stuffed with Hansards. This was immediately followed by the barest perceptible whine in Jonty's ear. Jonty's exasperation was intense.

"Fully automatic bullshit!" he said aloud, to the kiosk.

"What was that?" asked Lacestone, as clearly as if he'd been standing beside him. "Who's speaking?"

"Oh, you probably won't remember me, Mr Lacestone, but I came to see you when I left school. My name's Jonty—"

"Hello, operator, hello... Yes, there's something wrong with this line... what... no..."

Jonty stopped listening. He took a deep breath. A juddering, ear-splitting, jaw-breaking battalion of pornographic impossibilities, boots thudding, vibrated in the ether for some distance around. Lacestone's voice broke through again.

"Perhaps you could trace it. There's a man using the vilest language imaginable. What? Oh, wait a minute! Something's happening!"

Jonty had begun to physically assault the telephone equipment. Regardless of his own personal safety, he was subjecting the coinbox to a series of vigorous slappings, thumpings and elbow jabs; he followed up with one or two knee movements and then tried to sever the cable with a toecap; during which he kept shouting "Hello, hello, hello!" into the mouthpiece.

"Don't shout! I can hear you. Lacestone speaking."

"Good morning, Mr Lacestone. We seem to have been cut off by some maniac swearing on the line, somewhere."

"I thought it was you! Who's speaking?"

"Certainly not!... Not my style! Maybe you won't remember: I saw you about three years ago."

"O—o—oh?" Drawn out long, with extreme caution and deep suspicion: the gnat-like element had detected the presence of an aerosol somewhere.

"Yes, I saw you about a job, when I left school."

"Oh, I see, I see." His voice recovered its usual eunuch-like pitch and the jovial quality returned. "Then, that's quite different, isn't it?"

"Is it?"

"It is. What did you say your name was?" Lacestone began to clear his throat again. Jonty winced.

"Arnold Jonathan Godley."

"Oh, I see, I see. Arnold... Jonathan... now let me see, Godley...."

Lacestone went on saying it until Jonty felt impelled to stuff the receiver into his armpit and commence jabbering like Cheetah the Chimp in the Tarzan films, but he restrained himself with a great effort, and replied calmly.

"Yes, Arnold. Jonty. A little chap with fair curly hair and glasses. No moustache then, of course. Ashpit Grammar School. Wanted to be a pop singer."

This last clause was uttered with all the scorn Jonty could get into his voice. He modelled it on an actor in one of the endless soap-operas they set loose every Wednesday afternoon on Midland radio, gambling that Lacestone would be a fan. It worked.

"Oh, Jonty! Yes, yes, I remember now. Arnold Jonathan Godley, of course. You wanted to be a pop singer, didn't you? Big chap with black hair, if I remember rightly."

Well, it had worked after a fashion: Lacestone now FELT that he remembered Jonty, and had signalled his readiness to respond as if he did. One had to be thankful for small mercies, didn't one? But Jonty was affronted. He had thought at the time that he'd given Lacestone an experience he'd never forget, and here Lacestone was, as large as life, with no recollection of him whatsoever. Where had he gone wrong? Jonty had a frantic desire to shout into the mouthpiece:

"You must remember me! You must! I'm just like all the other little green Martians that keep popping into your office, but I'm the one with the black eye patch on."

What he actually said was: "I was wondering if you could give me a bit of help, Mr Lacestone."

"Help?"

Lacestone's castrato sounded jubilant, coming through full and clear as he began to recognise familiar landmarks again. "Help?" he repeated, more piercingly than ever.

Jonty winced. It felt like a hot gimlet pushed into his eardrums. He really must try to get hold of some Alka Seltzer.

"Yes, Mr Lacestone."

"Well, we'll try, we'll try. That's what we're here for, isn't it, Mr— Mr—"

Jonty had entertained very serious doubts from first acquaintance about what Lacestone was there for.

"You see," said Jonty, "I'm making an application to the Local Education Committee for a grant—to go to University, you know. And I was wondering, Mr Lacestone—"

Jonty heard his intake of breath. "That isn't our Department, I'm afraid. Just can't touch it."

This pronouncement was followed by a noise that suggested Lacestone had turned on a tape-recording of jet engines warming up, and then, just as suddenly, turned it off again.

"DAREN'T touch it! More than our job's worth."

The noise came again, causing Jonty to jump nervously.

"Is there something wrong with your phone, Mr Lacestone?"

"What? No, of course not!"

Jonty had a recollection of Lacestone sucking in air through pouched lips and shaking his head vigorously to register horror of some kind. He remembered that it was one of Lacestone's conventional weapons, at such moments.

"No, I quite understand, Mr Lacestone. I just wondered if you—IN YOUR CAPACITY AS YOUTH EMPLOYMENT OFFICER—"

Jonty capitalized the phrase with his voice, "—could say a word or two in support of my application. You see, you have details of my—of my—"

He felt strong trepidation about using the word 'record', but on the instant he could think of nothing else.

"—of my record, Mr Lacestone."

"Well, only details of your school and character, you know. That's hardly going to be much – er – is it?"

"Yes, that's all I wanted really. Just for a bit of help, you know. See what I mean?"

"I see. Yes, I do see," said Lacestone in a voice that indicated clearly not only that he did not see, but also that what Jonty was trying to make him see wasn't worth seeing.

Jonty could hear him lighting another cigarette and puffing out the smoke. The warning pips started up. Jonty swiftly inserted the coin he had at the ready. He wasn't going to let it catch him on the hop again.

"I've written to the office, and I'm still waiting for a reply. It's been about three weeks, now."

"Well, they're always snowed under with applications at this time of the year, you know. I shouldn't set too much store by the time lapse, if I were you."

Jonty couldn't prevent his thoughts from racing. 'Listen, Lacestone, you're not me, are you? And, Cripes, man, I don't set much store by anything, or even any store by anything. I just want you, in your capacity as an official clipe, to put in a bloody word for me. And that's bloody all. Why can't you just bloody do it?'

This morning, Jonty was conscious of having to restrain himself above the usual. He must have soaked up a little more of Crehan's Bass than he remembered. Oh! where was the nearest chemist? He replied politely.

"Yes, I quite realize that, Mr Lacestone. But time's getting on for writing for places and I was hoping to jolly them up a bit."

"All right! I'll tell you what we'll do for you."

'Oh, so we're back to the royal 'we', are we? That's more like it.'

"If we get any enquiries about you, we'll put in a good word on your behalf. How's that?"

Judging by the shocks being administered to Jonty's eardrums, Lacestone had started flicking at his mouthpiece with a finger, or tapping on it with a pencil, and Jonty could just about prevent himself from telling Lacestone how 'that' precisely was.

"Well, to be quite honest, I was hoping for something a little more positive than that, Mr Lacestone."

The blows to the receiver continued. Was Lacestone trying to induce permanent deafness in his left ear, or simply trying to get him off the line?

"Afraid we can't do more than that. They'd think we were trying to interfere with the running of the—er—works. You do see, don't you? Our hands are tied, afraid so, very much afraid."

Jonty couldn't think of anything better—preferably with leatherhide thongs that would tighten in the sun. His left ear began to feel numb.

"So you can't hold out any further hope for me, Mr Lacestone?"

"That's about the size of it. Why don't you give Mr Jarrold a tinkle and put your gentle enquiry to him? I can give you his number, if you'd like it?"

'Gentle-enquiry him! If he's anything like you, Lacestone, he wouldn't respond to a half-hour peal on the Bournville carillon, never mind a tinkle!'

"What did you say his name was, Mr Lacestone?"

Jay – ay – double ahr – and – oh! – ell—Dee-for Dolly. Shouldn't think he'd mind; but be tactful, old chap, he's – rather – er – a severe sort of man. Used to be a Chapel Minister, somewhere. Doesn't approve of smoking, et cetera. Got somewhat definite—er—views on Modern Youth."

Lacestone gave the high-pitched yell that stood in place of a laugh.

"And, of course, in my job, with these top brass, you can't be too – . That okay? Don't mention I suggested the phone call, will you?" he added quickly.

Lacestone had started the tiny vibrations of a warning bell in Jonty's mind. And he could quite understand Lacestone's trepidations.

Judging by the small byng of pure ash that he kept at the corner of his desk, his throat must have resembled the inside of one of those very tall chimneys you see sticking up over Wolverhampton brick factories. Anybody in Jarrold's position, who disapproved of smoking, must have struck a pang of terror deep into his packet of Woodbines, and irritated his smoker's cough.

"No, I won't tell him," said Jonty, compassionately.

"That's all right! Extension 666, Main Block. Here's hoping! Goodbye, then. Goodby-y-y-e-e!"

The emphatic click at the other end of the line signalled Lacestone's relief in managing to pass the buck so thoroughly. Thus, there was no succour coming over the waves from that direction! Jonty hung up.

Whither bonny boat? What should he do, or not do, now, or later? He could follow Lacestone's suggestion and give this unfrocked bureaucrat a bell; or he could write again, inquiring if his application had been mislaid; or ask why it had been conspicuously ignored? Or he could forget Jarrold entirely. If Lacestone was right, Jarrold was a full General in the O'Grady Volunteers, and better avoided. Or he could turn his face in the other direction and start a fresh essay. On who? Sorry – on whom? But the prospect of sorting out some partially-literate logorrhetic flannel-minded English, Scotch or Welsh poet to write on, and submit before January, to Sir John Shrike and his cronies, filled him with absolutely no enthusiasm. Car-parking might even be better. On the whole, he decided that the best policy was to stop thinking, do nothing, and go for a pint of best bitter in The Woodman, where something might well present itself to his fancy. If not, the beer would console him.

He went.

22

A few days later, Jonty went again to the bar of The Woodman, this time for his lunch. He had managed, in the interim, to hold to his decision to be indecisive about his future, and the bitter they sold there had helped him to abide in his decision amiably.

He lifted his tankard. A cold, live, lancing delight played over his taste-buds. And for only two shillings the pint! It was a bargain! He regarded the liquid appreciatively. He could do it again, too; God knows how many times he could do it with this noggin. There must be a lot of taste swirling around in a pint of beer. He had to hand it to the brewers! How they got that much taste into that much beer was marvellous and the best tribute you could pay them was to do it as often as his Dad.

He sighed and put down his now half-empty glass tankard on the dark oak table. Look at it! A good strong handle that you could put your whole fist through! Why was it that beer with handles was always so much more drunk-making than beer without handles? Or, to put it another way, why was beer in tumblers so much less juiced-up than beer in tankards? Did one glass-making process foment more alcoholic properties than another? Or increase the specific-gravity of the beer? He could write to the brewers – Bass, Guiness, Ansell's, Macewan's – and suggest a heavy research programme. After all, a question like that was vital to all beer-drinkers. Why not? But, for the moment, he'd accept it as a fact of experience, and rejoice regularly in that fact. So thinking, he matched deed to conclusion by taking another sip of the oblivion-bringer and another bite from his cheese roll.

This was different in kind, nature and substance, from the ones they sold in British Railway buffets, which he preferred to talk to, rather than to eat. This one not only managed to look like food, but to taste like it. However, you couldn't be too careful, even so. It might still be a trick: something dressed up to look like it, and to taste like it, but which, nevertheless, wasn't it. These days, they—a different set of 'theys' from the brewing theys—could even synthesize protein from anthracite coal and effluent. But this was fresh, at least, and had no suspicious smell, so it was probably all right. Throwing caution to the winds, he took another bite, a large one. It was delicious!

While he munched, he looked about him.

At least, there was no poker-work notice over the bar about the purity of the consumables: GENUINE ARTIFICIAL ROLLS SERVED HERE. While Jonty was amusing himself with his fancies, Barry Crehan walked in. Despite the fag-and-drag appearance he conveyed to the naked eye, Jonty had learned by now that Crehan went in for girls, and this girl was clearly something to go in for. Jonty had been compelled to see that Crehan's campness enjoyed producing imitation-camp, and that his long hair, his immaculately-kept hands, and his Carnaby Street gear, were all part of the take-off. It was one reason Jonty liked him. There could be no doubt about the direction of Crehan's sexual impulses and behaviour – despite the considerable doubt about his unsexual behaviour. And there was no doubt of any kind about the girl.

Crehan did not notice Jonty sitting alone in a cubicle. They went to the bar and got onto high stools. Jonty waited until he heard Crehan picking up his change, then, putting his head round the edge of the oak partition and assuming a heavy North-country accent, he called:

"Hey up, there, hinny!"

Crehan looked round to see who was being called by whom, and seeing no-one, turned back to the girl, shrugged his shoulders and made an "It's-nothing-to-do-with-me" face at her. She smiled at him, and they both drank in unison.

Jonty put his head round and tried again, but Crehan caught some sound of movement and turned swiftly to see Jonty's face growing out of the corner post, mediaevally.

"Look who's here! The Green Man!" he exclaimed. He put a hand on the girl's arm and said something to her; they got off the barstools, balancing their drinks, and walked across to join Jonty in his cubicle.

"Welcome!" he said. They sat down on the opposite bench.

Jonty looked across the table at the girl. He found it quite painless but something disastrous seemed to be happening to his stomach. It began to rotate like a washing machine. If he'd had a little round window in his navel, he knew she would have seen the knotted wad of his cheese roll rising and falling in a detergent froth of best bitter. He put both hands on the table and gripped it hard. If he didn't watch out, he'd start to vibrate all over as well. Crehan looked piercingly at Jonty and, after a moment, said: "Oh, sorry! This is Sofia. Sofia, Arnold or Jonty! Whichever!"

She nodded and said: "Hello."

Her voice was just as nice as it should be: he classified it as olive green.

"Hello."

A girl like that couldn't help having a beautiful pair of ear lobes, he knew, but her hair, which was very dark, almost black, hung over her shoulders to about mid-spine, and hid them. Pity!

"What are you staring at? Never seen a girl before?" asked Crehan.

The questions took him off guard. That was the second time Crehan had beaten him to the draw in the last few minutes. He'd have to watch it.

"I was wondering—," he said, which wasn't true, as his mental processes were almost at a standstill. Jonty found himself passively sitting there, absorbing all the signals the girl couldn't be blamed for sending out. But he gathered himself enough to finish his sentence: "—what kind of detergent she favours for her smalls?"

Sonia laughed, half amusement, half satisfaction.

'She knows what she's done to me,' thought Jonty.

"He's off!" said Crehan. "Don't mind him, Sonia. I keep telling him to keep off that brand of Meths he favours."

Crehan twirled the stem of his gin and lemon between thumb and two fingers, musing, watching Jonty closely. The girl had a tall glass of orange of fluorescent intensity before her. It accentuated the dark speckled plum colour of her woolly gaucho suit. Jonty guessed that she was a student from the College of Art. On the bench beside her was a huge tapestry-leather bag, with some Greek-looking designs on it, nearly big enough for him to go to sleep in. He looked at her breasts and decided they were firm, prominent and functional. They made him feel as if his alpha-waves had been interfered with. He tried to reassure himself by taking a large pull at his Bass. It worked well enough.

"That's better! I've resolved to do more of that in the New Year."

"Why wait?" asked Crehan.

"You've got something there. Make it a pint!" replied Jonty.

"That's not what I meant! But have one, anyway."

While Crehan was at the bar buying Jonty a pint, he began to study Sofia in earnest. Her eyes were brown and large, with the brown mirrored back on itself and then outwards again, giving them such opacity that he couldn't see reflections in them. They were heavy-lidded and dreamy and suggested shortsightedness.

Jonty was surprised to learn, while he was talking, that he'd decided to apply once again for a bursary; and, furthermore, he was just about to complete a third or fourth draft of his essay. This was the more surprising as, only a short time ago, just before entering The Woodman, he distinctly remembered telling himself that he had a good mind to acquaint the whole bureaucratic bunch of them at the Education Office, and Jarrold in particular, with where precisely they could put their bursary.

"What's the essay about?"

Her lips were splendidly full and moved in a way Jonty could not recollect seeing anyone else's move. However, he was glad she'd asked the question, as he was also very keen to know. He waited to see what he would reply.

"Well, it's a toss-up, you know, between that thirties group with the social conscience, and an obscure Welsh poet with about as much of it as a barrel of Guinness."

"Which thirties group?"

"I suppose group is the wrong word. More like an amalgam, really—going under the logo of Lender, Dauden and Lay Spewis. They've never been the same since General Franco got Spain back."

"What funny names! Oh, you mean—!"

She clapped her hand to her mouth and giggled. "But—if you've nearly finished, how is it you're not sure who it's about?"

"Ah, you see, that's the point! Most of my remarks are fully interchangeable. They can apply either to the Social Amalgam or to the Guinness poet, or even to both. Doing it that way was a very interesting challenge. But I'm not sure what that lot at Oxbridge know least of, at the moment. That's my problem! What's yours?"

"I haven't got one just now."

'That's what you think,' thought Jonty. 'You just wait, that's all!'

However, he was very pleased with the way he seemed to be emerging from the conversation as a person of acumen, subtle sensibility, and a man of decision. It wasn't convenient, but something inside him seemed bent on impressing her, whatever he thought he thought. If only Sofia's complexion hadn't been quite so attractively dusky, Jonty felt he could have been even more decisive. That particular shade of duskiness seemed to do something to his volition which he wasn't clear about.

At this point, Crehan returned with his pint.

"What's he been telling you?" Crehan asked, as he sat down beside her and put the bitter in front of him. Jonty took it promptly and said: "Here's to whatever!"

Crehan nodded slightly in acknowledgment, put his arm round Sonia's shoulders and leaned his head sideways against her temple, gently. She liked it, and told him so. Then she told him briefly about Jonty's project, and only then did Crehan speak. "More power to your elbow, old hen."

"Ah, yes. Cheers!" said Jonty, taking another swig at his beer.

"Och, man, I meant with your essay."

"Oh, that! Yes, I hope so," he said vaguely.

The re-appearance of Crehan had done something subtly destructive to his acute, man-of-decision role. He felt his shoulders easing back into his querulous-anarchist role. Not that Crehan was, at the moment, in any way antagonistic towards Jonty; he was full of bonhomie and affluence—the two things being mutually supportive, and probably crucial in Crehan's successful quests for these dishfuls of stomach-churning femininity.

"What happened to your application for a grant?"

"Nothing!"

"Extraordinary! I wonder why?"

Jonty did not find Crehan's question half as interesting as the one taking shape in his mind along the lines of: ''When are you going to take your arm away from that dolly?' He found this question followed rapidly by another that asked: 'If he doesn't hurry, should I lie on the table and blow froth up those nasal gratings of his?'

He realized that he was being quite irrational and told himself so. But self-injunctions of this sort never seemed to matter much in situations of this kind. Why not? That old Greek, Plato, had some half-baked notion about people always following The Good when they saw it. He had regretted he couldn't send the old sage a short stiff note pointing out his mistake and telling him the best place for errors of that kind, together with the whole of his Republic. Anyway, was 'the Good' what Crehan was doing to Sofia, or what Jonty wanted to do to Crehan? Come on, Plato, answer me that!

"I've no idea!" said Jonty. "Maybe the Secret Branch has passed a file over to Jarrold about my partiality for *The Weekend Mail.*"

"What's the next step?" asked Sofia.

He nearly blurted out: 'Well, the chances are, if you sit there much longer doing that, I shall turn into a homicidal maniac!'

He found it hard to understand why he felt so proprietorial about a girl who hadn't been invented until a short while ago. And Plato had nothing to say about that, either.

"I'm going to phone up the Education Office after lunch!" he said.

This decision surprised him most of all. After the conversation on the phone with Lacestone, he had come away with the firm intention of forgetting everything in the shortest possible time. Yet, here he was, telling Sofia that he was going to follow it up! Surely, there couldn't be something wrong with the bitter?

"Well, my dear, if you ever make use of the griff I passed on to you, don't tell them you got it from me, eh!"

Crehan took his arm away from Sonia's shoulders and reached for his drink.

'That's much better! Now I shan't have to fight you for her,' he thought. He said: "I won't. But it's all a plot to keep men of talent and poverty permanently poor. This old chimney who calls himself a Youth Officer was saying…"

They were both amused and sorry at the outcome of the talk with Lacestone.

"What's this Jarrold-bird like?"

"No idea, really! According to Lacestone, he hates alcohol, detests smoking, and used to be a preacher. Still is, by the sound of it. That's a very suspicious set of circumstances! If you add to THAT the fact that his phone number is 666, well, it's obvious what's going on."

"Is it? It isn't obvious to me."

"Ah, well, it wouldn't be, would it, a nice girl like you?" Jonty leaned across the table and stage-whispered: "It's the mark of the Great Beast! You know, Aleister Crowley building up some kind of secret religion in the gloomy recesses of the Education Offices."

Sonia registered her scepticism, and Jonty tried a little more of his spiel.

"Look at the material he's got! All those funny little men and women who scurry about the cloisters. It can't fail. You just keep your eye on the Sunday papers, that's all!"

"Who's Aleister what's-his-name?"

"Crowley," said Crehan, " He was a countryman of mine."

And he described some of the more colourful and appealing exploits of the Great Beast, skilfully omitting references to the orgies and sexual excesses that were all part of his magic.

"But this—er—Jarrold doesn't wear a kilt and carry a wand with a star on in the office, does he?"

"Ah, that's all part of the disguise!" said Jonty.

Sonia pulled a wry face at him.

"Anyway," said Crehan diplomatically, "you keep working on that essay. That's your best bet."

"Thanks for the vote of confidence!"

"Not to mention! You deserve it! Incidentally, Alexis says no letter has gone there for you, old hen! If she gets one, I asked her to bring it round to your house."

"Oh, thanks. But she couldn't, I'm afraid."

"Couldn't what?"

"Bring it round."

"Look, old hen, you're talking a lot of—"

"No, truly! We don't have a house, anymore. I'm living in a plate-layer's hut. Stratford-on-Avon line."

"Oh Gawd!" moaned Crehan, "Is this another of your—?"

"No! Cross my heart and hope to die!"

Jonty told them about the fire.

"Bloody awful, old duckie! But that doesn't explain how—"

"—Then this Housing Inspector came round, heard my father was in the Bin, and that was it! You know, all the old crap—housing crisis, waiting lists—all that Council stuff. I'm single. Couldn't see how they could let me have a house on my own. Et cetera."

"But, your father!"

"Well, they said they'd reconsider—if and when he came out. But this old hut's all right. It's quiet, no traffic, lines torn up ages ago. No rent. For now, it's just the job!"

Crehan laughed.

"What a marvellous idea!" said Sonia.

"Oh, do you like it?" asked Jonty, brightening up considerably.

"It is rather," Crehan smiled dubiously.

"No mod cons, of course. But it's home. You'll have to come up and see it sometime—both of you."

He took a chance on looking straight into her eyes when he said this. What he feared might happen happened; his rinsed-out cheese roll fell into the spin dryer. What was he going to do? She smiled at him. Instantly his circuit fused and he juddered to a standstill. He found himself gazing at her in mute admiration, like an out-of-condition Airedale... This kind of thing wasn't on, was it? It wasn't Jontyish!

Crehan looked at his watch.

"Sorry, folks! Have to be getting back to the studio. I'm up to here in it, at the minute."

He indicated the level by holding a straight hand just below his eyes. As he rose to his feet, he picked up his glass and finished it at a gulp, and then looked enquiringly at Sonia.

"What's the time?" she asked.

"Getting on for two."

"Oh dear, is it? I must go."

She began patting her large ornamental bag into shape.

'She can do that to me any time,' thought Jonty.

"Got a life-class at a quarter past."

Crehan and the girl stood up. Jonty remained at his post.

"'Bye for now."

"See you."

"Cheers!"

She wasn't tall, about his height, or maybe an eyebrow less. Neither was she slim; nicely plump seemed to be the right expression. He watched them walk to the door. Neither of them looked back. She was wearing cream coloured-boots, and, in a way he found impossible to define, he was strongly aware that they were—No, not sexy, or sexual. Sexist! No—Sexistic! That's got it!

He watched her rump disappearing through door of the bar. The way those boots emphasised the slight wiggle and roundness of her bottom was amazing, something the manufacturers had gone to great pains to build into the heavy duty zip-fasteners, it seemed, a trick of the trade that would remain a well-guarded secret.

'What a piece of whatever this girl was a piece of, wasn't she?'

He gulped down the last mouthful of his bitter and sat looking sadly at a few small bubbles in the bottom of the tankard. Aloud, he said: "It's all right for you. You can burst."

23

Jonty closed the books he had had scattered on the table before him, made a small pile of them, leaned back in his chair, sighed and looked round the large high nave of the Reference Library with satisfaction. Books and the odour of books! Waterhouse Gothic, and Jonty loved it. It was like a large womb, warm and comfortable, even when it was bitterly cold outside.

It hadn't been a bad day's work! Except for the counter-assistant, who, at every request slip he had written out, studied his longhand and watched him. Pity, that Havelock Ellis title on sexual perversions had been the first thing he'd wanted!

He picked up the pile of books, holding them in place with his chin, and returned them to the counter. The assistant, a pale girl with acne, was miserably filling in chitties with a ballpoint pen. She looked up at him with distaste, and seemed on the verge of calling for assistance to throw him bodily down the stairwell, when Jonty forestalled her with a cheery "Good night!" She did not respond in any way; but he felt relieved she hadn't threatened to withdraw his reading card. He went through the spring-door much too quickly so that it banged against the jamb. This prompted her to get up, walk round the curved counter, and watch him descending the stairs. He waved happily to her.

Ever since he had met Sofia, he hadn't been the same. For instance, he found himself working on his essay with something near to interest and with an energy that was quite out of proportion to the worth of the topic. Even when it was finished, it was going to be a toss-up between disposing of it down one of the Niagara-like public lavatories they had in Stevenson's Square, where everything disappeared in a tremendous whoosh, or by dispatching it to Sir John-o'-the-fens or to Lord David-o'-the-spires, where it would disappear with a gentle sigh, just as effectively.

After the fire, the thought of starting again had filled him with a sclerosis of fatigue. He had worked out his chances of collecting a bursary on natural ability as about zero zero five per cent. If you added national competition, it was an overestimate. But he seemed to want to finish it for the odd reason that he had told Sofia that he HAD finished it. With Sofia in the offing, if only in the mental offing, he kept finding out things about himself that he hadn't considered belonged to him. That sort of thing had never bothered him before. But there it was, and there it seemed to want to stay. It was upsetting.

Not only that, he felt sure in his own mind (a) the chances were he would never see her again, and (b) if he did, she wouldn't show the slightest concern about his essay. But what else could explain his spaniel-like urge to wrap up specimen pages of his penmanship in cellophane and red ribbon and offer them as a token of his esteem and affection to her? And why, knowing what he knew about the execrability of his script, did he want to do this? The only solution he could come up with was yet another question, much more succinct: why don't you get your head examined? The answer to that one was unambiguous: he certainly wasn't going to get that done: his admiration for the well-known quip about 'anybody who goes to a psychiatrist needs his head examined' was much too strong to allow it. Yes; it was a predicament.

Something had dilated inside Jonty, like the pupil of an eye. Was it the entropy of lust or love revealing these new psychological postures to him? He had had glimpses of this love-thing with Alexis, hadn't he, and look how that had worked out. Or had it been the lust-thing? Whatever it was, he had developed a good head of steam, and been forced to let it hiss away through the Dummock-valve.

Wasn't this love and fidelity stuff a bit out of date? If so, HE was out of date, but this chugging fumey engine of his feelings kept pulling him along the track. There seemed to be no doubt, in today's world, lust was all right. There was more widespread doubt about this love-stuff. What could it pull? What was it for? There was general agreement about the pulling power of a nice bit of lust, and you knew how far it could take you. In that sense, it was reliable and safe. But love! You had to watch it: you never knew when your boilers would blow.

He leaned against the bus stop, pushing away his doubts, and waited, as blankly as he could, for a number 44 to Tyseley. It was cold. He shivered. All the snow had thawed. The starlinqs were as unacceptable in their insults as always. The library clock showed four-fifteen: he should be in good time to catch Alexis leaving work. He looked across, wondering why it managed to look so much like the Parthenon AND the soot-covered Town Hall at the same time. Surely, it could have been more subtly built in the shape of a blast furnace, surrounded by statues of men in sweat-scarves and string vests, raising fully paid-up Union cards in rude triumphant fingers at the nearby statues of the Chamberlain family? The Parthenon, indeed! Whatever next?

The bus arrived in due course and he stood aside while a rubicund, puffing woman with parcels manoeuvred herself onto the platform. The conductor stood and regarded her thoughtfully, and continued picking his teeth. Jonty waited until she was mid-platform before he began to move. He stepped towards the bus. Quick as a flash, the curd-faced conductor lunged at the bell, turned to the stairs, and disappeared to the upper-deck. The bus shot away as if fitted with two or three Rolls Royce jet engines. Jonty saw the head of the puffing woman sink with great suddenness, and a brown paper parcel describe a neat arc through the increasing space between him and the bus, before exploding on the tarmac; but he had no time to retrieve it. He began to run and caught the bus easily enough. He helped the now purplish woman to her feet and handed her the rest of her parcels while she re-embarked inside the bus.

Jonty went upstairs and sought out his favourite long back seat. The upper deck was nearly empty. Curdface was at the front giving the only other passenger his change. That finished, he rocked and swayed his way back, swinging from handrail to handrail, like a thin ape wearing a conducting set. Then, he stood in front of Jonty, wagging on his feet, pendulum-like, and grinned. Only a conductor with prehensile toes and worn soles could have avoided falling over.

"Thought you wanted a number 87! Left it a bit late, di'n't yuh, mate?"

Jonty was about to give an impolite reply, when he found himself jacknifed over his thighs and held down by an invisible hand. The bus seemed to have run into an electro-magnetic space-field. A little gap had opened up between the end of his spine and the start of his skull. Then, the bus shot forward, and Jonty was thrown back against his seat once more; his head wobbled dangerously. It was fastened only to a thin elastic sinew that wanted to know how far it could stretch before settling back approximately into its former position. Curdface appeared not to have moved.

"How long's this maniac out for?" asked Jonty.

"Him! He's one of the best drivers they got, 'e is. Never 'ad an accident in 'is life, he ain't. Got a bit of a sensitive stomach, like, have you?" asked Curdface sympathetically.

Jonty noticed that his sentence rhythms were stereotyped.

"Not at all! Just a healthy urge to stay alive."

Jonty bought his ticket, and Curdface left, doing a good emergency fireman-slide down the stair rails and arriving with a thud on the platform below.

Jonty took out his copy of *The Weekend Mail* and tried to ignore the madman in the cab who didn't know his clutch from his brake pedal. He tried to stabilize himself by wedging one foot under the seat in front and jamming an elbow up against the metal bodywork at the side. There was another lurch that wasn't quite explained by letting in the brake pedal or stamping on the clutch. Perhaps the driver had a wager on with another inmate to reduce the double-decker to a single-decker by the time he took it back to the garage? Well, the odds were good; he could have Jonty's money any day! He re-positioned himself and continued his perusal of the paper.

He turned to the Classified Advertisements. Like minds were at work in these columns! Apart from the fact that much of the merchandise was unimaginably bizarre, if not entirely imaginary, their phraseology was devised in conference with an inebriated copywriter and a compositor who was high on printer's ink. They were usually good for a few laughs, but, this week, they seemed exceptionally funny. They reminded him of the three letters he had written recently on behalf of Herbert Smedley Dummock, the effects of which should have reached him by now. Jonty hoped sincerely that he wouldn't run into Dummock while he was waiting for Alexis. Jonty had no desire to be made a spectacle of: Dummock wouldn't cool down his resentment this time by allusions to Jonty's jeans, jazzed up by references to his chains and beads, and orchestrated by grace-notes on his button front vest. His reaction would be immediate, less subtle and quite unmusical.

Jonty was once more jolted back to the prosaic, or the frenetic, according to the way you looked at it. The man's driving technique was impossible to ignore. It consisted of jet-smooth supersonic accelerations—with passengers pinned helplessly against the backs of their seats—followed by rapid sequences of leap-frogging rushes, varying from the minute to the enormous. Jonty's spine felt as if it had been dismantled by a navvy and reassembled by an osteopath who not only didn't know his job but wasn't interested in learning it. When Jonty looked out of the window, he noted with surprise that the performance had produced negligible gains in the traffic queue. There was still a little way to go before he reached his stop.

Jonty went down the stairs gingerly. Curdface was on the platform. The bus came to a halt with a brain-paralyzing jerk. As Jonty stepped on to the curbstones, wondering if he would be able to walk without a stick for the next week or two, Curdface broke into an expression of sympathy.

"Still suffering a bit with your stomach like, are you?"

Then the bus shot away into the stream of traffic, but not before he had managed to lean far out from the platform, hanging on to the rail as if he'd been crewman on a racing yacht, and to yell:

"Try Milk of Magnesia, mate!"

"Thanks!" Jonty shouted back. "Tell that dozy bastard in the cab—Purple Hearts!"

Curdface waved, and stood looking through the rear windows, grinning.

Jonty began to walk slowly towards Burke's, Charles & Long's. As he neared the double green doors, he saw, as expected, Archie Casbolt airing his big stomach in the chilly chemical breezes of Tyseley. For Archie, wrapped in the fat allowance of three or four overweight men, it was always summer, and, in Summer, Archie suffered hell. At present, he would regard the weather as fair to balmy. He stood with his arms folded in the small of his back, his customary position on such days, and looked down the road, at nothing in particular and everything in general, without his Works Policeman's cap on.

As Jonty approached, he decided to drop into his role of a lifelong arthritic, which today he found easier to fake. Archie heard his footsteps and turned round, blocking the middle of the driveway, like the Colossus of Rhodes.

The bland mandarin smile that Archie normally wore dissolved, and his eyes peered craftily from their little mouseholes of fleshiness. A look of surprised horror formed. His arms unfolded from behind him, and suddenly, he threw them upwards as if he didn't want them. Jonty half-expected them to slip their shoulder moorings, slide out smoothly from Archie's sleeves, rise to a few thousand feet, and disappear in the direction of Acock's Green. When his podgy fists halted at a fixed height over his head, waggling and waving, Jonty felt a faint disappointment.

"Give us strength!" moaned Archie, "I thought we'd seen the last of you."

His arms dropped like Archie's arms dropping. The weight of his fists jerked his three chins together in a brief merger before diversifying again. Archie was Tory through and through: even his chins believed in individual initiative; and it also explained, as Jonty had so often told him in the past, why he was a policeman.

"People like you lost us the Empire," Archie would growl at him.

"What's the Empire ever done for you and, more important, what've you done for the Empire?" was a stock reply that would turn Archie into a choleric policeman with a flair for obscene language. Anything more un-Mandarin-like was difficult to imagine. But today, Jonty was playing for sympathy. It wouldn't suit his plans in the least to be frog-marched by Archie — which he could do on his own — back to the bus stop.

"Hello, Archie! Nice to see you! I'm on the Box again. Arthritis!" Jonty patted his hip. "How're you?"

"No better for seeing you," growled Archie.

He stuck out his plump lips in a pout.

"Now, don't be like that, Archie! I mean it."

"Like a pig's ear you do! Remember, I've seen you before."

Several platoons of rejoinders presented themselves at the ready in Jonty's mind, as required by immediate conditions and the strategy of guerrilla warfare. What was it to be—grenade, plastic explosive, or ground-to-ground missiles? But Jonty managed to keep to his resolution and went for a negotiated peace.

"No, honest!"

Their running skirmishes were features of a long-established ritual they had both agreed to take part in. Jonty liked Archie and today he just had to convince him that the Pax was genuine.

"Look, Archie! Fingers crossed. Barley! I've come on business. See?"

"What business? They booted you out weeks ago."

Archie was suspicious, believing that Jonty might have found a new tactical weapon.

"I know that, silly! But they never gave me my National Insurance Card. You know! Stamps! The new employer wants it. I've come to fetch it."

Archie needed time; he was ponderous in marshalling his ground forces. He didn't have any air forces. That was another reason, Jonty had once told him, he was a Works Policeman. Eventually, he said: "Oh? Well, I'd better phone up Mr Chase and ask him, first, hadn't I?"

Archie turned his bulk to the little green door in the big green door, and prepared to squeeze through. Mmm, quite a shrewd move of Archie's, that! But it was the last thing Jonty wanted him to do.

"Well, you can if you like, Archie. But it'd save a lot of trouble if I just popped along and got it, wouldn't it? Won't take a minute or two. I know my way around, don't I?"

"You bleedin' do! That's what worries me."

"Oh, come on! What could I do in a few minutes? Don't be daft! Look! I'll tell you what! Give me five minutes at the outside, and I'll be back here all shipshape and Bristol-fashion. What about it?"

Archie deliberated on it. Jonty was conscious of ponderous motions deep inside him, but he was managing them without audible clankings and visible pain. At last, Archie said: "All right! Just this once. But no more'n five minutes, mind, or I'll be on that blower quicker'an you can say knife. Go on, bugger orf."

Archie held open the little green door and Jonty went through it on the double.

"Thought you'd got arthritis!" said Archie, with deep suspicion.

"Eh? Oh, I have, I have. Didn't you notice?"

"Buggered if I did."

"Oh, well, it's there all right, Archie, don't you worry," replied Jonty, patting his hip again, and limping elaborately off.

Archie watched him falter his way through the archway into the Delivery Yard and hobble right in the direction of the Personnel Office. As soon as Jonty estimated that Archie had turned willingly away to resume his untroubled vigil of the street, he stopped limping, reversed his direction, and tiptoed to the corner of the entrance under the archway to peer around it. The little door was in the act of closing. Archie would be settling himself into his favourite stance for grinning at the Universe again.

Jonty went quickly through a short corridor and found himself in the Reception Foyer. There was no-one in it, not even the receptionist. He made at once for the door of the male Staff Toilet that led off the hall. He was in luck: It was empty. He opened Treblitt's favourite cubicle and went in, locking the door carefully. Straight away, he scanned the panelled sides to find the place where the graffiti with the bawdiest sentiments were scratched in most prolifically, found it, and fixed a sticky holly-bordered label above it, bearing the salutation: A MERRY CHRISTMAS TO ALL OUR READERS. That done, he let himself out and returned hurriedly to the Foyer. His luck had held. It was still empty.

The next objective was the large notice board used mainly by Top Management personnel. Jonty took a small scroll of manila card from his pocket and unrolled it. It was nearly a metre long and about three fingers wide, just right to provide a central heading for the board itself. He fixed it with drawing pins at both ends and stood back to admire his handiwork: OBSERVE STRICTEST OCCURACY IN NOTISES AT ALL TIMES. SINGED: MAJOR H.B.KNOWLES. D.S.O. WORDS MANAGER.

Very satisfactory! Very good advice! The lettering was beautifully executed, black, majescule, and punctiliously illiterate.

Jonty smiled with pride. However, he could not afford to hang about. The receptionist could come back at any moment. Or a rep from another firm could drop in. Or worse still, Dummock, or one of the draughtsmen, might want to make use of the facilities. He'd have to go. He made for the door. In the short corridor to the Delivery Yard he had a moment of panic: had he remembered to bring his National Insurance Card with him? He searched through his pockets, and, yes, there it was, in the back pocket of his jeans, warm and nicely curved to the shape of his buttocks. He flattened it out and waved it vigorously in the air to cool it. Then, he limped back to Archie as nonchalantly as he could.

He waved the green card in the air at Archie, as it was still slightly warm.

"They had it all ready, Archie. Thanks!"

Archie grunted, still suspicious. But he said, amiably enough: "You'd best be orf, then, hadn't you?"

"I'm going. Cheerio, Archie."

That partially restored the grin to Archie's face. He reverted to his oriental universe-watching posture, with his arms in the small of his back, and put his broad posteriors between himself and trouble. Two fingers in the region of Archie's kidneys jerked vigorously at Jonty in the well-known obscene salutation. "And to you, mate!" said Archie, over his shoulder.

Jonty let him have the best of the exchange and, without a word, walked a little way further along the road to wait for Alexis to come out of her office at the knocking-off hooter. It was still cold.

Jonty was people-watching again, one of his favourite pastimes. Alexis wouldn't be long, now. The hooter had hooted and the road was full of the usual humanity and the usual lack of it. Most of them wore blue overalls, with jackets and mufflers over the top of them, and caps over the top of *them*. They came out of the near distance like blue ants on the march, the main body going steadily in one direction while the outriders, scouts and stragglers ran nervily this way and that. The office workers would follow and the main troop would soon become multi-coloured.

Except for his factory wear, a man passed him who looked exactly like Thomas Carlyle rushing home to Cheyne Row and another chapter of 'The French Revolution' and his wife Jane pinning up a few more postcards on the screen in the sitting room. It was all in his face. Then a lot of people he didn't know went by. Then some girls he wished he did know went by. And then—wait a minute—isn't that—? Why, of course, it's Edith Sitwell going strong in a maxi-skirt, with the most recent book on the last of the Plantagenet monarchs under her arm and a pearly-white dewdrop under her Plantagenet nose. Then a group of anonymouses and a few pseudonyms followed, trailed by what he took to be real people, going through life under their proper names. Interesting! Thousands of people never find out they are the look-alikes of luminaries of the past or the present. Millions never find out who they really are at all. Millions find out too late, and some never stop using aliases. A funny world!

A toolmaker he knew, named Sylvester Tripp called Bert, passed Jonty on his bicycle. He waved.

"Hi, Sylvester! How're things?"

"Bert!" the man called back.

"How're things, Bert?"

"You wouldn't understand," said Bert.

'That's Bert's problem,' thought Jonty. 'He won't admit he's Sylvester.'

Fancy wanting to be called Bert! Calling him Bert, Jonty felt he had committed an act of treachery disguised as friendship. That was bad enough! But calling yourself Bert when your name was Sylvester must be exhibitionism of a pathological kind, mustn't it? If Bert just passed himself off as Sylvester with a merry laugh, nobody would notice it; well, not after a few introductory guffaws, anyway. But insisting people call you Bert, as Sylvester did, wasn't that inviting gossip and notoriety?

"There goes Bertie! Know what his real name is?... Sylvester! Ha, ha, ha!"

What about that other famous Bert, David Herbert Lawrence? Would he have asked his friends to call him Bert if he hadn't grown up with it? No wonder he wrote *Lady Chatterley's Lover*; it was to draw attention away from the fact that he was generally known as Bert. I bet if his name had been Sylvester Tripp he wouldn't have written it at all! It's pretty clear that Lawrence's problem was of almost an opposite kind from Tripp's: Lawrence wanted to make people forget his name was Bert; Tripp wanted to make them remember it was. I wonder if I can work an idea like that into my study of that obscure Welsh poet? Who the hell did he think HE was, anyway?'

"Well, well, well! Look what we've got here! You're just the one I've been wanting to meet, you bastard!"

Jonty woke with a jolt out of his reverie. Dummock's hand fell like a criminal arrest on his shoulder. Dummock, in a long-skirted highwayman's coat and bespoke shoes, stood glowering down at him. Jonty glimpsed Alexis's suede and fur creation approaching a little way behind Dummnock. Even in his extremity, Jonty noted with appreciation that she looked good enough to ravish him again.

"Hello!" said Jonty.

"I'll hello you, you bastard!"

Dummock doubled his fist under Jonty's nose. His triangular beak was white at the wings. He was furious.

"Who is this attacker?" asked Jonty, looking at Alex.

Dummock grabbed the unzipped edges of Jonty's windcheater and twisted his fist, pulling him forward, the way they did in Tough Movies. Then he pushed him roughly backwards into the coalyard gateway. Jonty had known, if he encountered Dummock, that he would be totally unmusical. But why had he gone soprano? Was he giving up his Orson Welles voice for good, or was it a temporary measure only?

"Never mind the funny stuff! You just bloody well tell me what—"

Alexis put a restraining hand on Dummock's arm.

"Don't Smedley. Don't start a brawl here. Please!"

'It's Smedley, now, is it? Christ, that's worse than Bert!' thought Jonty.

Dummock was now, unaccountably, trying for the soprano's top C.

"But you know what he did, don't you? He—"

"Don't screech! People are looking at us. Yes, I know. But I shall walk off and leave you and never speak to you again if you start making a fool of us here."

"That's right!" said Jonty. "Don't you touch me, or—"

"—Or what?" shrilled Dummock.

"Or she'll walk off and leave you," said Jonty mildly.

"I'll bust you wide open, the trouble you've caused me!" said Dummock, lowering his voice an octave or two, and letting go of Jonty's windcheater, and stepping back, and breathing like a spavined steeplechaser.

'That's better,' thought Jonty, 'more like the register of the old Orson Dummock, that is.'

To make sure that hostilities would not resume, Alexis stepped between them, so that all three were standing in a tight huddle just inside the coal yard of the railway junction, out of the mainstream of workers on the pavement, with the loaded trucks lined up on the sidings behind them.

"What're you doing here, anyway?" asked Alexis.

"It's Dummock's fault. He pushed me in."

"No, silly! Here! In Tyseley!"

"I've been waiting to see you."

"What about?"

"There's an eavesdropper," said Jonty.

Jonty looked at Dummock, who was still simmering.

24

"I'm not an eavesdropper," growled Dummock. "I'm a Godley-dropper."

He began to edge round Alexis's shoulder.

"And before you do anything at all, I've got things to ask, and when I've got the answers, THEN I'll drop you, bloody hard!"

Alexis pushed him away.

"Smedley! Why don't you just go and wait for me in the car. I shan't be long."

He ignored her.

"Who gave you my address, Godley, eh? That's the first thing."

Jonty looked hard at Dummock. He really was extraordinarily skinny. His already thin cheeks, nose and skull seemed to have shrunk under the tension of his anger. If he wanted to keep up the appearance of a natty dresser, he'd have to watch it; he was already beginning to look more like a well-dressed butcher's cleaver than a beau.

Dummock had started slowly advancing again. Jonty began going over Karate moves in his mind. But watching Dummock's eyes for any giveaway signs, he realized that his head was at exactly the height to butt Dummock under the chin and make a run for it. Trouble was, Dummock's chin was so sharp that Jonty visualized his head falling into two neat halves, like a split walnut; and running away would clinch Dummock's suspicions that Jonty was gutless and he didn't want that confirmed just yet.

"Would you mind telling me what you're talking about, Dummock?" he enquired politely.

This made Dummock go berserk. He started hopping, dancing, whirling about, and spluttering with sheer rage and frustration, while Alexis tried to drag him away. They were both talking at once in an incomprehensible stream. Jonty stood listening and watched them.

After a while, Jonty said: "Well, when you've finished this interesting exhibition of Morris dancing, Dummock, maybe I could have a private word with Alex?"

For some reason Jonty could not fathom, this remark persuaded Dummock to make an effort to contain himself and he quietened down. He said something to Alexis that Jonty missed and then stepped forward to hiss softly between his clenched teeth at Jonty:

"If Alex wasn't here, I'd tear you apart, tiny limb from tiny limb." And then, loud enough for Alexis to hear, he said: "I suppose you meant my wife to go crazy at me, eh? Did you?"

"I hope you're managing to keep up your readings of De Sade these days?" Jonty enquired artlessly.

Jonty had decided that the safest ploy, and the one that would give him most satisfaction, was to admit nothing and answer Dummock every time with some new taunt.

"You see!" Dummock turned to Alexis in great wrath. "He's too craven to admit anything."And then, as an afterthought, he added: "The bastard!"

"Well, why don't you leave it? What's it matter?" replied Alexis with annoyance.

"WHAT'S IT MATTER? God in heaven, you'd have known if you'd been there. I only told you the half of it. HE knew what it would do, this—this—this—"

"Bastard?" suggested Jonty helpfully.

Dummock turned round to gaze on Jonty: in some subtle way, his incredulity made his eyes move closer together. After a moment, Dummock turned to face Alexis again.

"He wanted to break us up AND get back at me by getting at Doris. The dirty little bastard! You know what he did first, eh?"

He went on without waiting for Alexis to answer.

"The first thing was this great thumping envelope full of questionnaires—FROM A BLOODY MARRIAGE BUREAU. Addressed to me! Marked 'Highly Confidential'! Doris opens all our mail, has done for years, and you should'a seen what happened. My life wasn't worth a plastic button. 'What you write there for?' 'Got a bit on the side, have you? Who is it, then, eh?' The third degree for days and days on end."

He suddenly turned back to Jonty.

"You know, don't you, Godley?"

"Who? Me?"

Jonty could imagine the black bold print of the envelope in his mind's eye, and remembered the *Mail's* advertisement written by the drunken copy-writer and a doped-up compositor in their inimitable English:

LONELY?

Choose your partner by **COMPUrER.** Scientific marriage. Punchcards and questionnaires. NATIONWIDE. <u>Absolutely</u> <u>Confidential</u>. Details sent under plain cover. No obligation.

"I haven't the faintest idea what you're talking about, Dummock," said Jonty, opening his eyes very wide. "Read any good books on the opening gambits of the Masters, lately?"

He remembered writing to the Marriage Bureau a real sob story on Dummock's behalf: no wonder they'd bombarded him with vast quantities of propaganda!

228

Dummock turned to Alexis for support and sympathy.

"Five years of a happy marriage, and then this? What could I say to her? It'd be a shock to any woman, wouldn't it, Alex… Alex?"

Dummock seemed unaware of the effect his sentiments were having on Alexis: she'd gone a little white round the gills, but said nothing.

"And then, when I'd just managed to smooth her fur back, WHAM! another packet comes through the letterbox. Of course, she opened it pronto, and the first thing that fell out was this little plastic beaker, with a label in purple bloody letters: FREE CONTAINER FOR URINE SAMPLE, staring her straight in the face. Christ save me!"

He put a hand over his eyes for a moment and shook his head. Then, whipping his hand away, he swivelled fast and held it, clenched, under Jonty's nose.

"You know what that was, don't you, Jonty?"

"No! Let me guess!"

Jonty knew all right. The headline had said: 'Pregnancy Testing, Confidential Service,' and a lot more of the usual guff.

He said: "Is your budgerigar off-colour? No longer bouncing with lust? I mean, if it turned purple, it needed a urine test, didn't it?"

In contrast with his budgie, it really was incredible how pale Dummock could look. He had a complexion on, at the moment, somewhere between slug-grey and flour-white. His fist, still poised under Jonty's nose, was beginning to tremble; he seemed to have something inside him that vibrated, making him quiver all over, like a City of Birmingham bus.

"Yes, you little bastard, you knew what Doris'd think, didn't you? What any woman would think?"

"Not so much of the little, Dummock! Let's change the subject! You've got bastardy on the brain—which, in your case is natural enough—but, how're the crosswards going? And Treblitt? And everybody in the Drawing Office? Give 'em my regards, won't you?"

Alexis stood by, watching them, content at this stage to say nothing as long as they did not actually start hammering each other. She had an expression on her face that might have been pleasure, the kind a woman feels who is as vain as Cleopatra and who's listening to two men fight because they have wanted her and have had her and one of them now has to step back. But to give her credit, she seemed anxious about the effects of Jonty's latest sally and kept looking quickly from one to the other.

Dummock was undergoing some kind of alchemy. He seemed to want to turn into a puff of that pure whiteness they put in washing powders; he became almost transparent and evanescent with anger. Then, changing his intention, his arms seemed to be fusing to his body, and gradually, by the sheer concentration of his outrage, he was becoming a white-hot blur of whiteness just about to melt into thin air, like something in a television space odyssey. The surprising thing was he did not actually disappear. Jonty closed his eyes and wished. When he opened them, Dummock was still there.

"Hello! Are you still here?" said Jonty. "I thought you were preparing to go somewhere?"

De-materialization now seemed imminent. Alexis put a hand on Dummock to restrain him.

"Don't!" she said. "You know what he's like! He wants you to make a fool of yourself. Just get a grip, Smedley, that's all."

'That's an unfortunate sentence!' thought Jonty. 'The verb's got no object! Though Dummock might give it one.'

Dummock, with an immense effort, began to cool himself, regaining a shape and definition more like his usual incarnation and, with it, his powers of speech rejoined him.

"The final straw was when these free samples came! Everything from straight Gossamer to a Japanese Tickler. Besides those plastic gadgets... And she's Catholic!... She nearly killed me! I just couldn't convince her."

'Well, naturally,' thought Jonty. 'How could you?'

"I'm sure you'll be able to make use of them, somewhere, Dummock," said Jonty.

Dummock made a step forward; his face was murderous. Alexis gave a short, compressed, in-drawn, gasping little scream, and put her hand in front of her mouth. She seemed to have no doubts about what Dummock intended this time. It was scarcely audible more than a couple of yards away, but it had the desired effect on Dummock. He stopped and said with concentrated fury: "My turn will come, Jonty! You'll see!"

"That's very moot, very moot, indeed!" said Jonty. "Why don't you go home, Dummock, and count your samples and read your catalogues, while I talk to Alex?"

"Yes, go on, Smedley. I shall only be a minute or two."

He debated with himself for a moment before saying: "All right! But if you're not there in four minutes, I'm coming back to—"

"—Go on!" said Alexis. "Don't be silly."

He walked out of the gateway of the coal yard and turned towards the car park. Jonty, with relief, looked at Alexis. Now, he could really concentrate on her. She was just as beautiful as he remembered. He openly admired where she was most beautiful, and not only because he liked it but also because she expected it.

"Hello!" she said, as if they had just met. "How have you been?... Never mind. What do you want?... Hurry!"

"Have you got any letters for me?"

"Letters? Oh, yes! I forgot. Now, where did I put it?"

She opened her cosmetic toolbox.

"I think it's in here, somewhere. I didn't want him to—Ah, here you are! They said you'd moved. I wasn't sure how to find you."

Jonty took the buff-coloured envelope.

"Thanks! How long?"

"How long what?"

"You had the letter?"

"Oh, not long. Two, maybe three days. Not long."

"Look, Alex, I don't like asking, but I'm—"

"—You want to borrow some money, is that it?"

He nodded.

"Okay. How much?"

"A couple of quid will do."

"Here's one! Got to be off. 'Bye. See you!"

He watched her running up the hill to the car park. What did she see in Dummock? Her reactions puzzled him: he had not expected the money from her. Why did she do it? True, she was hard to provoke; he had liked that about her from the start. He thought how different she was from the library assistant with acne, and wondered what he would have had to say to Alexis before she felt like fetching help to throw him out of the Reference Library. Ah ,well! Now, he could, at least, buy the latest issue of *The Weekend Mail.*

As he walked to the newsagent's, he mused on the variations in the two girls, Alexis and Sofia. In ways that were plastic and tangible, they had similarities he appreciated very much. But he sensed that Sofia was very different from Alexis; by how much and in what ways, though powerfully felt, were not obvious. He just hoped that circumstances would offer him a chance to find out, that's all.

Jonty looked up at the imposing facade of the building of the Local Education Authority.

If he had left his expedition to Burke's, Charles & Long's any later, it would have been too late. The letter instructed Mr Arnold Jonathan Godley to present himself for interview with Mr Jarrold, Assistant Education Officer in Charge of Grants and Bursaries, at 1100 hours the following day. Jarrold had been so long in replying, and had only been induced to do that through Jonty's persistence, that a conviction had been growing in his mind that this was to be his first, last, and only chance to impress the said Mr Jarrold. Jonty felt as though he had been invited to his own execution, a premonition made worse when he recollected the immense awe with which Lacestone had pronounced Jarrold's name.

Jonty stood hesitantly tidying himself up in front of the steps, which were none too clean, and which the sheer number of feet with fallen, unfallen, falling and about-to-fall arches, had caused to dip in the middle. Jonty looked about him for the notice that instructed you TO PLEASE ADJUST YOUR DRESS BEFORE ENTERING, but it was either absent or hidden. Strange! There should have been one in huge back lettering on a pure white background. Despite this omission, Jonty felt under a compunction to smooth down his Wyatt Earp moustaches, zip up his Winston Churchill windcheater, and settle down the Colonel Cantwell whisky flask in his hip pocket, purchased for his Edwardian father on his next Twentieth Century smuggling jaunt to the Palaeolithic hospital. Oh dear! The piddling things that officials seemed to care about.

Jonty took one or two tentative paces towards the entrance, but again his heart quailed. He knew that he was in need of another shot to 'psych' him up a little more. What should it be? Perhaps he should go off and come on again, dressed in a way that would cause any secretary to blench to the roots of her corns and bleached hair, scream soundlessly, and dial 999 for the arrest of a man wearing nothing but an unfastened mackintosh? No! better to find a Gents and put a clean piece of string through the belt-loops of his jeans, in the circumstances. This interview was an outside chance and he had to make the most of it.

Feeling a little better, he swaggered up the steps; but stopped to assess his reflection in the double swing doors at the top. First, he took off his glasses, polished them, put them on again, and peered at himself quizzically in the smoke-tinted glass. Then, beginning to smooth down his hair, with his nose about a centimetre away from the door, he soon became aware that something else was hovering at about the same height in the aquarium gloom inside, on the other side of his mirror. Jonty peered harder. He felt like Alice trying to penetrate the looking-glass over the fire-place. He discerned a cap-like shape, then a hand that appeared to be wagging out of an ear, and, yes, a dim face, but nothing else. Jonty wagged back, in the same way.

Suddenly, the glass door was ripped open, and Jonty found himself, still in his peering posture, staring straight into a pair of bleary eyes under a peaked blue cap in a blue piqued face—the same hue as school blotting paper—beside a hand that was scratching vigorously at an ear.

"Morning," said Jonty.

It was a janitor. From the open door exuded the gentle but unmistakable odour of damp bass brooms and embalmed Egyptian mummies, although Jonty wasn't quite sure of their nationality.

"Go on! Clear orf!" said the janitor. "You shouldn't be 'anging about 'ere. It's public property."

His hand started wagging again, this time in a dismissive gesture. Jonty straightened himself up. "And mimickin' a public officer ain't to be tolerated, nei'ver!"

"I thought this was the entrance to the Museum. I've come to feed the mummies," said Jonty.

"None o' yer lip, nei'ver! If you ain't got proper business 'ere, you ain't wanted."

"Are the bass brooms embalmed as well?" enquired Jonty.

"Eh?... What?"

Jonty changed his mind about twitting the janitor, who was small, not very robust, and getting on in years. He was no match for him: Contest Cancelled. The code of the Godley's didn't allow them to oppress the oppressed, harass the harassed, or impoverish the poor. They left all that to the O'Gradys.

"Never mind. I've got an appointment at eleven o'clock with a Mr Jarrold."

The janitor's anxiety ebbed, and the pique left his face and somehow got into his cap, which seemed to grow in importance.

"Oh, well, tha's different, that is! Why di'n't you say so?"

"I just said so!"

"I mean before! Aggravatin' a body like that. Dealin' wiv the public ain't a easy matter, mate. Room 666, four'f floor, straight up the stairs an' turn right on the four'f. See?"

"I see. Thanks!"

The janitor received Jonty's thanks graciously, and resumed scratching his ear. Jonty had a feeling that the code of the Godley's wasn't going to impede him in any way in his dealings with Jarrold.

By the time he had climbed the stone stairways to the third floor, he was inhaling more strongly than ever that peculiar stomach-sinking odour he always associated with his first day at school. He remembered it only too well. He had screamed for two hours, from assembly to morning break, when the teacher, now at her wit's end, tried to console him with a bottle of milk and a straw, which he had blown-into instead of sucking-out-of. He just couldn't get the hang of it at all, but he had sat uncomplainingly in milk-wet trousers until he was able to run home, sore but triumphant, and dry off before the fire without telling his mother.

He felt a bit like that now: Authority had never stopped having that effect on him, and it was quite extraordinary how the local Department of Education had managed to blend the balm of the tombs of Egyptian kings with the bouquet of the half-open cupboards of British charwomen, and to build the odour unmistakably into their schools and official buildings all over the city. Jonty, breathing steadily, reached the fourth floor, turned right, as the janitor had instructed him, and walked along the corridor until he reached a door that said Room 666. He mused for a moment before the Mystic Number. Was he going to meet an embodiment of the Great Beast, or, worse still, a specimen of the Local Watch Committee?

Jonty knocked on the door and, without waiting for an answer, went in. There was a large man sitting at a desk talking into a telephone, but he wasn't wearing a kilt or holding a wand, and there were no obscene murals on the walls with mottoes under them. The odds were now slightly in favour of a Watch Committee representative. When Jonty entered, he looked up at him, astonished in a very astonished way. Clearly, Jonty had not been expected. Jonty sniffed the distinct odour of self-denial and a liberal dash of coal-tar soap, which would also fit in with this individual being a member of the Local Watch Committee. Then, Jonty detected the faintest tincture of bass-brooms and cerements, although—not to put too fine a point on it—the man did have a large face and lobose ears, AND they were mummy-coloured.

In almost the same moment that Jonty had recorded his impression of the man, he noticed a girl in the corner of the office, who was anything but mummy-coloured. She was crouching on the floor and putting a pile of papers together. She was peach- coloured, small and mammose, and exposed a lot of what she exposed without seeming to mind. The man had leaned into a posture that kept his eyes away from her, something not easy to do in that rather small office. This had been the moment Jonty was struck by the strong odour of self-denial. As soon as he saw the girl, Jonty felt totally disinclined to follow the man's example. She looked up at him and smiled as he came in.

"Hello," said Jonty.

She said nothing, but opened her eyes wide and lifted her eyebrows slightly in acknowledgement. Jonty wished she hadn't done it in exactly that way, as it looked somewhat like an invitation to go up to the next floor with her, which he wasn't free to accept at the moment.

The man said "Shush!" at him, and waved a long plump hand.

"No, sorry! Not you. I was talking to somebody in the office," he said into the telephone.

Jonty sat down without invitation and watched the girl. She seemed to be more essentially feminine than a lot of girls he had seen lately, and, judging by the overflow, in an amount about equal to that he had seen on Sofia, although he couldn't be sure without weighing them both, pound for pound. It was a nice beginning to an interview that was going to be hazardous, so he made the most of her, while he could.

Jonty felt he had made the right decision as soon as the man put the phone down and said: "All right, Margaret. You can go now. It'll do later." His voice was deep and tired and he sighed between his words, so that what he actually sounded like was: "All right – (sigh) – Margaret... you can leave – (sigh) – now, it'll do later – (sigh)."

"Yes, sir."

She stood up (which she did very nicely) and walked across the room (which she did even better) to the door and went out (which wasn't a bit nice).

"I suppose—you're Mr Jonty," he said in his deep sighing voice.

Jonty's eyes swivelled to the large mummy-coloured jujubes the man was wearing in place of ear lobes, and wished he hadn't done it so suddenly. Not only that, Jonty caught a clear whiff of coal-tar soap, which, in a way, he was glad of, because it eliminated the slight doubt he had had until then that it might have emanated from Margaret.

"No, I'm not," said Jonty. "Are you, by any chance, Mr Gerald?"

"You're not! " The man sat up dead straight in his swivel chair. "Well, who are you? I'm expecting a Mr Jonty."

25

He sighed, and picked up the telephone and spoke into it before Jonty could reply.

"Oh, Styles, bring in the—folder for the eleven—o'clock interview, will you?"

He put back the receiver and scrutinized Jonty. He knitted his brows, but Jonty noted that he didn't do it very well; he left one lower than the other. Pearl one, drop one! Jonty watched the man's gaze loitering piece by piece over his clothing and hurrying on with distaste and pulling up its coat collar and muttering.

"I'm afraid—it isn't customary for me—to see anyone without—an appointment. I can't—"

Styles came in with the folder: he was small, oppressed-looking and blotchy. He put the folder on the desk in front of the man.

"This is the one, sir."

"Right! Now let's—see."

He opened the file.

"Not this one—Styles. This is somebody—called Godley. I'm looking for—an applicant named Jonty."

"That's the one for eleven o'clock, sir, Godley."

"That's my name. G — O — D — L — E — Y," he spelled it out, emphatically. "Godley!"

Styles pivoted to face Jonty fleetingly before turning away. It gave Jonty the impression that a timid little rodent, maybe a squirrel, had squinted through the twin peepholes of Styles's eyes for a second; and then, not seeing in Jonty anything to soothe its fears and suspicions, had popped back into its nest again.

"Oh?" said the man, in a tone that suggested it was a felony to admit your name was Godley. "That's peculiar!"

'It's no worse than Jarrold, is it?' thought Jonty.

Jarrold searched among some papers on his desk. "I've got it written—on a memorandum—somewhere. Jonty. Jonty. Yes, here it is. Eleven o'clock!"

There was a note of triumph in Jarrold's voice.

"That's the time for MY interview," said Jonty. "I've got a letter—"

Jonty handed it across the desk. Jarrold took it gingerly in one corner, between thumb and forefinger, as if it might be infectious, and placed it in front of him. Then, he regarded it for a moment, sternly, before perusing it with a deep suspicion.

"Mmm! It certainly says—eleven o'clock. And the name—is—" He appeared to search the page for it.

"I didn't forge it," said Jonty.

The fearful little rodent peered out of Styles's face for an instant, and then popped back again.

"That's very strange, very strange indeed!"

Big sigh. He handed the letter back to Jonty.

"Well, just look—for this Jonty's folder, Styles—will you?"

"Yes, sir," said Styles.

Jonty had a strong hunch they both knew that there wasn't any Jonty folder; but, nevertheless, he wasn't going to be accepted here as anything less than an impostor who had managed to get in on an appointment that properly belonged to somebody else.

"You'd better sit down, Styles." Jarrold sighed, "And we can begin interviewing Mr—Mr—er—Godley. I'm accustomed—to working to—a rather tight schedule—so I'm afraid—Ah, yes! That reminds me."

He leaned back in his swivel chair, balanced his elbows on the armrests, and placed his fingertips together—as if he were about to launch into a genteel prayer for deliverance from Godley's presence. In his now established sighing mode, he began: "I want to turn to—"

'—Hymn number 24 in Moody and Sankey?' wondered Jonty.

"—the question of a telephone call—I received the other day— purporting to come from—ah, Mr Lacestone's office—" He pronounced the name with distaste.

"—on behalf of—you, Mr Godley."

"Who?"

"You!"

"I'm Godley!"

"Oh, yes, of course."

"Maybe it was on behalf of this Mr Jonty!"

"No—in the circumstances—I'm inclined to think it was—on your behalf, Mr Godley. It was rather a—curious call, and I wondered—if you knew—anything about it?"

Jonty had been observing Jarrold closely during this exchange, and, on consideration, had decided that he didn't like the spongy way Jarrold's finger-ends went in when he pressed them together, which he was doing fairly continuously. They had a good half centimetre's give in them. Furthermore, his shirt cuffs were washed in that detergent with the built-in whiteness, and they came out of his worsted thornproof sleeves as if they knew it. Added to which, his shirt was also very, very clean. Usually, these things would not have fazed Jonty—although they were disturbing ENOUGH, in themselves,—but what Jonty just couldn't abide was the phony defence Jarrold's face, ascetic expression and self-denying manners were putting up against the dandified witnesses of his manicured hands, immaculate cuffs and impeccably pressed suit.

'Ladies and gentleman of the jury, this man's manner, aspect and dress must indicate something, mustn't it? Yes, it must. I rest my case.'

Jonty had deliberately kept Jarrold waiting for his answer. He now looked at Styles, to see how he was responding to the lull in the firing. Styles was studying the end of his poised ballpoint with terrifying attention, and doing his best to look as if he didn't go to bed in his clothes. Jonty mused on the trouble that phone call to Jarrold had caused him: apart from the usual tussle with the coinbox in the kiosk, there had been the trainee operator who had kept putting the plug in the wrong hole. However, at last, he had made the connection.

"No, I don't! What was it about, Mr Gerald?"

Jarrold pressed together his sorbo-rubber fingers, and tried to imitate it with his lips, but there was no give in them.

"Jarrold!" he said, haughtily.

"What?"

"Ja-rrold!" he repeated, slowly with emphasis; and then, normally, "Pronounced Jarrold."

"I see," said Jonty, pronounced Jonty. "May I make a suggestion?"

Jarrold inclined his head slightly forward and a little to one side, like royalty from a motorcade. He supposed that Jarrold meant him to assume agreement. However, Jarrold didn't wave formally to the onlookers, so it could have been a signal to a hidden security man to mean: 'I am about to arrest you as a deserter from the Respectable British Public, in the name of Queen Elizabeth the Second, Our Gracious Sovereign and Emperor, Defender of the Faith, Guardian of Public Morals, and generally known V.I.P.'

Jonty took a breath. "Wouldn't it be better," he asked, "if you attended to Mr Styles first?"

Jarrold's spongy fingers stopped their pressing movements and stiffened visibly. "I'm afraid I don't quite understand your meaning!"

'Don't you don't quite me! Either you don't understand at all or you understand only too well. And stop sighing like that!'

"Well," said Jonty, "I'd rather discuss my affairs with you in private, if you don't mind. If you could attend to Mr Styles, I would feel I—"

Jonty ceased in midflow. Jarrold was obviously under stress: he had stopped pressing and leaned over to look hard at the papers on his desk in front of him, and a tincture of plum was beginning to suffuse the mummy colour of his earlobes. Had Jarrold taken out letters patent on the use of the word 'I', or something, and was becoming angry because Jonty had used it three times in his last statement, without Jarrold's permission?

"You—" said Jarrold in a deeply strangled voice and sighing heavily, "—are not in charge—of the routine of this office—I am glad to say—Mr Styles WORKS here—he is here to take notes."

'So that's what he's here for, is it? And the best of luck, Styles!'

"I see!"

Jonty glanced at him: he was bent even lower over his ballpoint, watching its tip in terror. Jonty waited to see if Styles's squirrel would peep out, but it was probably curled up safely in its nest, fast asleep: Styles didn't raise his eyes a fraction. Then, a short pause ensued, in which a muted, but distinct, mewing sound was audible to all. Jonty was startled by it when he supposed for a moment it had been made by Styles's squirrel, before recovering himself and dismissing the idea as absurd. Styles had given a little start and began doodling with great rapidity on his pad. Jarrold coughed quickly, to camouflage the sound and to try to persuade Jonty that he had been mistaken, riffling noisily through the papers on his desk, and then leaning back hard in his chair so that its springs complained loudly, and said: "Perhaps we could—return to the question—of the telephone call.—You wished to know.—Well, one day last week – I had — a call purporting to come from — Mr Lacestone's (distress signs) — office —"

'So that's what purporting means, is it? Well, I did a nice bit of it there, all right!'

"—It was clearly false—a hoax, you might say—In brief, Mr Godley—this person—," Jarrold managed to show by his intonation that to be called a person was thoroughly reprehensible, "—did his best to speak highly—of your—er—application to this office—for a grant. I telephoned Mr Lacestone – (more distress signals) – later—and he knew absolutely nothing about it."

Jonty waited for Jarrold to continue, and Jarrold and Styles waited for Jonty to reply. Jonty said nothing. Jarrold inspected his manicured nails, alternately curling and straightening his fingers, and twisting his wrists to observe his palms. After a while, almost nonchalantly, between sighs, he said: "I thought it sounded—very much—like you, Mr Godley."

This remark prompted Styles, on the edge of his chair, to try rolling himself into a ball, while Jonty did an impersonation of Jonty shewing injured surprise.

"Me! I! Whatever gave you that idea, Mr Gerald?"

'If you can Jonty me, I can Gerald you, Jarrold!'

Jarrold did his best to continue examining his hands calmly, but he was ruffled, as Jonty knew, by observing the slightly plum-coloured earlobes paling back into their normal healthy mummy colour. Then came another mewing sound. Styles, having given up his efforts to become spherical, shuffled his bottom on his leather chair in manifest embarrassment, and nearly slipped off.

'Sounds like a kitten,' thought Jonty. 'Have they got it shut up?'

He looked at the row of cupboards under the heavy mahogony bookcases behind Styles, but detected nothing suspicious.

"Well, as a matter of fact—YOU did," said Jarrold, recovering himself, expertly.

"Oh, why?"

"Because it sounded like you — Mr Godley — it sounded like you!"

Then, when Jonty did not respond to this reply, he added, from clear irritation, in his best Watch Committee tones: "Come, come, Mr Godley! Let's not act about it!"

It was the first time in the interview that Jarrold had looked straight at Jonty, who noted with some surprise, that his eyes were navy blue. Were they unique, or did he wear tinted contact lenses?

"Who's acting about it? Is Mr Styles acting about it? Are you acting about it?"

Mr Styles, once again, was scribbling furiously on his pad.

"Very well, Mr Godley—I see that there is—no more to be said under that head."

'Gerald, I do wish you wouldn't rhyme things like that. It sounds simple-minded.'

Jarrold resumed: "I suggest we turn to—"

'Oh, no, not another hymn! What about this kitten you've got shut up, somewhere?' Jonty silently protested.

"—the matter of your—application—er—proper."

Pat, pat! Jarrold palpated Jonty's folder, lying on the desk before him.

"Now, I might say at once—that there isn't a chance in—that the Committee has considered your—application, and, after spending— more time on your case—than is usual, we are not— in a position to offer—assistance."

'It's a mystery why all these sighs make the bastard sound so regretful,' mused Jonty.

"Why not?" asked Jonty abruptly.

Jarrold's navy-blue eyes came to attention and gazed over Jonty's right shoulder. Faint scuffling sounds came from Styles's direction.

"I beg your pardon!" Jarrold had lost all interest in his manicure. "I suppose you are aware, Mr Godley, that the Selection Comittee is not accustomed to giving its reasons for its decisions?"

He said this in one breath and let out a large shuddering sigh as he finished, leaning back tiredly in his chair, and allowed his eyes to stand at ease.

"Well, never mind THEIR reasons, Mr Gerald, give me the real ones."

Jonty could sense Styles dithering soundlessly on his chair behind him. Jarrold's eyes flicked instantly to attention, and then wavered as a plaintive little mew, followed by a homely gurgle, was heard. This time, Jonty decisively placed it as having come from the direction of Jarrold's chair.

"Styles," said Jarrold, with a deep sigh, "I think it is time—you brought in my tea and biscuits. It is now—precisely eleven fifteen a.m."

"Yes, sir."

Jonty nearly broke into a wolf-howl of derisive laughter, but managed, just in time, to change it into a spluttering cough. Styles scuttled gratefully out with a surprising turn of speed, and closed the door silently behind him. Jarrold was flicking through Jonty's file again. Eventually, he took out several sheets of paper, and held them in front of him while he spoke.

"Since you seem to feel that there might be—er—partiality in the decision, Mr Godley, —I might inform you that the record states—the Committee cannot justify—in your case— the expenditure of public monies. Your academic record—is, almost (to be kind), non-existent— and this report from your headmaster—" He waved a sheet of paper at Jonty. "—tells us that you were expelled—for persistent truancy."

"There were good reasons for that!"

Jarrold looked once again directly at Jonty and gave him an imitation of a smile. His teeth were large and horse-like, all the same size.

"There are always good reasons, Mr Godley, for that kind of behaviour."

A very rude response rose to Jonty's lips and it was providential that Jarrold's stomach chose that moment to send in a strong, vocal complaint to head office. First, there came a drawn-out neighing tone from some way off, followed by the nearer sound of a stable door slamming, or even two planks smacking together. Then, close at hand, came a long low groan, like heavy wooden doors closing slowly on un-oiled hinges. Jonty hoped that it was actually Jarrold's diaphragm sinking permanently to the bottom of his stomach. Its insistence diluted neatly the malice of Jarrold's reply and the triumph that was beginning to form in his smile. Jonty and Jarrold found themselves actually looking at each other without the power of speech, the one lost in a whirling sense of consternation and embarrassment, and the other in pure unimpeded joy.

Jonty began to admire Jarrold's stomach; it really had put up a most incredible performance. He could almost certainly get into show business with an organ like that. 'The Incredible Talking Stomach. Speaks Six Languages. Amazing Volume. Tonight at the Albert Hall. Free Seats to the Deaf.'

Jonty felt he could stand up to Jarrold's arguments but he wasn't sure about his stomach's. A good old trooper that was! There was certainly more to Jarrold than met the eye. It was with great difficulty that Jonty dragged his mind back to the matter in hand.

"I'm keen to get on, Mr Gerald, and take a degree. All I need is the chance, you see."

"Keenness, I'm afraid, Mr Godley, isn't enough. It has to be backed up – by a fully adequate academic – performance, which, in your case, – you have not got."

'Which in your case, you have not got. And the japonica glistens like coral in all of the neighbouring gardens. All right, I know!'

"The Committee wished that I should—see you, and give you their decision personally—only because the innumerable letters – we have received from you—were an indication of—er—some earnestness. The Committee thought—a personal explanation would—"

'—Put a stop to them. I know!'

"—be better all round," Jarrold concluded, inconclusively.

'All round what? The mulberry bush? Ham Hall Power Station? The Wrekin?'

Jarrold leaned back again in his chair, re-composing himself. The patriotic naval colour was returning to his eyes which, when his stomach was on the wire, had seemed to pale a little as if bleached by service under hot foreign suns. He appeared to think that the worst was over.

"The Committee," he went on, "wished me to—offer you a little useful advice—and that is—"

Styles returned as quiet as a squirrel carrying a tea tray. Jonty saw at once that it was set with one cup and saucer, a plate, and a pile of arrowroot biscuits in a glass jar. All the crockery matched and had pink roses embossed on it. Jonty craned his neck to see if their biscuits were embossed in the same way, but Styles was moving the tray.

"Ah! Thank you, Styles. Put it there. Yes." Jarrold gave his attention once again to his candidate. "And that is, Mr Godley—"

Styles crumpled onto his leather chair and once more took up his crouching position behind his pad, holding his ballpoint in two hands as if it might be a nut he was about to nibble at.

"—perhaps you would be best advised—to enrol with the University of the Air—admirable scheme, admirable—and we think it exactly suited to your—kind of student needs, Mr Godley."

'Oxbridge, indeed! Crap, Mr Godley, crap! We don't want your kind at our older establishments, do we, Gentlemen? Furthermore, we don't want you at the redbrick or even the white-tile universities. On the other hand, this University of the Air – shall we say, Hot-Air? – is just the thing for you. Agreed, Gentlemen? Agreed. Next Business.'

"That's not what I'm looking for."

"It could be your answer, Mr Godley."

"Some answer! If I got a first, it might get me an introduction to the manager of Joe Lyons's Teashops, I suppose."

"Think about it! It could solve your problems, Mr Godley."

But Jonty had already given up thinking about it. Watching Jarrold help himself to tea and biscuits was making Jonty feel hungry; besides, in some subtle way, it seemed to emphasize the far from subtle fact that he wouldn't get a sausage out of the Local Education Committee for his plans, and that, personally, Jarrold wouldn't give him the droppings of his nose, never mind a half cup of tea or a broken piece of arrowroot biscuit.

Jonty was beginning to feel desperate.

What he was up against wasn't just Mr Jarrold, Assistant Education Officer, himself. Oh, no! It was the immovable, unshakeable, invisible something that Jarrold stood for. Jonty wondered if, instead of talking to Jarrold, he should not give vent to a more characteristic urge that was clamouring for release, and leap up onto the corner of Jarrold's desk, assume the posture of an ithyphallic satyr, and piddle gently into Jarrold's teacup while leering coyly at Styles hiding behind his ballpoint. But he didn't. He continued to sit in his chair, caressing the bulge of the flask of whisky in his hip pocket and wondering what his next move was to be. Suddenly, he rose, said "Excuse me!" to Jarrold, and went across to whisper in Style's ear. Styles got up, opened the door of the office and pointed along the corridor. Jonty nodded and went out.

246

He had no doubt in his mind, now. He wasn't dealing with a priest of the Mystic Order of the Golden Dawn, but one of the most formidable representatives of the Local Watch Committee anybody could have the luck to meet.

26

When Jonty got back to Room 666, Jarrold, still at his desk, was working his way steadily through the pile of arrowroot biscuits and starting on his second cup of tea. Jonty felt sorry that HQ wouldn't receive any more dispatches from Jarrold's stomach this morning. Jonty was about to sit down when Jarrold said: "Don't bother to sit—Mr Godley! The interview is now over. My schedule—is very tight, so I'll—bid you Good morning."

Jonty thought quickly. It was clear that Jarrold had made up his mind about Jonty before he had entered his office, just as—to be fair—he had made up his mind in advance about Jarrold. What could he do now to soften the cavity where Jarrold should have kept his heart?

"Perhaps I could—" Jonty began.

But Jarrold held up a white, pneumatic palm, like an effete policeman.

"Before you say anything further, Mr Godley—please go with Mr Styles—He will tie up any loose ends for you. Good morning!"

He lowered his hand and popped another arrowroot biscuit into his mouth.

Jonty watched the steady champing of Jarrold's jaws with a kind of horror. Self-denial, my Aunt Fanny! Styles-denial, yes! Jonty-denial, yes! People-denial, yes! But Jarrold-denial, my Royal English arse! Of course, that explained the little sex-kitten with the gorgeous fur he'd caught bending when he entered Jarrold's office. Jarrold had probably ordered Margaret to do the filing on the floor every day. Look the other way, my eye! No wonder he's a member of the Watch Committee; he likes watching!

"Are you having difficulty—in understanding me, Mr Godley?"

"Not at all, Mr Gerald. I understand you only too well!... It's simply that you don't have full details of my—of my peculiar situation."

Jarrold took the biscuit that was half-in, half-out of his mouth and said, unclearly: "Oh? What's *peculiar* about your situation, Mr Godley—that I am not already aware of?"

"Well, I don't suppose you get many applicants who live in a plate layer's hut on a shutdown branch of the Earlswood line of British Railways, do you?"

When this had absolutely no braking effect on Jarrold, who continued to eat his biscuit, Jonty added:

"With an invalid wife." Jarrold munched contentedly on.

"And three sickly children," added Jonty. Jarrold's rhythm was in no way impaired. "And an arthritic mother-in-law to support."

A bit of biscuit went down the wrong way and Jarrold reached out swiftly for his cup. Minus his usual brand of genteel grace, but with signs of a more primitive gluttony, Jarrold swallowed a mouthful, coughed, and discharged a little spray of morning tea onto Jonty's file in front of him. He swallowed another before he was satisfied that the obstruction had been cleared. From behind him, Jonty heard a slight Phut! He took this to indicate that Styles had succeeded in getting into another dimension at last. Jonty turned to verify it. No! He was wrong! Styles was there, still in his material self, and still in his outdoor clothes that doubled as pyjamas. He refused to meet Jonty's gaze.

Jarrold sat bolt upright again in his swivel chair. The slight tinge of plum was back in his earlobes. He pushed his tea things away from him on the tray and proceeded to give Jonty the full treatment from his navy blue eyes. Jonty looked at him steadily in return.

"Are you telling me, Mr Godley, that you are married, with several dependants?" he said all in one breath. The tea had done him good.

"Because if you are—" he paused and laughed, showing Jonty the pink inside of his mouth, like a yawning cat.

Jonty continued to watch him and said nothing.

"I needn't tell you, I hope," Jarrold went on, "that the question of financial support—is quite impossible. It is not—the policy of our Committee—to provide Social Security payments for the families— of—of people like you, Mr Godley. Not only that—these—er—facts were not included in your original—er—application...."

Jarrold continued along these lines for some time.

Jonty let his eyes wander over the furnishings of the office. Why was it that the Local Education Authority favoured a decor that was predominantly merde-coloured? Did it show systemic scatological tendencies, or did it express a fundamental philosophic view of life? Jonty had given up listening to Jarrold's messages, but judged by the spasmodic gestures he was now making with his head and hands, it wouldn't be long before he gave up expounding the subtleties of the Committee's discussions on social dropouts, and resorted to a succession of succinct commands, such as: "Trim your nails. Get your hair cut. Stand to attention when you're spoken to. Get out!"

Jonty waited for a lull in the firing and then sent in a brief salvo of his own.

"My family has always been poor. My mother died when I was fourteen. My father is in the bin. I am unemployed and showing signs of incipient addiction to Welsh poetry. Surely my circumstances are more than enough to—?"

"—Indigence and misfortune are not qualifications for academic achievements, Mr Godley," Jarrold cut in with suppressed fury.

He was going to have the time of his life relating to the Selection Committee later how he had been insulted in his own office by an upstart who didn't know his place. Et cetera.

"Furthermore, Mr Godley, if your ambitions are academic—as you say they are—you have—if I may be permitted a personal observation—you have been more than a little feckless—wouldn't you say?"

Jonty, whose mind had been wandering again, found his attention snatched back by something in Jarrold's last pronouncement. Jonty regarded him quizzically. The plum colour had now suffused most of Jarrold's face.

'Did you say – "F...less"? You couldn't have said that, could you? No, of course you couldn't! But if you did, you couldn't be more wrong. I've had some— . Oh! FECKless! That was the word, was it? Feckless! That's different. A word like that is a plain insult. What right have you got, Jarrold, to pass judgment on my extra-marital-sex-life, eh, Jarrold?'

"Well," said Jonty, falling into the pronunciation he used for his Troglodyte act. "Fings ain't wot they used to be, you know. Plenty students my age are married men wiv li'bilities, not to mention fings like pot an' grass an'—"

"POT! Are you admitting to smoking—?"

"—I don't admit to anything, Mr Gerald," said Jonty in his usual accent. "Not even what you think I've admitted to. Just putting a case, that's all. Hypo-thetical!"

"Hypothetical!"

The realization, which for Jarrold was awful, that Jonty had been having him on, injured his dignity so forcibly that he got to his feet, displaying his well-cut thornproof suit, his height, and some signs of strain. Jonty, still standing, was a head shorter.

"It is time this interview came to an end. Not only have you wasted my and Mr Styles's valuable time—"

'The last stages of the nervous breakdown that Styles is in can hardly be described as a waste of time, Mr Jarrold; but then charity isn't your strong point, is it?'

"—but you've also given false information—in order to solicit public monies on your own behalf—"

"Hold on, Gerald! Remember: the poet doth not lie for he doth nothing affirm, as my brother Sydney was saying the other day. Anyway, it was true for you!"

"WHAT?" shouted Jarrold.

Then he leaned his two closed fists on the desk, put his weight on them and looked at them. He was in the closing seconds of a gruelling fifteen round contest. He looked done in. Jonty even felt a little sorry for him, but he recovered himself just in time and went on:

"Because from the moment I put my foot in your office, you had made up your mind I was some kind of deadbeat, hadn't you? Maybe a sex-fiend or a drug-addict? You'd already sentenced me, hadn't you, if not to life imprisonment, to a good stiff course of Lifebuoy and the Gideon Bible every Christmas. See! Facts! Your facts. I hadn't got a dog's chance, had I? I gave you what you wanted—to justify your decision. Right? Right, Gerald?"

Jarrold said nothing. There was now no trace of colour in his skin. Jonty was a totally new experience for him. Never before had anyone dared to speak to him in such a fashion. Styles was squeaking mutely behind him.

Jonty had intended to leave with the crescendo of his question still resonating Jarrold's earlobes. But he suddenly remembered what Crehan had told him about nepotism. Why not unleash that on Jarrold as well, while he was still groggy? Jonty decided that he had been on his feet long enough. He sat down uncaringly on the chair in front of Jarrold's desk. Something on the seat cracked under him as he did so. Jarrold watched him, powerless, like a man in a nightmare. His colour was changing in a way that was difficult to define.

"Furthermore, Mr Gerald, is your Committee aware that there are irregularities—?"

But Jonty didn't finish. The ripe and unmistakable aroma of Scotch whisky pervaded the office. It was beautiful. Warmth and wetness began to circumambulate Jonty's buttocks and crawl along his thighs. Jarrold's eyes had suddenly presented themselves in full naval uniform and he had begun twitching his nose. He took a breath. Was he about to give Jonty two weeks spud-bashing for insubordination?

Jonty stood up.

Instantly, three pairs of eyes went down to the sizeable stain spreading over the velveteen seat of Jonty's chair. Jonty fancied he could detect a sensation of unimaginable luxury in the area of his genitals. Styles's face was a picture painted by an artist of caricatures. Horror began to grow in his features as his eyes fixed themselves on the increasing zone of darkness around Jonty's flies. What was the matter with Styles? Had he no sense of smell? Or was he a Band-of-Hope teetotaller?

Jonty decided not to wait for the answers: he made for the door. As he was leaving, he caught sight of Jarrold studying the chair, now looking a little tipsy on its Victorian legs as the velveteen seat continued to change its colour for the worse. There was an expression of righteous self-justification and triumph on his face; at least, that is how Jonty interpreted the turtle-like thrust of Jarrold's neck, the glowing eyes, and the half-open mouth.

'Faces need Slurp,' thought Jonty, with his hand on the doorknob. 'Well, some do! Others need a demolition job.'

Was it a quirk of Providence, or sheer relief, that prompted Jarrold's stomach to choose that very moment to begin complaining again? Jonty had stepped across the threshold when he heard the empty echoing sound of it; it was like a load of house bricks being dropped in a long tunnel. Jonty felt the final bell had marked his victory, and left jubilantly.

Jonty went straight to the Public Conveniences and removed his jeans. He extracted the splintered remains of the flask and dressed again. They were still damp, but never, in his whole life, had he smelled so rich and opulent. As he descended the flight of stone steps, he caught sight of Margaret disappearing into the Ladies. The urge to rush in after her, and tell her what he had felt when he had first set eyes on her plentiful bosom, and her other abundancies, was strong. First impressions were very potent things. But because he felt uncertain what she would want to tell him, after setting eyes on his jeans, he didn't. You couldn't be too careful, could you?

Jonty reached the smoke-tinted double doors at the entrance. The janitor was standing outside, taking care of a blink of winter sunshine and smartening up the pedestrians with his eyes. As Jonty went by, he touched the peak of his cap over his piqued face with the hand that wagged.

"Mornin' to you, sir," he said.

"Good morning," said Jonty.

As he went down the last flight of hollowed-out steps to the street, Jonty could feel the janitor's eyes boring into the wet patches on his backside. All at once, Jonty felt a surging swell of exhilaration. He turned round and called to the astonished janitor: "They don't make mornings much better than that, do they, old gaffer?"

The janitor refused to reply and looked at the passers-by in hurt dignity.

'Never mind!' thought Jonty. 'What happens next is bound to be an anti-climax.'

♣

A few days later, Barry Crehan called. Jonty was at home, in his platelayer's hut, working on his essay. He had offered Crehan his other chair, the ricketty straw-bottomed job, while he sat on his straight-backed one at the green-baize card table he was currently using as sideboard, office desk and dining area. Jonty was about to read his horoscope to Crehan from the current issue of *Vanity*.

"Listen to this! *'Are you losing control? Yes. Much as you like to decide things, this month others run your life. ALL the action planets are opposing your sign, even your own sex-arouser, Pisces! Little electronic breakdowns? Your stereo goes PFT! Your car loses its lights. Even your heated rollers won't heat.'* "See! That's me! All the time, I get trouble with my heated rollers. And that tangled mess in the corner, full of jumble, is what's left of the stereo after it went PFFT!"

"I wish I could help, old hen!"

"Oh, you have, you have! Dropping in like this!... 'THIS month', it says, 'others will run your life'. What a laugh! They've been running it ever since my first spoonful of Cow & Gate. Now, along comes Jarrold, I ask you?"

"Yes," agreed Crehan, "he sounds like a real Scots Dominee, the kind that chains the swings up on a Sunday."

He threw back his head and laughed. Jonty caught a glimpse of two large, hairy nostrils before Crehan took a long pull from his can making them disappear. His shoulder-length locks swung backwards and forwards.

"Sorry, laddie! It's not funny, I know. Wish I could show you a light on the horizon."

"Well, you have! A green light! Telling me about Sofia was a big help. More than you'll know."

"Yes, good! I thought you looked smitten. And I just wanted to let you know about 'the other'."

"Yes. Jolly dee of you, that was!"

Jonty had been working by lamplight when the interruption came, trying to get his paraffin-heated brain to the point of making intelligent and non-obscene comments about the Welsh poet he had finally settled upon to study. It wasn't easy: the particular combination of properties. Difficult to invent, in the mood which had stayed with him ever since his encounter with Jarrold. It was, therefore, more than light relief Jonty experienced when Crehan knocked on the planks of his door, wearing a suit that was too tight under the arms, across the shoulders, round the biceps, over the quadriceps, about the hips, under the crotch, and all round the seams. Jonty had managed not to laugh. He hadn't wanted to hurt Crehan's feelings.

The only thing about the suit that was unhampered was the check, which was woven emphatically into it in squares the size of a navvy's palm, with colours that positively hallooed at you from the middle distance. Also, he was displaying, under the suit – God knows how! – a high-necked sweater plaited from ship's hawsers (Barry, be choosy about knitwear!) and, at the end of his arms, a pair of shiny black driving gloves, which he had now removed, and which had glistened in the lamplight.

Besides telling Jonty that Sofia fancied him, Crehan had brought 'the other' information: (A) Herbert Smedley Dummock had been promoted to the position of Production Manager at Burke's, Charles & Long's; and (B) Crehan himself was now knocking off Alexis. Jonty thought he should write to Major Knowles and suggest that, in the former case, a more appropriate title for Dummock might be Reproduction Manager. And, in the latter case, Crehan would have been more accurate if he had said that Alex was now knocking off Crehan, or even, with greater precision, he was himself now being knocked off by Alexis – which formulation Jonty felt did greater justice to her skill, experience and appetite in these matters. But, out of friendship for Crehan, he forbore to say so.

Of course, (A) and (B) were not unconnected. Oh, dear, No! Dummock, being Dummock, would HAVE to keep up, in material and outward signs, with his new-found status; and, conversely, the outward signs would have to keep up with the status he felt he was worth. It was a situation with built-in negative feedback, and there was plenty of room under the arms for later broadening out. Dummock would know exactly how to broaden it. Dropping Alexis would be his first move. Later, he could throw away his wasps and flies and start playing with men and women in cages specially designed, tooled-up and produced by Burke's, Charles & Long's. Jonty could already see the panel in the *Weekend Mail*:

VACANCIES

WANTED AT ONCE: MIDGETS OF BOTH SEXES FOR PLAYING CHESS WITH. NO KNOWLEDGE OF GAME PREFERRED. APPLY IN WRITING: MAJOR H B KNOWLES... etc.

And soon after that Dummock would be seen in public with the bigger, more powerful, quieter, limousine-type of concubine, complete with portable telephone, two-ended Hi Fi, and one-ended cocktail-shaker. Oh, dear me, Yes! Dummock would go in for status consistency in a big way, would Herbert.

However, Jonty could see that Crehan seemed glad about the new arrangements and Jonty, for the moment, was glad that Crehan was glad. But, Jonty knew there would come a time when Crehan, with a very tired expression and bags under his eyes like potato sacks, would be only too ready to take an uncharacteristic interest in a quiet life. He would not simply lose enthusiasm and become non-glad; no, he would become positively un-glad. The predominant mood would be woe of a significant order. Alexis's kind of appetite would finally – Jonty felt – have that effect on all but a libido in the heavy-duty category of H S Dummock's. Furthermore, Crehan was displaying a lack of regard for what natural endowments he had actually received by wearing garments of the ilk of his plaid suit. As Jonty reached this point in his cogitations, Crehan chose that moment to cross his legs in the rickety straw-bottomed chair and Jonty winced visibly. Crehan, apparently not in the least uncomfortable, smiled indulgently at him. Jonty, inexplicably, felt sorry for Crehan.

"Shall I read you your Horror-scope?" Jonty asked with compassion, picking up the current copy of *Vanity* from his green-baize dining table.

"Chr-r-rist, man, No! I never want to know what's in store for me. It would spoil my life."

"Drink another can of this lab-specimen, then?"

"Thanks! That thing I will do!"

"Having things good, like you, I can sympathize. Any change would be for the worse, I s'pose." Jonty sighed. "Thus, no zodiacs."

"Something like that. Surprise packages are more in my line, old hen."

Jonty went over to the orange-box he was using as his pantry, and took out another can of a well-known brew, returned and gave it to Crehan. He had to bend; the chair Crehan sat in was very near to the ground. He straightened up and looked about him.

"Whereas in my case—" he said, and swept his arm round in a grandiose gesture, like a monarch indicating his domain. His outstretched fingers accidentally caught the oil-lamp hanging from a hook in a crossbeam and set it swinging crazily so that the shadows stretched and squatted, fattened and thinned in a bizarre dance. He pulled his fingers away in a jerk and tried to shake them free from his knuckles. Then he blew vigorously on them. "Bugger that!" He sucked one of his fingers. "See what I'm up against?"

"I do indeed, old hen! How's the digit?"

"Only a third degree burn. It's all right!"

"Well, my offer still stands, if you want it."

"What offer?" asked Jonty.

When Crehan did not reply, Jonty said: "Oh, that one! No, thanks! That's not in MY line. This—living here—on a branch track to nowhere—has its advantages: no neighbours, no noise, hawkers or canvassers; the occasional dog. You know!"

"No lavatory! Ah ken verra weel," answered Crehan, parodying himself.

"True! But the space outside is very spacious, and inside, look around, one down and none up, the flat is—er—compact. I've got an unlimited rent-free view of tarred wood and corrugated iron. Not everybody can live like this, you know."

Crehan wriggled his bottom again—and on that chair, and in that suit! The latest models under the Hernia logo! He really was careless.

"Aye. Well, it gives you a guid chance to get on with your *magnum opus,* doesn't it?"

"Oh, that!"

Jonty pushed a sheet or two of notepaper away from him on the green baize, in disgust.

"Why? What's the matter with it?"

"I suppose, not much really."

"There you are, then!"

"Except details—like me having nothing to say about the subject under consideration! To whit, one Welsh poet."

"You? Nothing to say! I can't believe it!"

"And a subject who's got nothing to say about anything, not even Wales, and writes as if he had learned English through the medium of Urdu. And pushes his ballpoint with both hands."

"It can't be as bad as that, old hen!"

"Can't it? You should read it."

"Okay! You're on! Give it to me!"

"You couldn't decipher my scrawl! I'll read a bit out loud, if you like, and you'll see what I mean."

"I like."

"Listen to this then:

"'To examine this poem analytically...' Christ! How else could you examine it? '...is to discover how the imaginative process involved in the making of a poem. ...' The WHAT process? Of this poet? '....discovers itself through the agent of its purpose....' That's assuming it has any purpose, which is far from certain. And assuming it has an agent. If it has, he should send it back to the poet. .... Et cetera. Want any more? There's loads of it!"

"Sounds fine to me!"

"Wish it was! That's the first passage I'm taking out. Haven't even got to the poetry, yet! What an unpoetic prospect that is!... Let's talk about something else, shall we?"

"Okay! There is something else I want to mention. I'm having a bit of a Mingle in a couple of days. You know, Regge music, lots of birds in suede and leather, and all that sort of thing. What about it?"

"It's not going to be full of painters and sculptors with see-through souls, is it? And characters based on Joe Orton and Bernard Levin, is it? And hashish-eaters, is it? Because—I mean, I don't mind the birds."

"Can't guarantee there won't be! A few of these, and a few of those. You know, a pot-pourri!"

"Doesn't sound like me!"

"Sofia will be there, of course. That sounds like you!"

"How nice of you to invite me! Of course, I'll come."

"Thought you would! Next Thursday, about eight. See you there."

Crehan stood up. It appeared to be painless. Jonty, however, felt sure that, if Crehan blinked just then, the suit would divide itself nattily down the middle, falling apart as aptly as scissor blades. Would he feel embarrassed to have his mutilations, wounds and deprivations revealed to public view? But Crehan didn't blink; his eyes were wide open as he carefully put down the familiar red can on the basket chair.

"Thanks for the jug!" he said. "By the way, Alex asked me to remind you about the cash she lent you."

"Oh, did she?"

"She did. She thought you could bring it with you on Thursday, old hen."

"Nice of her to remind me! I'll try. But you can see the way things are, can't you?"

Crehan nodded sympathetically.

"Anyway, do your best, hey? Cheery-bye!"

"Hey up!" said Jonty.

He watched him disappear from the overflow of lamplight along the embankment until he had merged with the darkness. The only sound was the crunch-crunch of Crehan's plastic-sided Chelsea boots on the ex-British Railway gravel, once drenched by the johns of the commuter trains all puffing and creaking towards Earlswood Lakes, punctually behind schedule. The era of steam was leaking away; but it had given Jonty his hut. That was some consolation! He hoped the gravel wouldn't spoil the gold reinforced seams on Crehan's boots; the man cared about such things.

Jonty went back inside and looked around, critically. He had managed to salvage a number of items from the fire: his father's folding bed, the card table, the old suitcase and some clothes, a couple of leather bags, a few saucepans, and the idiot-box – standing eyeless and disconsolate in the corner, wires in curlers, readying itself for a future coming-out ceremony.

"Not a pretty sight! Worse than a junk store in the Rag Market."

He felt in need of a fillip, something to relieve his feelings. The booze had gone; it would have to be some other solution. What? Of course! Jarrold! He owed him a letter at least, didn't he?

The sooty throat of the iron stove rose in front of him. Just the thing! He rubbed his fingers over the carbon film on its surface, and examined them. He blew on them to remove the excess and then tore a clean sheet of lined writing paper from an Exercise Book with a red cover. He inspected the results: faint smudgy prints with dark edges, like watermarks, had appeared on the paper.

"Lovely!"

He seated himself before the green-baize surface and began to write in a backward-leaning illiterate hand with an HB pencil he had managed to filch from under Treblitt's watchful eye. First, the address.

ELDORADO

Home for Unmarried Mothers

Bornville

BIRNINGHAN

Should he date it for the first of April? No, it was only January: too obvious. He wanted it to sound authentic—at least, on first sighting. No date at all would be better. He thought for a moment, and then began to write fluently.

Dear Mr Jarrod,

Can you advice me how to get money out of your Committy?

I am a poor and anxious student and I've heard if you get to know somebody what works at the Educayshun Office you can get grants out of them easy as winking.

A freind of mine has gave me details of one or two fiddles lately, and I will gladly supply them on demand and an S.A.E.

I'm a cuddly 39-24-36 eighteen-year-old who wasn't born yesterday. If you want to see me personally in your office to talk things over I'm always avaleable.

Yours in hope,

Henrietta Cooper.

P.S. In decimal currency my vital statistics are 100-60-90 but it sounds awful. Perhaps I oughter warn you I always get a bad headache after sex.

Jonty read it through and thought it would do. Let Styles put that in his folder marked BURSARY APPLICATIONS! Jonty was sorry that he wouldn't be in the office when it arrived. He leaned back in his chair and pictured the scene. Jarrold would get so hot under the collar that his sorbo nose would droop, give a little evil-smelling wriggle, and fall blackly onto his blotter, like a burnt string. This feat would be accompanied by applause from his stomach, whose acme of appreciation would be an office-shuddering belch, while Styles disappeared in a puff of smoke to the sound of no band playing. Afterwards, Jarrold would collapse weakly in his swivel chair, concealing the site of his missing nose, and bluster hysterically:

"Shape up, man! Arid get my tea and arrowroot, for God's sake!"

Jonty's daydreaming had restored his equanimity of mind. He made sure that the fingerprints would be useless to any police laboratory, put the letter in an envelope and sealed it. For the price of a stamp, it was a cheap peformance. It would start Jarrold's week beautifully for him.

Now, it was time for bed. He removed his suedes, hung his windcheater and shirt on a chair, got onto the folding bed and pulled two army surplus blankets over him, and an ex-army greatcoat over that. He would finish reading *Vanity* before going to sleep; he hadn't quite got through the horoscopes.

After a moment or two, he looked up and stared morosely round the hut. He groaned loudly, It looked like a film-set for one end of Fagin's kitchen. Even if he got as far as asking Sonia at Crehan's party if she would like another mustard-and-cress roll, how could he ever hope to bring her here? He tried to ignore the speculation and read manfully on. His eye fell on an injunction to:

> *'Work on a crochet bedspread or crochet shawl. You*
> *could sell the design.'*

He tossed the magazine aside, and pulled the blankets over him.

"Not for this bed, I couldn't!... Anyway, I've lost my crochet hook."

Jonty, falling asleep, suddenly felt a stab of pity for his father, although it was not in the code they had evolved for each other. Am I becoming susceptible to filial feelings, for some unaccountable reason? Maturity, or the influence of women? He consoled himself by promising to give himself the treat of a good long hot soak at the Municipal Washing Baths on the day of Crehan's party, and tried to dream that he and Sofia would live happily ever after.

About the Author

Roy Holland was born in Birmingham. He went to Africa in 1966 to teach in the universities of the Boleswa countries. In 1971 he went to Greece for three years. He and his family lived on the island of Levkas for six months, the Gulf of Corinth for a similar period, and in Corfu for a little over two years. He wrote full-time until 1974, when he returned to the U.K. and worked on a research project until returning to Africa in 1977. Thereafter he lived in Southern Africa and worked in universities in Zimbabwe, Lebowa and Venda. He was Professor of English at the University of the North, the University of Venda, as well as Dean of the Faculty of Arts in the later 80's. He retired early to write full-time, and now lives in Ledbury, Herefordshire.

www.ingramcontent.com/pod-product-compliance
Lightning Source LLC
Chambersburg PA
CBHW020823260626
47169CB00003B/802